THE SECRET DIARY OF A CONMAN

Vish Dhamija is a bestselling author of crime fiction, including The Rita Ferreira Series (*Bhendi Bazaar, Doosra* and *Lipstick*), *Unlawful Justice, Cold Justice, The Mogul, The Heist Artist, Prisoner's Dilemma* and *Déjà Karma.*

Vish's books have been published in India, the United States and France. *Glimpse* magazine has called him 'India's John Grisham'.

An Amazon Prime-sponsored screen adaptation of his bestselling novel *Bhendi Bazaar*, with Bhumi Pednekar slated to play DCP Rita Ferreira, is currently in the works.

Vish lives in London with his wife, Nidhi, and his dog, Simba. *The Secret Diary of a Conman* is his twelfth book.

THE SECRET DIARY OF A CONMAN

THE SECRET DIARY OF A CONMAN

VISH DHAMIJA

PAN

First published 2024 by Pan
an imprint of Pan Macmillan Publishing India Private Limited
707 Kailash Building
26 K. G. Marg, New Delhi 110001
www.panmacmillan.co.in

Pan Macmillan, The Smithson, 6 Briset Street, Farringdon, London EC1M 5NR
Associated companies throughout the world
www.panmacmillan.com

ISBN 978-81-19300-86-0

1 3 5 7 9 8 6 4 2

Typeset in Adobe Garamond Pro by R. Ajith Kumar, New Delhi
Printed and bound in India by Thomson Press India Ltd.

This book is dedicated to Simba, our lovely furry baby.
He made ours a truly blended family.

It's a privilege to be your hooman dad and be able to call myself
Vish 'Mufasa' Dhamija.

The QR code below will lead you to a Spotify playlist that I've put together for this story. Each diary entry is accompanied by a song that resonates with it. You could either listen to the track first and try to work out where the next entry is headed. Or you could listen to the songs as you read along. Or save the playlist for later. Whichever way you choose to tune in, I hope you enjoy the book. And the playlist too!

PART ONE

ONE

'Boadicea' – Enya

THIS IS A WORK OF FACTION: FACTS INFUSED WITH FICTION, and a bit of fantasy. Any resemblance to actual persons, living or dead, or any actual event is most definitely intentional.

For a few months now, this rather crazy idea of chronicling my life story has infested my mind like termites on wood, eating up whatever little brain I have left. I think the seed got self-pollinated when I was in prison. Haven't a lot of people written journals while they were in prison? Jeffrey Archer, for example? When he got out, his diaries were published and people across the world paid to read them. Though his imprisonment was for an altogether different reason, he and I have one similarity: we both went to prison.

Of course, if I had asked for a pen and paper to write while I was inside, I'd have been laughed at. Maybe even got kicked in my gonads for making such a request. To be fair, I am not some missionary or an actor or an author or a rock star or a cricketer or even a politician who's held a public office. What have I done in my life that's worth anyone's time? Who would want to read it? And if, by chance, someone did, the next question is *why*?

Believe you me, though I have a feeling this diary will be read by others, I am writing it for myself. It is for me. It is my diary. I want a record of events in case I get Alzheimer's in my old age. I am told it runs in my family. I already fail to remember if it was my mother or my father who told me, you see.

Is it a diary if I don't write in a dated notebook? Or will it be referred to as notes? I'm not going to be fussed about mentioning dates, but I'll still call it a diary.

My. Not-so-secret. Diary.

And since it's for my own gratification, I can say what I want. I can break chronology, I can write from my imagination – though it might be untrue. I can embellish a banal anecdote to make it sound earnest, even admirable. I can reminisce about what never existed, I can romanticize a particular figment of my life. I can draw doodles or make pencil sketches, go off on tangents or invent references. I can start a fresh page whenever I like. End one when I want. Readers must interpret it at their own risk. You may make assumptions or hazard a guess – that is up to you. I won't deny or defend or elaborate. I won't apologize either! No one should have to apologize for telling the truth or half-truths even, if you ask me.

I must make you aware, dear diary, that I have a good memory. Not a photographic memory alone – that is such a cliché: '*Oh, I have a photographic memory*'. No. If I have a conversation with someone, I can later transcribe it word for spoken word. I am one of a kind, smart. The rest of the world are dummies; they don't see me as a polymath. Pity! Some people have even accused me of being a narcissist – you can't please everyone, can you?

By the way, would I be labelled as a total loony if I talk to my diary as if it were my friend? You can call me anything: a fraud, liar, squirrelly, outlandish! You may classify me as an unreliable narrator, someone totally unmoored from reality, but remember: I'm writing this for me. If and when someone accidentally comes across it, I'll leave it up to them what to believe.

As Salvador Dalí – yes, the celebrated Spanish surrealist known for his outlandish paintings – once said, 'I have Dalí-nian thought: the one thing the world will never have enough of is the outrageous.' Taking heed of the big man's wise words, I promise you one thing: my story – call it a diary, notebook, notes, gibberish, whatever – will not read like some dystopian account. I'll keep it interesting and bizarre.

As a footnote, I must clarify that although I'll be writing my diary in English, there will be an occasional word in Hindi or Urdu, which I'm sure you'll understand or look up. One Hindi/Urdu word I love using, and for which I haven't found a suitable alternative, is *hazaar*. It translates to 'thousand', but when the noted nineteenth-century poet Mirza Ghalib wrote '*Hazaaron Khwaishein Aisi*', he certainly didn't mean a thousand desires; he meant numerous, infinite longings. I find hazaar to be one of the best synonyms for 'unlimited'. You see, this is what I mean when I said I tend to stray from the narrative. Bear with me.

One more thing, my darling diary … did you notice the title of this entry? I think I might keep doing that. If you know the songs, hum along!

All the best!

TWO

'Amar Akbar Anthony' – Eponymous OST

HELLO, MY NAME IS RAHUL MAHAPATRA AND I'M A CARD ARTIST.

I can do artful tricks with cards. I am good at deception. I have mastered legerdemain when it comes to cards. I can manipulate them, cull them, bottom deal, second deal, middle deal, Greek deal, false shuffle, riffle shuffle, count cards, make cards disappear and reappear, make players cut cards in a manner to suit me, false cut … all of it and more, and without my fellow players noticing anything.

How? Well, I just told you I'm a card artist. I can also do a few tricks with coins, but I'm not a sorcerer. I have no juju. I cannot cut people in half and join them again, I can't make a dove disappear from under a handkerchief, I cannot pull rabbits from a hat – oh, hold on, maybe I can.

Hi, I am Saurabh Mathur, and I'm a musician. I say musician, but I'm not in some rock or jazz band, nor do I compose film scores. And, as a matter of fact, I haven't had any professional training – I'm what they call an autodidact, a self-taught person. My instrument of choice is the violin, but I can play most stringed instruments. I perform at dinners and parties, where people invite me to entertain their guests. I am not a celebrity performer so the money isn't great, but it's okay. I get by. Money shouldn't be the goal for an artist. Sometimes, I get paid less than the tips I receive.

Oftentimes, as a second act, I perform some card tricks for children – for free, just to entertain them. It gets me bigger tips if the parents are impressed, and when I leave a mark, the kids tell their parents to invite me to more parties.

Hello world, you are supposed to call me Dimpy Raja, though not many people know me by that name. I was born in a small town in Uttar Pradesh that remained a part of UP when the state split into two. Tangential info, but I thought I'd still let you know. I come from a lower-middle-class background. I say 'middle class' but if I'm being honest, and if they based the classification on financial status alone, I'm pretty sure I'd be classified as an underclass. But hey, why bother?

Loser

I failed in school simply because I could never give a concise answer to questions asked in examinations. I detest people who merely want the basics, no frills. I mean, your life isn't just the essential bits; it's the flourishes, the embellishments, the asides … are you with me?

Just a little piece of trivia: the three of us are the same person.

Let me put it in simple terms for you. I am a conman. Con has several synonyms: scam, rip-off, sting, hustle, swindle, flimflam … you get the idea, so take your pick. The term originates from 'confidence trick', shortened to 'con trick' or 'con game', further shortened to con. And the person being conned is called a mark, rube or gull (short for gullible). Remember that.

Another thing to note is that there are short cons and long cons. While a short con takes seconds or minutes, a long con is something that unfolds over an extended period of time – weeks or months – and involves a script, teamwork, sets, stages, costumes and props, among other things. It also involves large sums of money. Will you remember that too, please?

THREE

'Free Bird' – Lynyrd Skynyrd

2 December

Three months out of prison

I'VE SEEN AND LEARNT A LOT IN MY LIFE (HALF OF WHICH I don't remember) and yet, I know there's still a lot left for me to see, to learn, to practise.

At thirty-two, I am already what they call a relic. Relic, you know? A surviving reflection of what I used to be in my heyday. I used to be a legend among my peer card players, con artists, swindlers, scammers, grifters. There were many who aspired to be me. I'm serious. Unfortunately, those days are now long gone. I'm finished now. Over with, done. And that isn't because I've lost any of my skills or my panache or my looks or my dexterity. Not at all, not one bit. My conning career is over because I was caught and arrested by the police. Once. And that's one time too many in this line of work.

Mud sticks. Once the façade cracks, it's checkmate and game over. In my case, I was convicted by the court and sentenced to a three-month incarceration. I'm now an Arthur Road Jail graduate, so to speak. My reputation is besmirched. And for someone like me, that's the end of your career. Once the police know you, recognize you and are suspicious of you,

you are a marked man. Other people – the posh, rich and so-called respectable – don't trust you anymore; they don't allow you to sit at the same table with them.

I don't agree with those who might call me conceited, since I'm actually handsome: five eleven, clean-shaven, with a full mane of slightly wavy, dark hair and a prominent jaw with high cheekbones. I'm told I have very expressive eyes. Of course, I'm no Dwayne Johnson, but I worked out regularly at the gym before I went to prison – and while I was in it. With my fast metabolism, I'm not flabby or out of shape even now. In my younger days, a few photographers had even approached me for modelling assignments. This was before film stars and sports personalities took over the entire modelling industry, but that's another story. Without getting side-tracked, I have to state that modelling didn't interest me one bit, since it would have afforded more recognition to my face than I fancied. My interests lay elsewhere, and recognizability wasn't helpful in the line of work I had picked.

I am what people call a petty criminal. That is not how I see what I do, and I do it purely of my own volition. I enjoy it. It's thrilling. It keeps me going. It makes my adrenaline rush. Much like a gambler in Vegas – although the odds of me winning are a lot higher than a punter in those professionally run casinos. And I have won more than I've lost. But over time, since I was found out and the police nabbed me, I've become a loser.

At the private, unlicensed card parties at clandestine locations in Mumbai, where I used to be invited and paid to play, I was a king. Strike that. I was an ace. I was the ace of spades. Sleight of hand, counting cards, manipulating cards, card flourishes, you name it; Poker, Blackjack, Texas Hold 'em, *Teen Patti* – with its hazaar variations – bring it on.

Some people call professionals like me cardsharps or card sharks – both nicknames mean the same thing: that we cheat at card games. I call it cardistry, which is a portmanteau of card and artistry. And I've perfected the art to a science.

I can also do card tricks. Four aces is my favourite one: I place – in a room full of people – sixteen cards in stacks of four each. Anyone from the audience is welcome to come and check the cards to ensure that none of the sixteen cards is an ace. Then I give the cards a shuffle, place them back and presto! At the bottom of the four stacks will be the four aces from the pack. It is a matter of skill; a simple sleight of hand.

However, I don't do these tricks when I'm at a card table. That facet of my life has to remain unbeknown to the high-stakes gamblers I play against, or I'd be kicked off the premises immediately. Gambling and magic tricks don't mix, for obvious reasons. Once in a while I'll perform card tricks, pro bono, to entertain a room full of kids; but my foremost reason for being at those weddings or parties – and for which I'm getting paid – is my violin playing.

Fortunately, these two aspects of my livelihood have never had any overlap. I am always careful when I accept an invite to showcase my musical talent for money; if there is even the slightest possibility that somebody from the gambling world might be there, I don't take out my deck of cards. I always do my research well, irrespective of what or where I perform, and long before I arrive at the scene. If it is a party, I must know the host and possible guests. If it is a high-stakes card game, I make sure I know all the punters. It's the only way to survive for as long as I did without getting caught: eight long years. That, and a very good memory.

I have other skills, too. I can shake your hand and pocket your wristwatch. It's quite simple if you wear a metal watch bracelet. Leather straps are a lot harder, often unyielding. There were times I survived in Mumbai making good cash selling high-end watches. But that isn't a capability which is of much significance these days, what with most people relying on stupid smartphones to know the time.

How does one take off someone's wristwatch during a handshake? Well, speed has to be your partner in crime. You should move at lightning speed. I don't need to emphasize that if you are slow, you will get caught and bear the consequences right there. You'll be slapped or kicked, maybe handed over to the police. Essentially, you should be faster than the time it takes the other person's eyes to send a signal to the brain. Before the mark realizes, the con should be over and you, out of their reach.

The same principle applies to misdirection. To succeed, you must suspend morality and imagine that you are married to the Siamese twins – Miss Speed and Misdirection. You cannot do without misdirection any more than you can do without speed. Hide something in plain sight and people don't even notice it. Most people instinctively focus on the wrong things. If not, it is *my* job to misdirect them.

In the four-ace trick I told you about just a while back, I invite people from the audience to validate that there are no aces among the cards I've laid out on the table. Usually, a curious few are itching to come forward, to touch, to see, to confirm. Obviously, I keep the number of people to a minimum – one or two, maybe, since I don't intend to let the whole crowd come close to me. The whole point of the exercise is to let those scrutinizers pick up the cards, look at them, count and recount them to verify if each stack is four cards, and the total cards are sixteen. These detectives relay to the crowd that there is not a single ace among them, let alone four. The aces are not in the deck either, but their focus is on those sixteen cards, and sixteen cards alone. The aces are with me, and I place them at the bottom of those four decks before these detectives get back to their seats, before I begin the trick. The shuffle I do when I am, supposedly, performing the trick for them, is deceptive. It's called a false shuffle in card parlance. I place all four packs over each other and shuffle the sixteen cards vigorously without moving a single card from its place because I do not want to disturb the cards that I've already put in place for the grand reveal later. How? You might ask.

It's speed.

It's misdirection.

And.

It's practice. If you honestly repeat a sequence hazaar times, you will hone the skill to perfection, no doubt about that.

Concentrate. Repeat. Rinse. Repeat. Cheat. Repeat.

I practise with mirrors surrounding me. You never know who's looking at you and your hands, and from which angle, do you? Practise until you become so adept, so flawless, that you can even fool yourself. Precision is crucial to what I do. Like an archer with his arrow – Arjuna in *Mahabharata* – hitting the eye of the bird by seeing its reflection in the water. You should be able to do it with your eyes closed, in your sleep. That's when you have the proficiency to become a pro.

Speed. Misdirection. Practice. There's your Royal Flush: Ace, King and Queen.

Back to the card table.

I can deal the cards in the order I want. But I ensure I never deal myself a set of aces. That's what an amateur would do. And that's why the amateurs get caught. Never, ever do that. You should get the best cards only when someone else has dealt the hand. I'll tell you more but, at the moment, I have to take a break because I'm required elsewhere.

I have a cat. Or should I say the cat has me? Dogs have owners. Cats have staff. They say some hazaar years ago cats were worshipped by humans. I think the cats still believe that. I know for sure that if this was her flat, she wouldn't let me in. But I still love her even though *I* am *her* pet, which I have come to recognize after she accepted me as her companion. She's one of those hundreds of stray moggies that inhabit Mumbai. They have bulletproof immunity, and don't get vaccinations to endure common ailments like high-priced, pedigree pets do, all the time. With no neutering programme, these cats are forever procreating and multiplying in numbers. They survive by scavenging on leftovers that people throw in the bin. Someone once told me that there is a statistical relationship between stray cats and cities that have high fish consumption. On that front, Mumbai is not alone; Kolkata has its fair share. Maybe Chennai too, I don't know. It doesn't pique my curiosity enough to ask around or even Google it. Just when did the domestic cat go into the sea to fish for itself? But I've digressed again.

Well, you will have to bear with me at times. I have this nasty habit of deviating, of segueing into related, sometimes even unrelated subjects. It's like what fiction writers call a side plot, but here's the problem: sometimes my departure from the point I'm making might sound utterly irrelevant to you, and I leave it up to your judgement to ascertain what's pertinent and what's extraneous. In my defence, asides are something that come with the territory. I use them for misdirection at card tables, while performing card tricks and, ergo, it comes naturally. I can apologize for this in advance, but I warn you that nothing shall change in my telling of the story.

Anyway, coming back to my cat, she's called Zeenat. I gave her the name since she had no tag, and no one ever came looking for her. Why Zeenat, you may ask? Well, my mother always made snide comments to my father that he was too friendly for her liking with our neighbour's wife, Zeenat. She would call her a witch, a *churel*. There is yet another reason that might make things clearer, but I shall reveal that at an opportune instance.

For now, let's get back to the current Zeenat. Funnily enough, her response to my calling out for her is dependent on whether she needs something from me at that moment or not. Zeenat adopted me one day without any kind of forewarning. She's ginger in colour like the famous cartoon character Garfield and if she were left to her own devices, she'd probably be as fat. I bet she could eat an entire blue whale in one sitting. Moby Dick, if you're reading this, beware! Zeenat always carries a fork-and-knife set in hopes of finding you.

So, like I was saying, two days after I returned from prison, about three months back, this tubby tabby just jumped into my second-floor apartment through the open window and made herself comfortable, politeness and privacy be damned. Are you curious as to how she got to the second floor? Cats can scale buildings with the help of drainpipes. I know it since I've seen Zeenat go in and out countless times from the very window she first used to enter my dwelling. She hardly ever knocks at the front door for me to let her in, and I have no cat flap. Hence, unless she holds a broom between her hind legs and flies up and down, there is no other explanation. Although, knowing her, I wouldn't put it past her.

For the last few minutes, Zeenat has been purring insistently and scratching my leg. She wants something to eat, and rightly so. It's nearly seven in the evening, and she's been out all day. Maybe she got something to eat outdoors, but one look at her face makes it seem like she didn't. I can never be sure. Right now, she's pretending like she's a helpless, famine-struck cat that's been abandoned. She's an extremely consummate actor when she wants something. I'll be right back.

♣

Did I tell you I live on Pedder Road in Mumbai? Yeah, posh or what?

I can guess what you're thinking now. How come someone who plays cards and the violin at weddings; has been to prison and lives with a stray cat can afford to live in a two-bedroom apartment that is worth well over eleven crore rupees? It's a long story.

Zeenat has finished her dinner and is now standing at my feet, looking up as if to impress upon me that she wants a bite of mine. Just a few minutes ago, I had asked her, 'You want salmon or tuna today?' knowing she couldn't care less. If she could have her way, she'd have had both. She's a real *bhukkad*, if you know what I mean. While tearing open the salmon pouch and emptying the contents into her bowl, I had realized I was hungry, too. Some might find the smell of cat food nauseating, but I find it appetizing.

A look into the fridge revealed that there was bread, there were eggs, there was beer and there was milk. And that was fine by me. I never learnt to cook. I'm not a gourmand. I eat to live and not the other way around, like some other folks. If I'm cooking, it's bread and eggs, or else there's always some frozen food in the freezer. Tonight, I decided to bake the frozen cheese and garlic bread, dressing it with some olive oil, crushed red chillies and sea salt flakes. After grabbing a Kingfisher, I brought my dinner to the sofa in the living room to continue writing in my diary.

As I eat, Zeenat has switched on her charm, licked her lips a few times, running her long tongue over her nose, too. I've told you before – she's incorrigible!

FOUR

'Our House' – Crosby, Stills, Nash & Young

MY APARTMENT ON PEDDER ROAD IS ON THE REAR SIDE OF THE building, which, despite its market value today, is dilapidated, lichened and weathered, much like every other building in Mumbai, unless it is owned by the likes of Mr Mukesh Ambani. If I step out of my building and look to the right, I can see the concrete monstrosity that has come to be known as one of the most expensive private residences in the world. But hey, whatever floats your boat; who am I to judge? Anyway, back to the point: how do I live in such an expensive property, albeit on rent?

I go by the name Rahul Mahapatra here. I have a whole backstory to go with it. Born and raised in Delhi, I moved to Mumbai to manage my family business – which is commodity exports, by the way. I have a large team based around the world, so my work goes on 24/7. Of course, none of this is true; it's all fabricated to lend me gravitas and attract respect. What else would I tell people? That I'm some kind of part-time bandmaster at weddings and parties? The guy who plays music at parties and entertains kids with magic tricks is Saurabh Mathur. I don't advertise, I get word-of-mouth referrals and that's enough.

Rahul Mahapatra plays cards. But I don't play for myself or with my own money. I have two patrons. Both are compulsive gamblers, both loaded up to their necks. Fortunately, they play in different circles so there are no crossovers between them, nor with the other players they take me to play with.

Gambling in Mumbai isn't legit.

But stockbrokers can buy, sell, short sell, play dirty, speculate and still call theirs a recognized trade. According to me, speculation is no less than gambling. When the banking industry brought the world to a standstill in 2008 by ignominiously engaging in hedge-fund trading, they didn't send all the bankers to prison. Not that I know of. Nasty bankers, nastier governments! Didn't someone once say that money made the law, and the law now protects those who have the money? Don't even get me started on that one …

I got diverted yet again, but I won't apologize for it. You know that by now, don't you?

Gambling in Mumbai happens at private residences. I'm talking high-stakes gambling, not what friends play at Diwali get-togethers. This is serious business. The biggest I won in one night was close to ten lakhs – just my share – so you can imagine what I'm talking about here. Another question you might want to ask now is how do I play games which require such deep pockets when I am a bleeding pauper?

The two patrons (read: gamesters or gamblers) I used to work with were Roshan Godara and Jinendrabhai Patel. It's not like they need the money like I do. It is an addiction for them. It's about one-upmanship. So they used to pay me to play with them as their friend when I was, in actuality, playing *for* them.

So that I didn't overexpose myself, I only played ten or twelve times a year – enough to live a grand lifestyle in a two BHK on Pedder Road and drink the twelve-year-old Macallan whenever I wished.

As I write about it, I'm getting reminded of everything that has led to this point in my life. Oftentimes, I regret the day I met Roshan Godara. And even more so, I regret the last game we played together.

♠

I was still in my PJs one February afternoon, relaxing, which was typical of my days back then. I have never held a nine-to-five job in my entire life. I wasn't made to work for others, or to succeed my father in the business he ran to support our family – I will tell you all about it a little later, but I fear that you will accuse me of veering from the subject again. Zeenat wasn't in my life then, and my girlfriend of two years had walked out on me the previous Christmas for reasons I shall explain in a while, too. By the way, my ex's name is Zara, and that is another reason I christened my cat Zeenat – to please my inner child by naming her with the same first letter. Despite being confident and mature in my professional life, I can be ingenuous at times, I know!

Where were we? Oh yes, I was at home when I got a call from Roshan Godara. Roshan is a third-generation industrialist. His grandfather owned several textile mills in Lower Parel, and when his father took over the business, he diversified into retail. Roshan inherited the business early on since his father had been on board the unfortunate Air India flight 182 from Toronto, which exploded over the Atlantic Ocean on 25 June 1985, due to a bomb planted by terrorists. Roshan was in his early twenties then and the only heir. He must be in his late fifties now, but his age is irrelevant. What is significant is that the silver spoon he was born with was placed more firmly in his mouth after his father's death. The business was big, there was professional management in place and hence, unlike ordinary people like us, he had no need to work his ass off. But along with money came boredom, which led him into the dubious company of other more-money-than-brains friends, which sired wrong habits – alcohol, womanizing and gambling, to name but a few.

I met Roshan about five years ago at a music gig I did at a birthday party. He spotted me performing card tricks for kids and seemed impressed. I hadn't yet gotten into high-stakes gambling when we met. He wore jeans and a navy blazer that looked expensive. He was short. A head full of almost-silver hair; a walrus moustache; sharp eyes behind gold-rimmed glasses; a prominent nose; straight, dental-polished white teeth; thick lips to complete the look. He looked moneyed and genial, not menacing. He clapped and walked up to me once the kids had gone away.

'You know some wicked tricks, man! I'm Roshan. Roshan Godara.'

'Saurabh Mathur,' I said, as I took his outstretched hand.

'Do you know any other magic tricks?'

'Not many, just a few with cards to entertain kids.'

'So you know other card tricks, too?'

'A few, like I just told you,' I smiled.

'Would you like to do something different?'

'Different, how?'

'Besides performing these card tricks at children's parties – which you do as a side job anyway, considering your main reason for being here is music, isn't it? Have you ever played cards for money?'

'What do you have in mind?' I have to admit that he had got me interested by then.

'Why don't we meet at my office and discuss it in detail?'

He opened his wallet, gave me a hefty tip and his business card, since other people were now within earshot.

I thanked him and he moved away.

Can you guess the first thing I did the next morning?

I'm sure you got it wrong. I cooked myself a breakfast of two over-easy fried eggs, buttered a toast and had it all with a strong black coffee. Although Roshan's little pitch had got me intrigued, I didn't want to give him the satisfaction by showing any desperation.

I called him the next day, but in the afternoon.

Until I met Roshan, I had never imagined I could use my skills so profitably at card games. Hell, I didn't even know about the existence of these private parties. However, he took the time to explain everything to me. The rules, the games, the stakes and the kind of people he typically played with. And then we became partners, in a manner of speaking. We brought complementary skills to the partnership – he had the money and connections, and I understood the math behind the cards, the algorithms. Cards aren't a game of chance. Those who take chances are morons. Cards are a game of strategy and sleight of hand, of confidence and probability.

Imagine that Monty Hall has you on his game show. He asks you to select one of three doors – there is a prize behind only one of the doors and nothing behind the other two. You pick door number one, but Monty doesn't open that. Instead, he opens door number two, and there is nothing behind it. If Monty then gives you the option of choosing between the remaining two doors, is it in any way beneficial for you to switch your choice now?

You might say no. I say yes.

I'll switch my choice and immediately double my probability of winning – from 33.33 per cent to 66.66 per cent. This is called the Monty Hall Paradox, and I've studied it, so let me explain. Bear in mind that your approach to solving the problem might not match the actual process but still, let me try. In Monty's show, there are three doors, behind which are a car and two goats. He asks you to pick a door, and you choose Door One. Monty instead opens Door Two to show you there's a goat behind it and asks you to pick a door again. Do you, now, stick to your original choice of the unopened Door One or do you switch to Door Three?

You might not believe me, but the odds aren't fifty-fifty. If you switch to Door Three, you will win 67 per cent of the time!

If I haven't done a good job of explaining, you can blame my teaching skills and look it up on the web. Trust me, I'm being truthful for once.

♥

Back to when Roshan called me in February this year and told me he had booked two seats for us at a card party. These parties were always held at one of the players' home or second home. Most of these rich blokes had extramarital flings going on, so owning a second home was almost mandatory. Well, it doesn't bother me – we all have our vices. The point I'm making is these parties were never hosted at hired locations or in hotel rooms. The police had no reason to intervene in private parties. In any event, these were respectable, rich, connected people who could pull strings should the police catch any scent and come snooping around.

With Roshan – as with Jinendrabhai – the terms were fixed. They put in all the money. At the end of the game, if we won, we first put aside the money we had spent that night and then divided the pot equally. If we lost, I earned nothing and the loss was theirs. They hired me for my skills, so I think it was a fair deal. However, losing was out of the question unless Roshan or Jinendrabhai *wanted* to keep others from suspecting that we were playing duplicitously. How else could someone always win?

Roshan told me over the phone who else would be at the party – I knew three of them already but one player was new to me, so I did my homework on him.

Roshan and I got to the venue after 9 p.m. It was a penthouse in Worli, owned by one Amit Gupta. As per our custom, Roshan handed the cash to a man at the door and we walked in. The other two men I knew were Jamshed and Robin; they were already inside. Amit, Jamshed and Robin were all fifty-plus businessmen – I never cared to ask what trade they were in to avoid being asked the same question myself. The new person that day was in the same age bracket as them; maybe fifty-two or -three, not a lot older. No one introduced us, and that was okay. I've been to many parties where some of the players chose to remain anonymous. He was dressed in casual khaki chinos, a powder blue open-collar shirt and tan leather loafers. He was clean-shaven, including his head. After exchanging hellos, two servers – one male, one female – served us drinks and some finger food and we got to the table by 9:45 p.m.

Seating was decided by lots. That day, Roshan sat to my right, which was always an asset since there were no dealers at these private parties. Dealers made it feel formal, while this felt like it was between friends and associates. We were all respectable businessmen at a friendly game here, not some convention of cheats. This was good, as the game could be rigged from the start by me, with my ability to deal cards at will. We dealt cards by turns, and if the person who cut the cards was in cahoots with you, you could stack the deck so your partner could cut it at the exact place you wanted him to. Convenient, isn't it?

'*Teen Patti,* with no variation in this round,' the host announced and started shuffling the cards.

Two rounds later: 'I've never met you.' It was the new player, looking at me.

'That's strange because I know about you.' I knew his name was Anand.

'How?'

'I can read people,' I responded.

'But I'm not wearing a name tag.' He looked down at his shirt pocket and smiled. *Smartass!*

'You aren't, but you gave a cheque at the door.' Instead of cash, which was peculiar for a host of reasons, I wanted to add.

'So you're observant, but that doesn't qualify as reading people.'

'You could say that.' I didn't want to get into an argument. The fact was he was right. I wasn't reading him. I had read *about* him. Slightly different, but I had read a flipping dossier on him. I knew his name – Anand Kumar. He owned a dozen petrol stations across Mumbai and had a wife who was gallivanting with younger men at the gym while he was dipping his pen elsewhere. No children – at least not between them. They lived in Cuffe Parade and hobnobbed with television actors. They were IPL fans – both Mumbai Indian supporters who always got box seats at home matches. Rutting Kumar drove a blue Mercedes and his cougar wife had a white Volvo. But, of course, I didn't say all that. Always do your homework, and always be prepared, but having info does not necessarily mean you have to use it.

Rule 101: don't show your cards until you *have* to, and unless you have to.

Back to our table, everyone!

JQK

The short conversation laced with my arrogance had been nothing but misdirection. My smartass comment had taken Anand's gaze from my hands to my face. That's all I required.

In those few seconds, I did a noisy riffle shuffle, culled the cards and started dealing. A card to the newbie Anand Kumar on my left, then one to Jamshed, to Robin, to Amit and then to Roshan, before I dealt one to myself. Three rounds, three cards each. Now everyone was focused on the game.

AAA

I hadn't dealt myself any great cards. I had dealt the best cards to Roshan and some cards worth betting on to Anand. Why? Because for Roshan to win a big hand, someone else needed to have good enough cards too, to raise the stakes. There's little point if everyone else folds. Got it? And as one after the other player folded, including me, Anand kept raising stakes and Roshan matched them. He knew he had to exercise control and not double the wager – that might've sent a signal to Anand to fold. The idea is to make the prey think he's leading the predator into a trap.

₹

That night we won thirty lakhs. Roshan had deposited ten lakhs at the door for the two of us, making our total winnings twenty, and my share a cool ten lakhs.

FIVE

'Folsom Prison Blues' – Johnny Cash

LIKE I TOLD YOU EARLIER, I WENT TO PRISON AND MY EARNINGS dried up; it's like the tap got turned off, almost immediately. No one hires a failure. It's almost a rule, isn't it?

Roshan and Jinendrabhai don't want me back in their circles so soon. Or ever. They have made crores using me, and they know I have the potential to make more. Maybe they want things to cool off for a while. Or maybe they have written me off, who knows? Who knows if Anand Kumar has put them under surveillance too, and is now looking for an opportunity to grab them?

Perhaps Zeenat and I should go travelling across the country. I have only ever seen two cities in my thirty-two years of existence. Saharanpur (where I was born) and Mumbai. That is, if you don't count the numerous railway stations in non-consequential cities where the train stopped when I was travelling to Mumbai eight years ago. Zeenat, I can safely assume, has never been out of Mumbai.

I have enough money stashed in various bank lockers across Mumbai. For those of you who don't know, lockers are vaults where you keep valuables without having to account for what you store in them. I have eight such lockers across different banks and branches. Trust me, no one cares. The bank managers who signed them off have since changed jobs, some may have moved out of Mumbai even, and no auditor has ever reconciled or come asking me about anything. For obvious reasons, I can't go to a bank and put all the money I earn through gambling into legitimate accounts. When I got arrested, I gave away the name of one bank where I had a locker, which had enough cash to satisfy the police that I had cooperated with them. As they say, there should be some element of the truth in a lie to make it sound believable. *Ardh-satya* is better than a blatant lie. Of course, I'm not stupid, I didn't tell them about all the other *benami* safe deposit lockers I held in other banks scattered across Mumbai.

Fortunately, in India, no one cares how you can live without any means of income so long as you stay off the radar, pay for everything in cash and do not flash your money around. I own nothing of value that they could raise an eyebrow at. No car. No property. I dress well, but that's because I can't turn up to play cards with businessmen in a wife-beater and boxers. I spend on The Macallan, a great Scotch if you like the sweet taste; I use air-conditioned cabs, I buy expensive cologne, I go to fancy restaurants, I watch theatre, but no one is adding up these expenses to see how much I spend in a week or month or a year. Yes, I own a few expensive paintings in my apartment, but they are in such shabby frames that even the police who came to search my apartment couldn't imagine they were genuine. I have loose diamonds, but they're secured in benami lockers, too. Both Roshan and Jinendrabhai helped me get these lockers under false names, but since they were equally complicit in the forgery, neither came forward to disclose that info when I got arrested.

I was arrested because that son-of-a-bitch Anand Kumar – after losing a small fortune on that fateful night in February in Worli – used his flipping police connections to put me under some kind of surveillance. I suppose he suspected we had cheated, but couldn't go after Roshan for reasons that don't need explaining. It would've been impossible to implicate him, so Anand found a scapegoat: me. The police caught me one evening in July with five lakhs in cash, which I couldn't provide a source for, and I was booked for money laundering. Luckily, I was permitted one call and I called my friend. One of my only two friends in Mumbai city.

Ranjit Bhatia.

You'd think his father must have hated him a lot to name him Ranjit – like the vilest villain in Bollywood ever. Period. Why would anyone name their only son Ranjit? But his father did. Ranjit was an unwanted child from an illicit relationship that he had on the side. Nonetheless, since Ranjit's father did not have any legitimate children, Ranjit inherited his entire estate and honestly, if you ask me, I'd be happy to be called Gabbar Singh if I inherited that much. But that's for another day – as usual I've wandered from the principal narrative, and I won't apologize for my verbosity. More about Ranjit later, hope you can wait a little longer.

Ranjit knew Roshan, and the only condition he had for getting me an advocate was to protect him. My former business partner had Ranjit by his shorts and curlies for reasons that I wasn't aware of. But if Ranjit told me not to mention Roshan's name, that was a promise I'd keep – even though on the night of my arrest I was carrying money we had won together. Funny? For all the warmth and camaraderie he had displayed, Roshan wasn't my friend; we were in business together. When I was arrested, self-preservation prevailed and he made himself scarce. I don't blame him; I don't agonize about it, to be honest. Shit happens! I knew the risks before I started swimming with the sharks. Once you're caught, you can't turn around and question why the shark has caught you and not the other fish.

Ranjit hired the best lawyer for me – Anita Bhambhani. Stylish, very stylish indeed. She was silver-tongued, and I liked her. She treated me well, not like a common criminal, and explained to me that taking the case to court might not be the best course of action. She said she could speak to the prosecuting advocate for me and, if I was willing to enter a guilty plea, she'd file for a lesser charge. Anita quite bluntly warned me that if we went to court and I pointed an accusatory finger at Roshan, she'd recuse herself. I appreciated her honesty and, while the prosecuting advocate was asking for a year, she got me a much-reduced three-month sentence. She told me that was the best she could do for me under the circumstances; Ranjit shared her opinion and I accepted it as my fate.

A significant condition I put in before agreeing to the plea deal was that my picture would not be released to the media. The public prosecutor didn't even blink an eye at that. A petty punter or a pygmy fish in the money-laundering Pacific, he couldn't care less about. He simply wanted to teach me a lesson and, insofar as he was concerned, he had succeeded.

You know the best part – if there can be one after getting incarcerated – is that Anand Kumar has no idea that I know he was the one who got my ticket punched. And I have no intentions of calling him up to let him know or to threaten him with dire consequences, like they show in B-grade films. I won't suddenly turn into Rambo and pick a fight with him. He is a big fish in Mumbai; comparatively, I am insignificant; a has-been as far as he or the police are concerned. If I pick a fight with him and the police start snooping into my affairs, I will indeed be in grievous trouble. I can't state or prove any source of income; I cannot even account for my rental

spending. Best to retreat and lick my wounds until I can do something.

Every dog of every breed has his day, they say.

P.S. I struggled with the dog's sketch because, unlike Zeenat, I don't have anyone to model for it right now.

SIX

'Papa Kehte Hain ...' – *QSQT* OST

I WAS BORN IN 1988. I GUESS THAT MAKES ME A MILLENNIAL or Gen Y. I don't think the term existed back then and if it did, it was certainly unheard of in Saharanpur, the small town in Uttar Pradesh where I was born. I was the only child and we still barely subsisted on the meagre earnings from my father's cycle repair shop around the corner. My mother supplemented his income by working as a domestic cook for four different families. Despite being a good cook, she was called a maid-servant – a *bai*, if you know what I mean – and therefore was also made to do dishes and cleaning and other petty chores around the houses she worked in. Men in these households even made passes at her – I know since I sometimes overheard her crying on my father's shoulder – but that is an inconsequential detail.

My father opened his shop at eight in the morning and closed at eight in the evening. Mum went out to work at eleven and returned home at almost the same time as him. We couldn't afford a television, and I'm talking about an era before the web and gadgets, so I had a lot of time to be on my own. I returned home from school at 2 p.m. and ate a meal that mom had prepared for me, wrapped in a towel inside an insulated basket to keep it warm. I used to finish my homework and simply waste time waiting for my parents to return. None of my school friends lived in the vicinity, and the well-off kids in the neighbourhood who went to private schools didn't entertain children like me. I tried a few times to join them while they were playing cricket on the side street, but they shunned me.

I was what you might call a latchkey child. I had to find my own amusement, my own toys, make up games, imagine friends and play with them. After a while, I was happy alone. Doing nothing. Fantasizing, wasting time.

Until I found real entertainment.

There was a *chillum*-smoking *madari* who lived at the end of our street. The neighbours wanted him gone – *not a good influence on our kids*, they said; *he stinks*, they said – but he didn't give a shit what others thought or said about him. He wasn't leaving the place anytime soon. Some days, he would go out, but most days he would lie in his room on the ground floor, smoking his pipe, with the main door to his dwelling ajar. Sometimes I'd see him juggling balls, and if I met his eyes, he'd pass me a smile. My parents had given me strict instructions that I go nowhere near him, come what may. But I was a bored twelve-year-old, so one day when the madari returned my smile, I walked closer and said, 'Hello baba.'

'What's your name, *bachcha*?'

'Dimpy Raja.'

'Raja?' He laughed. 'I never thought I'd meet a Raja in my life. Where is your kingdom?'

'My father's name is Raja, so he called his shop Raja Cycles and gave me his name, too. What's your name, baba?'

'You can call me anything you want, it doesn't matter.'

Up close, he appeared to be in his fifties, but I couldn't tell. Not that it mattered.

Thus started a clandestine friendship that would flourish

over the next two years. He was a juggler, a conjurer, a ventriloquist; he knew several coin and card tricks, and he owned a parrot that could repeat words. Madari baba was a street performer who earned even less than my dad – which was very little to begin with.

'Why do you come to see me?' he asked one day while we sat in his decrepit *kholi.*

'I don't know.' I seriously didn't. 'But something about you makes me wonder if there is life beyond normal—'

'What do you mean by normal? Do you think I'm abnormal, like the wayward asshole this world thinks I am?'

'Oh no baba, that's not what I meant.'

'Then what did you mean?'

I had difficulty finding words to explain. For the love of God, I was twelve, what did he expect?

He stared at me. My silence wasn't the response he was expecting. 'I'm waiting,' he said.

'I'll try,' I started. I didn't want this little bond we had built to end. If he eschewed me, I had nowhere else to go. Those lonely, wasted afternoons would return and that was the last thing I desired. Truth be told, my colloquial remark about normality had originated from my unfamiliarity with the lexicon. Most people don't want to be called 'not normal'. Not normal somehow equated to being abnormal, and while I had meant it to be a compliment, he seemed offended. I was struggling to find the words when—

Again: 'What did you mean by not being normal, bachcha?'

'Baba, you know I respect and adore you – you've been like a guru teaching me lots of magic tricks with cards and coins. I was only saying that … unlike my mother and father, you have a different lifestyle. You don't have to go to work daily to earn your bread, which, in our times has become a norm.'

'You are already a scion of a business empire. Isn't your father training you to take over?'

'Empire? He's got a shop and some days he returns without earning a paisa.'

'Hmm ... bachcha, I'm tired. I want you to massage my feet – they hurt. And you can leave after thirty minutes when you hear me snore.'

That was a *guru dakshina*, a fee owed to the master. It was Madari Baba who put me on the path of magic – I call it magic since he called it that.

'One day, you will do something great, bachcha,' he used to say. '*Tu bahut bada aadmi banega.*'

♦

Madari Baba died when I was fourteen years and two months old. It is very unfortunate and difficult when you cannot publicly mourn someone you loved and adored, who taught you so much. I didn't, at that point in my life, know that his teachings would fill my entire quiver of life skills. He was my only friend, but since no one knew about his role in my life, I had to stand there listening to the neighbours – including my parents – celebrate how a bad influence on society was dead. However cruel it might sound now, I kept my gob shut at the time.

There was little point in trying to explain the relationship we shared. He was my mentor, a guru, and he had never asked for anything in return. Yet, the belief most people in the neighbourhood held was that he was some kind of paedophile enticing young girls and boys, when I knew from experience that he was not. His biggest curse, I realized in time, was that he was penniless. Therein lies one of life's most jarring paradoxes:

we were poor – my family, our entire neighbourhood – and we endlessly criticized society for the class divide because those richer than us resented and kept away from us. Meanwhile, we did the same to those poorer than us. Go figure!

Madari Baba lived and died for his art and his skills, which never earned him any laurels or the money he deserved. But I wasn't going to tell these women and men that Madari Baba was a genius, and a decent man. I worried that if I showed any remorse, they might look down on me. I hated myself for not standing up for a man I truly loved and revered.

I know some people can compartmentalize various aspects of their lives. But my life was, and is, one big canvas where the colours mixed without my help. I grieved for a long time, and then life had to move on. Besides, what good would it do to Baba if I stood up for him after his death?

What would my parents think of me?

What would Puja Mahapatra think of me?

Now you will learn where I got my pseudonym Mahapatra from.

Puja was a girl who lived in the block opposite our dilapidated shanties; the block of houses where the rich and privileged lived. Her father was a mid-level manager in a paper factory. Paper factories were a dime a proverbial dozen in Saharanpur, exuding a foul smell across the city. Unlike my all-boys government school, where we turned up in wrinkled clothes, Puja went to a co-educational private school and wore the shortest skirt in her group. Truth be told, every time I saw her, it took me a while to look at her face. My eyes always went to her legs first and by the time I could look up, she had either sat in her car or the school bus. The few times I could catch her eye, she passed me a knowing smile, like she knew I was admiring her legs. Once – I kid you not – she saw me staring at her legs and rolled her skirt from the top, making it even shorter. She was gorgeous. She knew I came from across the street and maybe she was just teasing a slum-dweller, but you have no idea what the sight did to a fourteen-year-old Dimpy. That impression of shaved legs has stayed in my mind since then. Sometimes I wonder if she had been trying to send a message – though I know it is a fantasy – which never came to fruition.

In the coming months, I got to know that she was going around with a rich boy from her side of the road.

That boy was Ranjit.

Ranjit became friends with me solely because I had no inhibitions about buying cigarettes. He approached me, and not the other way around.

'It's more for my girlfriend than me,' he explained.

'Puja?'

'How do you know?'

'I've seen you both holding hands a few times.'

'No, how do you know her name is Puja?'

'Oh, I don't remember, someone told me …' I wasn't about to tell him that I fantasized about her, that I sometimes followed her from a distance and had once heard one of her friends call her name.

'She's hot, man … isn't she?'

What was I to say – that I was smitten too?

'So, she smokes?'

'Yeah, and I want to impress her, so if you buy a pack, I can give you half of it as a fee – win-win for both of us. What say?'

I wasn't stupid. I didn't smoke. I took the money, bought half a pack and pocketed the balance.

'If she's already your girlfriend, why do you need to impress her?' I asked.

'Simple. To get into her skirt, man. She's a nympho,' Ranjit's words, not mine, 'and if I don't get cigarettes for her, there are others – some of them older.'

That day onwards I took it upon myself to help Ranjit procure cigarettes for Puja, to ensure she didn't stray from my friend.

And trust me, I did my best.

I completely understood that Ranjit's friendship with me wasn't born out of altruistic reasons. His dad, Mr Bhatia, owned a few sugar mills and was one of the most talked-about persons on our side of the tracks, primarily because he had impregnated a woman outside of marriage – an extramarital romp. To the shock of us lesser mortals of Saharanpur, Mr Bhatia lived with the two women in the same house. Ranjit, being an illegitimate and only child, had more leeway with his parents than other children since he was shielded by both his mother and his *badi-maa*, Mrs Bhatia.

However, for whatever selfish reasons he had initially spoken to me, he was also the first person who had challenged the norms and become friends with me, someone from the other side of the tracks. He had no inhibitions coming to my derelict abode, or to ask me over to his plush residence.

He was my first real friend.

Still is.

The trouble was, being with him in his large house meant being with Puja, too. And she loved flashing her legs, which at that age was a turn-on.

But Ranjit and Puja came as a package.

One evening, Ranjit told me that he had finally succeeded in getting into her skirt. Not that I had any expectations – Puja was way out of my league, and there was little point in fighting a battle that you knew you could never win. You had to be a first-rate *chutiya* to do something like that, but I still felt a touch of jealousy. However, I wasn't going to let that affect our friendship in any way.

My father died when I was in class eleven. My mother cursed me, saying that his heart had failed him since his son was worthless. I admit I was pitiful at my studies, failed exams several times and was now repeating the grade with boys who were two or three years my junior. However, it wasn't like my father had believed I had a promising future after attending the government school I was in. If they ever made an alumni register at our school, the crème de la crème would be junior clerks and peons. Others might be running errands at local shops and restaurants. Some blessed ones might become business tycoons – cycle-puncture repairers, *istri-wallahs, dhobis*, vegetable vendors, *chai-wallahs*, *phool redi wallahs* – but to the best of my knowledge, none have come out with an IPO yet. Neither have they ever been featured in *India Today* or *Forbes*.

Truth is, I had no interest in my studies. Not the way they taught us anyway. The environment of the school and the teachers didn't even inspire me enough to cheat on the tests to pass. I just couldn't see the point of that education. I wasn't dumb; I had been a good student of Madari Baba. Whatever spare time I had after school, I used to rehearse the card and coin tricks I learned from him. I was scared I might forget if I didn't practise. Sometimes, I dazzled Ranjit and Puja with my performances.

A year later, I was still in class eleven – yes, failed again, but this time in science – when my mother passed away. Even though I never really loved my parents, I missed them. Children fail in school exams all the time. That usually didn't translate to their parents' untimely deaths. My parents lived an unnourished life; their life expectancy was never going to be the same as the Queen of England. Still, their deaths left a big vacuum in my life that I hadn't anticipated.

Life doesn't imitate a school or college – you don't have to pass one step to get to the next. For that matter, you can fail ten and then top the next hurdle.

The day after my mother was cremated, I began selling whatever little we owned – my father's little shop was rented, but it got me some goodwill money. The shanty went for fifty thousand rupees. In the end, altogether, I had seventy grand in cash.

I didn't want anything to do with Saharanpur anymore, but I didn't know where else to go. Delhi sounded right, and it wasn't too far, but Ranjit advised me to go to Mumbai.

'My dad's got an office there, and I might be moving there after college.' Unlike me, he was a good student, and while I struggled in school, he was about to complete his undergrad.

'But what will I do in Mumbai?'

'What were you planning to do in Delhi?'

'Find some work.'

'Then go and find work in Mumbai – I will call the peon in the office and ask him to let you in, so at least you have a roof over your head until you find some work.'

There was merit in this advice.

The Dehradun Express left Saharanpur a little after 4 p.m. Ranjit and Puja drove me to the station that afternoon and bought me a one-way ticket to Mumbai. Conscious of the fact that there was no pantry on the train, they also bought some snacks for me for the journey. I guess Ranjit didn't want me to spend money on the route. It was just another way to look after me.

Some thirty-seven hours and eighty-three stops later, I

arrived at Bandra Terminus. But the tedious journey was far from over.

♣

Ranjit and Puja got married after I left Saharanpur. They were only twenty-two, but Puja's parents were adamant they weren't going to send her to Mumbai with Ranjit if they didn't tie the knot. *'Koi oonch-neech ho gayee toh* what will people say?' Ranjit recited to me on the phone when he called to give me the news.

'I wanted to tell my mum that all the *oonch-neech* has already happened,' Puja said in the background. 'Sometimes I was under and he was on top, sometimes the other way around.'

Puja was funny.

'So, you're getting married?'

'Yes, and you have to attend the wedding, my friend.'

'I don't have money to travel.'

'I'll pay for the fare.'

'I have work here, I can't get leave.' I rolled out another excuse.

'Leave the job then. The three of us will return to Mumbai together after the wedding and sort something out.' Ranjit was insistent.

In the end, I explained to them how I felt: I'd be out of place in their crowd. Saharanpur didn't invoke any happy memories for me. I still missed my parents, and they would be coming to Mumbai after the wedding and honeymoon in any case, so we could meet up and party here.

They eventually relented.

SEVEN

'Love Story ... Just say "Yes"' – Taylor Swift

THE JOURNEY FROM SAHARANPUR TO MUMBAI WASN'T JUST A matter of distance. I was a simpleton, a philistine from a small town. I needed finesse to adjust. And finesse is difficult to come by if your entire education has been in Bhojpuri and no one's even taught you how to use a spoon, let alone forks and knives. We usually had rice and watery dal and pickles at home, and they were eaten with bare hands.

You will never move ahead if you let your past define you, someone once said. Right off the bat, I knew I would never belong as Dimpy Raja. I needed to move on and learn new skills. When I told Ranjit I wouldn't fit in, he was adamant that I try. He told me not to bother about the expense, and he stood by his word and sent me money. I enrolled in an English class to blend in. Bhojpuri would have got me a job as an errand boy in Mumbai, which wasn't what I wanted. I learnt to play the violin. Simultaneously, I picked up books on manners, etiquette, style, dressing up. I still, at most times, think in Bhojpuri, then translate into English in my mind before I speak. Not easy, believe me!

Real estate in Mumbai was exorbitant, but I was able to live in Mr Bhatia's office in Andheri East. It wasn't ideal, since I had to crash on the sofa in the reception, but I couldn't complain.

With all the quick-learning guides and private classes, I had spent most of my money, too and was on my last five-thousand rupees by the time Puja and Ranjit arrived in Mumbai.

They insisted I move into their Bandra residence with them and, notwithstanding my reluctance, they took me in as a lodger. It was awkward – them being newly married – hearing the high-spirited noises of *oonch-neech* and *aage-peeche* in the night, and seeing Puja in short cut-offs during the day. They made a lovely pair, and I always told them that if their baby turned out ugly, it was a sure sign that Puja had cheated.

I can be funny, too.

But it wasn't to be. Regardless of their active sex life – I only have audio confirmation from my initial days, but I know they weren't making those noises tickling each other or sucking on Naga chillies – they never had any children.

I played the violin at Puja's next birthday, and they were quite impressed. That was another turning point in my life.

'You should play professionally,' she said.

'You should, she's right,' said Ranjit.

'I can try.'

'In fact, I have an office party coming up. Why don't you play for us? There will be a lot of guests. I'm sure once people hear you play, you will get other offers, too.'

'I'd love to.'

'Could I give you some unsolicited advice?' Puja asked.

'Of course,' I said.

'I think you should change your name, too … don't get me wrong but if you ask me, Dimpy Raja sounds like a name from a run-down, tier-three town … sorry.'

'You make a valid point. So what should I call myself?'

'Something more common, humbler, which doesn't reveal where you come from?' she suggested, 'Maybe pick a common surname like Bhargava or Mathur or …'

'Mathur sounds good.'

'Saurabh Mathur,' Puja said.

'Why Saurabh?' I asked.

'Because before I came on the scene, a guy called Saurabh was desperate to get with Puja. Poor guy tried hard, I have to admit,' Ranjit explained.

Wordsworth once asked, 'What's in a name?' I know you are tempted to tell me that it was William Shakespeare and not William Wordsworth who said that. Same response: what's in a name? The name of the person who said it shouldn't matter. In any case, it was one of the Williams, right?

'Saurabh Mathur it is, then.'

Ranjit was right. After my performance at their company's annual function, I started getting offers to play violin at other parties.

I began earning decent money and decided to move out. I loved Puja and Ranjit to bits and I'd do anything for them, but I had started feeling like I was a serious intrusion on their privacy. I reasoned it out with Ranjit at his office because adding Puja to the debate would have meant a two-against-one I never would have won.

I moved to a small one-bed in Andheri East – near the office where I had initially camped when I came to town.

I met Roshan Godara a year later.

And 'Rahul Mahapatra' moved to Pedder Road a year after that.

♠

I met Zara at one of the parties where I was performing. She was quite a stunner, a Puja Bhatia née Mahapatra lookalike. Same physical build – both ectomorphs – petite, narrow hips, a wide forehead and auburn shoulder-length hair, with the well-defined square jawline, flattish chin and wide cheekbones that were classic hallmarks of what the world described as a square face.

For a second, I felt as if she was Puja's sister or a distant cousin, carrying the same genes.

'You're pretty good.' She came up to me as I was packing up after the party.

'Thanks.'

'I'm Zara Khan.' She pronounced it 'Z'ra', like Urdu for 'just' and not Zara like the fashion label.

'Nice to meet you, Zara. I'm Saurabh Mathur.'

'Where did you learn to play?'

'Well, just by watching others. How about you, what do you do?'

'I work for a private equity firm.'

'Who are you here with?' I wanted to know if she was single.

'Oh, this party is for one of our clients' fiftieth birthday, so I am representing my firm.'

Given the scale of the party, the catering, the cars in which other guests had arrived and the money spent by her client – also my client at the moment – it was evident that he was some big cheese at a foreign bank. And if she was representing her firm on the occasion, she wasn't some lightweight there either. Suddenly, my eyes took in her attire – it looked designer, her shoes spelt money, her jewellery was stylish.

At that moment I could see she was a better match for my other avatar, Rahul Mahapatra. Sadly, she had met Saurabh Mathur, a violin player for private parties. She was being polite, talking to me, but I knew that would be our first and last meeting unless I did something right away.

'Do you play any instrument?'

'Used to play sitar, but hardly get any time now.'

'Well, work-life balance is an art.' That was a smart one, even for me!

'It's easy for you to say, being an artist.'

'Do you believe in ghosts?' Why was I acting childish – what was the point of that question?

'No.'

'You just killed Phantom – the Ghost Who Walks.'

'Phantom wasn't a ghost.'

'You're getting technical. Do you believe in magic?' Was I misdirecting her without me knowing?

'No.'

'You just killed Mandrake, too.'

'Are you a magician then?' she asked.

I guessed it was time to stop. 'This,' I looked at my violin case, 'is my love. I have a full-time business to manage, but I do this since it is good for my soul.'

'Really? So, what do you do?'

'I own a large export house.' I recited Rahul Mahapatra's persona without using his name; the narrative I used to woo punters at gambling parties. I had promised myself I'd never mix the two avatars. But here I was, falling in love with one of the most gorgeous women, cast in the same mould as the first girl I had set my eyes on – what was the worst that could happen?

I could see she was impressed. 'Do you have a card?'

I did, but I couldn't hand her a card with another name. 'Not carrying one at the moment,' I apologized. 'Do you have yours at hand?'

'Of course.' She pulled one out from her expensive party clutch and gave it to me.

Zara Khan. Director. I was right.

'Why don't I give you a call sometime and maybe we can catch up over a coffee?'

'Sounds like a plan.'

I barely slept a wink that that night. Zara Khan kept pulling at my heartstrings. How corny is that line? No, you don't need to answer that one.

EIGHT

'Pyaar To Hona Hi Tha' – Eponymous OST

YOU MAY BE WONDERING WHETHER RANJIT AND PUJA KNEW about my multiple personas. They did. How else could I have explained my transition from a run-down one-bed flat in Andheri East to a two-bed on Pedder Road? They were the ones who suggested I use another name for the gambling activities. Ranjit explained that I needed to be vigilant at all times, stay under the radar and manage the money well. No flaunting, no ostentatious lifestyle, no attracting attention from neighbours. Who knows who might get suspicious and report me? Ranjit was a textbook businessman. He also advised that under no circumstances should I let my two personas mix, and that I should do my homework before turning up to either of the gigs.

Ranjit also told me he knew Roshan Godara, when he first proposed that we work together. 'He comes across as someone as straight as an arrow; he wouldn't even pee in the shower.' Those were his exact words.

'What is that supposed to mean?'

'Haven't you heard that there are just two kinds of people in this world – those who take a piss in the shower and others who lie?'

'Excuse me,' Puja stepped into the conversation, 'Showers

are supposed to be taken standing, and I am a girl, so what about me?'

'Technically, you can. It's not like your bladder snaps shut when you stand. It's not an impossible feat.'

'Oh, you're disgusting.'

'Well, at least I'm not a liar.' Ranjit chuckled.

'Thank you so much for your valuable insight, Dr Sigmund Bhatia.'

'So, what about Roshan Godara?' I wanted to know more about the man in order to decide if I should accept his offer.

'He seems to be a sincere guy on the surface. Goes by the book. Like he wouldn't do anything that makes him step outside the boundaries of the law, so I am amazed to find out that he gambles. Funny what you don't know about people you think you know.'

'What don't I know about you?' I asked in jest.

'Just what I told Puja. I am not a liar; I piss in the shower.'

'And from tomorrow, he won't be taking a shower in the ensuite,' said Puja.

'You're a liar then.' He winked.

Ranjit can be a crass comedian like that sometimes. Much like me. Which isn't strange. You can uproot a mango tree from Uttar Pradesh and replant it anywhere in the world; it may die, but if it bears fruit, it will be a mango. It's not so much about the soil as it is about the roots. Ranjit and I come from the same background, same town; we even liked the same girl. Once. If he or Puja ever knew about my feelings for her, they never showed it. Or did I miss the signs? Well, I was telling you this to establish Roshan Godara's credentials and look at me, I've been swept away once again.

'Don't get greedy, never get carried away, my friend,' Ranjit had warned me. 'Whatever happens, do not overdo it for any price. It's a small circle of people, a close-knit community – your reputation will precede you. Don't burn yourself.'

♥

And for a while, everything worked perfectly, like in paradise.

Do you know what the trouble with living in paradise is? Some dodo or egghead always ends up biting the apple. In this case, it was none other than yours truly. I had mixed my two identities to woo Zara.

Why was it so serious, I hear you wonder.

Because meeting Zara wasn't a one-time thing for me.

I would meet her again and again, and I couldn't simply walk up to her and say I had changed my name to Rahul Mahapatra now, could I? I should have – hindsight is always a good thing – stuck to being a violin player, and not claimed to be a businessman. One lie and I was already concocting more in my mind.

'You let your dick overrule your brain?' Ranjit laughed when I told him. We were sat in his office, sipping coffee. 'Let's call Puja, and ask her for a woman's perspective.'

Puja strongly opined that I should either forget about meeting Zara ever again or I should come clean. 'Tell her you lied about the business just to impress her.'

'I'm not sure she'll appreciate my candour.'

'Are you thinking with your brain or your dick?' she asked me the same question as Ranjit, point blank.

'Straight from the heart.'

'Is heart a new euphemism for dick?'

'There is a chance she'll never talk to me again.'

I think I've already told you that I had a crush on Puja back in the day. And now that I had found someone who so closely resembled her, it was like a childhood wish had come true. It was like being given a second chance. I wasn't going to mess that up for a little lie. I decided not to tell Zara the truth. Not immediately, at least. In time, if we got close, I'd break the news to her and explain to her why I did what I did. What I ignored was a lesson learned by so many before me – maybe Sigmund Freud had something to say about it, too, I don't know – every relationship needs truth before commitment. Else, you're headed for a downward trajectory from the start.

Well, for better or worse, I had made a decision and decided to stick to it.

I met Zara for coffee, a week later. We got along. I mean Zara Khan and Saurabh Mathur did. The violin-playing Saurabh Mathur with Rahul Mahapatra's business; it was a mix-up of personas from the start. My stupidity, my bad, of course.

◆

I introduced Zara to Puja and Ranjit, and we were able to catch up a few times. Soon, however, my friends got busy. Ranjit had diversified his family business – his father's sugar mills were facing harsh competition from other manufacturers and alternative sweeteners. They depended on sugarcane crops, and if a season was poor or the crop failed, the prices of raw sugarcane escalated. With fructose, sugar substitutes and all the crap that dieticians prescribed to lose weight, the family business wasn't bringing in as much money. Diversification became more of a necessity. And they got into a business where Puja could play a bigger role, too.

Ranjit's father bankrolled him into property development. This was Mumbai – anyone who had the money and could buy and sell property was a king. Ranjit started by buying small flats in various states of disrepair. He refurbished them, added modern interiors with Puja's input to drive up their value, and sold them at a profit. A few cycles of buying and selling – in the next three to four years – made them enough money to move to the next rung of the ladder. They became property developers: 'Bhatia Constructions' was small-scale, to begin with, but it was only a matter of time before they got into building small six- to eight-flat complexes. And then even bigger, more lavish and expensive ones.

There was no precise incident or moment in time, but Ranjit and I organically grew apart in the years that followed. I got busy, too, living several lives – gambling, playing the violin, performing tricks for kids and spending the rest of my time with Zara. She told me she had come to Mumbai from Hyderabad about five years back. Her parents were strict, and as such she had had no boyfriends before me. I preferred not to reveal that I hadn't had a girlfriend before her or that I once had a crush on my best friend's wife.

Zara was an anomaly. Okay, the whole debacle can be blamed on yours truly for being crafty, initially, and then being a chicken for not telling the truth, and I am more than happy to accept my part. However, Zara seemed like someone who wanted to break free desperately. A Muslim girl brought up in a conservative family in Hyderabad, she loved Mumbai. *Everything* about Mumbai – the place, her newfound freedom, her job, her rise in the corporate world that accorded her status and the fact that no one was looking over her shoulder and telling her what to do. She dressed flashily without inhibition and didn't have any unnecessary religious diktats telling her what she could or couldn't do. She drank, she smoked, she partied, she liked company. I was never brought up religious, so it didn't matter to me if she was a Hindu, a Muslim, a Parsi, a Jew or a Christian. I couldn't give a flier—I'm trying not to use cuss words in my diary as much as possible, but at some point, it might become impossible not to. Cursing is a part of life ... I have gone astray from the central narrative again, haven't I?

Where were we?

Yes, so Zara and I liked each other. Strike that. Zara and I fell in love.

Everything else remained the same. She was a banker or whatever in the finance industry, and I was a conman.

She was quite impressed I lived on Pedder Road. I was quite impressed she was interested in me. I mean I wasn't a tramp or a vagrant or a serial killer of some kind but still. For the longest time, we agreed not to quiz each other on our professional lives or how we made our livelihoods. Of course, I knew she had a steady income – a salary and quarterly bonuses – but I never asked anything more. Quite generous of her that she never questioned me either. Life was good.

But.

A lie is a lie.

And the truth is the truth.

And the truth is an asshole.

Every relationship needs the truth before commitment. Else, you're headed for a downward trajectory from the start. I think I've already mentioned that before.

I cannot blame it on anyone else.

I started on the wrong foot, whatever my justification was.

I ignored Puja's advice for whatever it was worth.

I carried on despite the odds stacked against me.

What did I expect? A miracle? A lottery? A freaking fluke of kismet?

NINE

'Love is a Losing Game' – Amy Winehouse

Lonavala was just over a two-hour drive from Mumbai. Zara picked me up in her gleaming black BMW X3. She had asked me why I didn't own a car while we were planning the trip, and I told her I was afraid to drive since my parents had died in a road accident. What else was I supposed to say? I couldn't tell her that all my income is unaccounted for and hence, owning assets is forbidden. And therein lay the dilemma. The lie I had blurted out to impress her constantly demanded further deceitful fabrications to shield it.

'So you don't drive?'

'I do, but only if I have to,' I lied through my teeth when, in reality, I would have loved to drive the Beamer on the scenic route, with Zara sitting beside me.

'I love to drive, I'll take you there and bring you back safe, don't worry.'

'Not worried at all,' I said, putting on my seat belt.

The drive was truly magnificent. It took us longer to get to Lonavala since we stopped for hot tea by the roadside. We left her car in the care of the tea vendor and walked along a trail across the plateau, holding hands. Zara was wearing a colourful fitted T-shirt and capris, and she looked stunning. I remember wondering if I would ever be able to come clean, considering how close we were, without the distractions of the city and her work schedule. We both wore walking shoes and as the route grew thinner and steeper, she walked in front of me while I trailed behind, watching her. In that moment, it occurred to me how fit she was. While she was willing to walk further – after a brisk five-kilometre walk – I was the one holding her back. I consider myself fit, but I couldn't keep up with her pace and energy. We returned to the car, savoured another over-sweetened masala chai and drove to our destination.

We stayed in a bungalow owned by the company Zara worked for. It was some kind of employee recreation facility. It had three bedrooms, a small swimming pool, and it came with a caretaker and a cook. I was elated when I spotted the barbeque by the poolside. Living in a flat in Mumbai, that was a luxury not many could afford.

Soon after we arrived, I gave money to the caretaker for beer and chicken, and headed to the pool. Meanwhile, Zara went to the bathroom for a shower.

I honestly thought that the time had come to tell her the truth, to own up and face the consequences. What was the worst that could happen? She'd leave me in my swimming shorts and drive back alone? Or kick me out of the guesthouse? As I always do, I had prepared a small script – I was an orphan (true), brought up under difficult circumstances (true), had a deprived childhood (true) and hence, had lied to her because I did not want to lose her. It sounds pathetic, yeah, I know! Like a Z-grade flop film script. But what would you have done?

Even that would only be confessing to half my sins. If she bought my story – which wasn't a total lie – the next part, the more difficult part to explain, would be to tell her what I really did for a living. That I was no commodities exporter who had offices around the world; I was a flipping conman, a cardsharp, and playing the violin was just a front in the event someone came asking how I earned my bread. That I wasn't a business graduate from Delhi University, but a school dropout from Saharanpur; that my parents hadn't died in a car accident, and the closest they ever got to any kind of vehicle was other people's bicycles that my father repaired; that I first liked her because I had a mad boy-crush on Puja and Zara resembled her.

How would she react to that?

Kick me in the rear and send me home, perhaps.

There is a fundamental problem in coming clean; for everyone, I suppose, and not just me. How far back should one go? How much truth does one reveal? How much can you add or subtract from the truth for it to still be true? Is a half-truth true? If you don't embellish the truth but omit certain portions, is it okay?

I was lost in my thoughts about how to start the conversation when Zara appeared. She had wrapped a white towel around her bust, over her swimsuit.

'I thought you'd be in the pool by now.'

'I was waiting for you.' I got up from the recliner.

That was when she dropped the towel, and I dropped all thoughts of revealing any truth I had been contemplating. She wore a white bikini, and I decided – I am quick at making decisions – that I wasn't going to ruin this vacation by boring her with mundane stuff like my real name, my past, my profession. She looked gorgeous. I had seen her without clothes before, but we were slightly conservative, so we generally made love in the bedroom, where the lighting was dim. The bright sunlight and the sparkle from the water highlighted her smooth and unblemished skin even more.

'Haven't you seen a girl in a bikini before, Saurabh?'

'Girls, yes, but never a goddess in the flesh.' You see, Mr Smooth again.

'Goddess, wow! You sure know how to make a girl feel special, even if it's by using cheesy lines.'

We remained by the poolside for three hours. In and out, resting on the recliners. The caretaker had got us beers and cheese and masala peanuts, so we didn't need to go in for anything. He lit the barbeque around seven and made tandoori chicken. Lip-smacking good. It might not be surprising that I never once got the opportunity to tell Zara about myself. Or maybe I had lost the inclination to confess.

We retired at nine and made love twice. Later, as we lay in bed naked, my left arm under her head, I have no idea what came over me. I can't explain.

'My father wasn't a good man,' I blurted out, not knowing why or why *now*. Misdirection?

'Why do you say that?'

'He was a drunk ... and at times he hit my mom. And me.'

'I'm so sorry. That must have been very difficult for you. What did you do?' She turned, lifting herself on her elbow, and faced me.

'I used to run away to a friendly old neighbour and hide at his place. He was single, an artist of some kind and worked from home most days. He never asked me anything, never expected anything in return. Over time, I grew quite fond of him.'

It was all true; my dad did occasionally slap us both – my mom and I – and the friendly old neighbour I used to run to was Madari Baba.

'Where is that neighbour now?'

'Unfortunately, he passed away long before my parents.'

'I'm sorry.' She bent forward and kissed me, and I could feel my manhood stirring again. 'Can I ask you a question?'

'You just did.'

'Okay, can I ask you another question?'

'You just did that too.'

'Make love to me.'

'That isn't a question.'

We made love a third time and drifted into sleep. I woke up a little after four in the morning; through the tiny gaps in the curtains, I could see the predawn light. I got up and tiptoed out to the poolside and lay down on the recliner. I pondered if it was a good idea to bare some of my buried childhood memories to Zara. I mean … when I arrived here, I had wanted to tell her the truth, hadn't I? And instead of coming clean, I was embroiling her in a further web of love and lies.

Lately, this feeling that I was betraying Zara had overtaken me. I was lying all the time. And with every lie, the probability of getting caught geometrically progressed. How was I to keep an account of what I had told her and what I hadn't? All liars need damn good memories. Like a new software upgrade, 2.0 shouldn't make the previous version redundant in any manner. Another thing: lies don't just add up, they multiply. The more lies you tell, the more efficient you have to be at keeping track, or you will contradict yourself at some point. Two lies always run the risk of getting entangled like iPod cables.

My double life was no exception.

I knew I'd be misunderstood when she came to know the truth about me. Or should I say I'd be understood for what I was, since I had been the one misinforming her the whole time?

♣

Love is beautiful. While they say real love blooms in an instant – much like Nescafé – it takes a while before you taste the real thing. But it also only takes a moment for everything to end. Like the mug of instant coffee slipping out of your hand, crashing on the hard floor – it's over.

In the end, I know one thing: you cannot hide forever. You will eventually make a mistake. If not you, someone else will make it on your behalf, trust me. There are enough nosy parkers in this world. And sometimes they aren't even nosing around. Circumstances bring them into play. I guess you just have to be unlucky. But to tell you the truth, I was becoming lackadaisical, careless. As you can imagine, it had become so simple – like second nature – for me to slip between my personas, to lie impromptu, that I stopped worrying about being caught out. I convinced myself that maybe the situation would take care of itself somehow. Yeah, like a rabbit closing his eyes when he sees headlights, I know.

I won and lost the love of my life. And I had no one else to blame.

Zara had been to my Pedder Road flat several times. She lived at Churchgate, and she was paying a fortune. She had hinted she could move in with me and even offered to pay, but I wasn't ready. That was my excuse, though it was more because I hadn't told her the truth. If I agreed to having her live with me, the truth would be out sooner than I wanted. She'd know when I went out to play cards, she'd know I wasn't born into wealth, she'd know I wasn't just a violinist, she'd know I was a freaking conman. See I avoided a cuss word again. Proud of me now, aren't you?

But the truth – pardon my French – is a real bastard.

Truth finds a way to escape into the real world, irrespective of how hard you try to keep a lid on it.

And it happened in a flash. When I least expected it. You see, I had gotten accustomed to my life. Zara and I. She came over weekends, we spent the entire time in bed; we loved each other, we found each other's company exhilarating. Our lovemaking – thanks to compatible sexual desires and needs and wants – was bliss. Heaven!

But this double life required a lot of effort. I ensured she never came to the flat in my absence. I hid all my post and any other evidence of two personalities living under one roof. I used to confirm, twice, when she'd arrive so I was at home, and no delivery in the wrong name arrived while she was there.

But even the best of conmen falter and fall.

Who was to know what would happen next?

Who was to know that Zara would have some kind of fallout with one of her clients for making unwanted advances, leading to an adverse ramification with her boss?

She left office at lunchtime in the aftermath of her not-so-friendly discussion with her stupid boss and decided – instead of going home – to drive to my place without notifying me in advance. Usually, I stayed at home in the day, since most of my engagements – irrespective of which role I played, violin player or cardsharp – took place between evenings to late nights.

You could call it forsaken luck or kismet or fate. I had stepped out to access one of my bank lockers – you might not know this, but some banks are pretty firm that if a particular locker isn't 'accessed' within a twelve-month period, it is deemed to be inactive, giving them the right to open it and claim all it contains; rogues of the first order. But it is what it is. So I had to travel to a small place in Versova to open and close the locker, and to complete some paperwork as its owner. If you know Mumbai, going from Pedder Road to Versova and back (with an hour to complete the bank formalities) can take a while. It took me four hours that day. The most damning four hours of my life.

In my absence, when Zara turned up at my Pedder Road flat and found it locked, she approached my neighbour. We just had two flats per floor and my neighbours were a Sindhi family called Daswani. Mr Daswani was out, at work, and so were the children, but Mrs Daswani took it upon herself to call Zara in for a tea. Over tea, she was confused by Zara's inquiries because no Saurabh Mathur lived next door to her.

'But it is Rahul Mahapatra's flat.'

'Who's Rahul Mahapatra?'

'The guy who lives next door.'

'There must be some mistake, I am looking for Saurabh Mathur, who—'

'No way, unless you're on the wrong floor.'

'Of course not, I've visited him enough times—'

'But I have signed to receive couriers for him a few times; he's Rahul Mahapatra.' Mrs Daswani was curious now.

'How is that possible? We have been dating for almost two years …'

'Are we even talking about the same guy?'

'You only have one other flat on this floor, right?' Zara asked. She described me physically and Mrs Daswani nodded and agreed – yes! That was what Rahul Mahapatra looked like.

'So we can't be talking about two separate people, can we?'

'No, we can't, unless I've missed the fact that the flat is shared by two men.'

'No way!' Zara exclaimed, 'Like I said, I've visited him enough times to know if someone else resided with him.'

'There has to be some mistake.'

'What kind of mistake?'

'I don't know, I'm just saying. The guy who lives in the

flat across from us is definitely Rahul Mahapatra, no question about that.'

'And the guy I've been dating for a few years, and the one who lives across your flat on this floor, is Saurabh Mathur. We can't both be right.'

'No, we can't.' Mrs Daswani was as flabbergasted as Zara, I suppose.

'So what do we do, how do we find out which one of us is wrong?'

'I have an idea.' Mrs Daswani raised her index finger like a teacher.

'What is it?'

'Stay here, make yourself comfortable. He will be back in a while … when he arrives, I'll step out and call him "Rahul". You can hear his response and make up your mind then – does that make sense?'

'Yes.'

'Now, how about another cup of tea?'

'That would be lovely, Mrs Daswani, thank you.'

♠

I got out of the elevator two hours later and Mrs Daswani stepped out of her house to greet me. 'Hi, Rahul … how're you?'

'I'm good, Mrs Daswani,' I responded, just before I saw Zara emerge through my neighbours' door.

It was over.

As much as I tried to explain that I used a pseudonym to perform at parties so that my customers couldn't identify me – and that the alias was taken from Puja's maiden name – Zara's ears and brain had already been closed to any sort of justification. And to be fair …

'You didn't think you should have told me this in all the time we've known each other?'

'I didn't think it mattered.'

'We spent days together, we went for a holiday together, we made love and you didn't think you could tell me the truth? When I was candid enough to tell you I come from one of the strictest families in Hyderabad, where girls weren't allowed to mix with men after puberty. And I gave you my virginity – seriously, have some balls to tell me the truth.'

Though my softened lies weren't helping, I knew the truth would, indeed, shatter her. What could I say in my defence? I had always known I'd be in real deep doo-doo when she found out; no comeuppance could expiate me now, but I tried.

'I was only trying to protect you from—'

'Who died and made you my parent? Why do you need to protect me? What a prick, you misogynist.' We were now inside my flat and she was getting louder by the second.

'Calm down, Zara, give me one more chance—'

'Saurabh or Rahul or whatever your real name is,' she said, and I didn't want to add Dimpy Raja into the mix, 'I will love you forever, but I will never trust you again ... and before you ask, yes, I can do both.' Her voice was laden with scorn. Umbrage. With that, she turned, dried her eyes and walked out of my flat and my life, leaving incipient tears in my eyes.

I wanted to stop her, to explain, but I knew it would be impossible to fix the broken relationship. Broken trust can be worse than broken glass – it might sound cheesy, but it's true.

But.

Would you condemn me if I said I felt a bit relieved?

Don't get me wrong, I was sad, but to be honest, also relieved. I never deluded myself. I had known this day would come.

An hour after the break-up with Zara – if it can be called that – I walked down from my flat to buy some alcohol. A bottle of Jack Daniels was required to ease myself into the new life of being single again. I felt let down by my own self.

As I walked back, a homeless guy was sitting on the pavement. He looked at me with beseeching eyes … he saw me approach, but he didn't say anything, didn't ask me for money. As I passed him, he said, in a near whisper, '*Offer nahin karoge sahib?*'

I turned and checked. Perhaps I had imagined it. '*Kuch bola?*'

He pointed at the bottle in my hand; although it was concealed in a brown paper bag, it was obvious what it was. I looked at the bottle, looked at him. He gave me a big toothless smile. He appeared over sixty, although seeing that he had lived a rough life, it was hard to tell.

'It's okay, don't want, don't give, sahib.' He sounded embarrassed. Maybe the previous guy he asked for a drink hadn't obliged, or had responded rudely. There are all sorts of assholes in this world. Like me, for example. I didn't want to sit there with that strange, homeless guy and share the contents of my bottle.

'We can share if you come to my flat, not here.'

'No the bother at all, sahib,' he responded in broken English. He sounded afraid this time. Maybe he had had a bad experience joining someone to share a drink at their flat; maybe he felt claustrophobic inside a room. 'I okay, no drink, you go. No problem.' He politely gestured for me to leave.

I pulled out my wallet, took out two thousand rupees – the cost of the bottle I had just purchased – and handed it over to him. 'You know where to buy it, don't you?'

'Yes sahib, good sahib.' He performed a mock salute. I walked on.

That night, I turned into George Thorogood: *one bourbon, one scotch, one beer* … although, technically, Jack Daniels isn't a bourbon but that is a minor detail we can overlook, can't we?

After a week of wallowing in my grief, locked up in my flat with my phone switched off, I picked myself up, dusted myself off and moved on.

Mr Resilient.

PART TWO

'The Axe forgets; the tree remembers.'

AFRICAN PROVERB

ELEVEN

'Duniya Mein, Logon Ko Dhoka …'
– *Apna Desh* OST

29 February

IT'S A LEAP YEAR. THEY SAY IT BRINGS ONE LUCK, NOT THAT I believe it. A leap year isn't what most people imagine it to be. It isn't that the earth decides to take a detour and spend an extra day going around the sun every four years. The earth takes longer than 365 days to complete its rotation and every four years, we tot up those accumulated hours and add a day to the calendar. How can a little arithmetic of that sort change fortunes? Even if, for a second, I agree it *is* lucky – who is it lucky for? It can't be for the entire universe. Some have to lose for others to win, don't they? Anyway, enough about leap years. I have other things on my mind. I've been out of work now for almost six months.

Money is the least of my worries. I have risen from that underprivileged, deprived life in Saharanpur where two meals a day was considered a luxury. Starting from scratch in Mumbai has brought its fair share of struggles, but fiscal worries are now in the past. I am not starving. My needs are still basic. I can afford to live on Pedder Road, paying the high rent without taking out any loans … who'd give me a loan anyway? And

Zeenat and I can survive on the money I have stashed for years to come. Some might think I am living in the lap of comfort, in paradise.

But I am a gamester at heart. And let me tell you that gambling is never about money. It's not about winning or losing either. If you ever have a heart-to-heart with a gambler, you'd know that gambling is about anticipation – when the cards are on the table, and you're playing blind, the adrenaline gushes through your veins as much as after you've seen your cards. It is because of the thrill and not the cards per se.

I have lost big in life, and it has been eating away at me. Anand Kumar seems to have gotten away with sending me to prison, and that does not sit well with me at all.

Being single doesn't help. Although, in some ways, I am glad Zara broke up with me when she did. Imagine if she had been around when I got busted. She was so agitated and shaken up when she found out my real name wasn't what I said it was. If she came to know that I wasn't a successful exporter but a failed gambler, she'd have gone ballistic. Picture that.

I am not alone; Zeenat lives with me – turning on her cunning Mona Lisa smile when she needs feeding or caressing – but the fact remains that I am still single. (As if she can read my thoughts, Zeenat has just walked up to sit next to me.)

;)

Before I forget, I want to ask if you realized that I skipped an entry in my diary? I jumped from Entry Nine to Eleven. I couldn't have done it if I hadn't engrossed you in that African proverb on the previous page. Bet you didn't even notice.

That, my friend, is called misdirection.

I might do it again. Remember, *Dhoka Kabhi Ho Jaata Hai!*

Let's not pretend to be saints and act moralistic, please. We all do what we need to, and we all have regrets. My regrets aren't about money. Oh no, not at all. I have enough to last a lifetime, like I said. On balance, I can leave Mumbai – or stay here without making any noise for the rest of my life – but the three-month prison sentence I had to endure still hurts me. It has been distressing me more since I got out. Why was *I* put there? What purpose did it serve for Anand Kumar? I met him just once, at that game night, and I wasn't the one who had swindled the money off him. From his perspective, it was Roshan who had won, it was Roshan who had fleeced him, so really, it should have been Roshan whom Anand had any grudge against. Perhaps he couldn't afford to go up against Roshan but … why me? The question has been bothering me to no end.

♥

I began just for the heck of it. Maybe it was to simply ease the demons troubling me, but I had to do it. No apologies, no sympathies. 'Sympathy,' I once heard from Danny Bhoy, the Scottish-Indian stand-up, 'is a word in the dictionary between shit and syphilis.'

Ergo, I followed Roshan for over a week. It is not difficult to follow someone without them knowing they have a tail, especially if you know their routine, their habits, their office, residence and car, trust me on this. Within a week I knew that Roshan bloody Godara and Anand Kumar were still buddies, and they still played together. That's when the fly in the ointment started to become a full-blown hurt.

They had conned me. Maybe it was convenient for Roshan to shake hands with Anand after he lost that night, or it could be that they had set me up. Roshan might have decided he wanted to end his partnership with me. Maybe someone had warned him; maybe someone had caught on to my moves?

In that event, what better tactic to get me out of the way? One man's loss is another's gain. People don't ever miss the opportunity to wish upon a falling star. If they can exploit your misfortune, they will. Roshan made me play with him, *for* him, until it suited him; made money using my talent, and then discarded me.

Am I overthinking this?

No, I'm not overthinking this.

Something isn't right.

Adding to my mental agony is the fact that Roshan hasn't answered any of my calls or responded to my messages.

Why?

Maybe I am getting anxious. Emotional, even. And this requires a cerebral response, not an emotional one. But I need answers, or I know this little dilemma will keep troubling me. I haven't met Ranjit and Puja since I got out – I've spoken to them on the phone a few times, promised them I'd come over to their place but cancelled last minute twice. It may be that I am embarrassed. Ranjit had come to see me when I was arrested, he was present in the courtroom, too, but I haven't seen Puja at all. As a matter of fact, I haven't seen Puja since Zara broke it off with me, which feels like another lifetime. We were so close once. And it isn't Puja who is to blame. It is my own foolishness. I feel ashamed not because Zara left me – well, that is there too – but because Puja had predicted it, forewarned me about it happening for the very same reason that it did.

Perhaps it is time to go and renew these old ties. They are my best friends. I am confident they will ignore my little peccadillo and accept me with open arms. We'll all laugh it off together.

♦

When I visited Puja and Ranjit a few days later, everything had changed since we'd last met. They now lived in a palatial penthouse in Worli. Dual-aspect glass windows overlooked the Arabian Sea, a vista one could only imagine in their dreams. I knew Ranjit had diversified and expanded his dad's business, so I should have expected it. He had visited me once in prison to let me know about their housewarming party, but I couldn't attend for obvious reasons. Just for your info, they don't let you out of jail to attend such events.

But there I was, in the here and now. Puja gave me a tight hug and held on to me. For the first time in my life since I had seen Puja or known her, there was a lack of sexual energy; I no longer felt the tension I used to whenever I was around her. The magic of having had Zara in my life lingered on. Maybe I was a Zara Man now and forever. Ha-ha! I too could love Zara and be without her. Like she had said, I could do both.

'How have you been?' Puja asked.

'Well …'

'You know, you don't have to answer that. I know you've been through a lot.' Puja was in shorts and a thin T-shirt, but instead of being attracted to her in the way I used to be, I felt the warmth of a friend. Call me soppy and old-fashioned, but I was emotional and could sense waterworks coming, so I held on to her a while longer until I was sure they wouldn't betray me.

'I'm good,' I finally managed to say.

'A lot has happened since we last met,' she said. 'I'm sorry I didn't visit you at Arthur Road' – I was glad she didn't say the word *prison* – 'I swear I wanted to, but Ranjit said it wasn't advisable considering the circumstances—'

'He was right.' Mr Understanding, aren't I?

'Ranjit is taking a shower, what would you like to drink?'

'Whatever you are having.' Her breath revealed that she had already had a drink.

'G&T?'

'Yes, please.'

♣

'So what are you saying?' Ranjit asked. We were six or seven, maybe eights drinks down – who was counting? – when he acknowledged my theory. After following Roshan for a while, watching him mingle with Anand Kumar, I had come up with a hypothesis: Anand must have gone after Roshan when he lost big that night in February, who, in turn, had blamed it all on me. Which made it all fair and square between him and Anand.

Ranjit revealed that Roshan had encouraged him to hire a lawyer for me; it could be that his guilty conscience was troubling him, or perhaps he just wanted to ensure he was kept out of this whole mess. Ranjit was also aware that Roshan and Anand were still – at the very least – friendly. The sleuthing I had done was unnecessary. He'd seen them together on multiple occasions, so in all probability they were still playing cards in the same circles. Which further advanced my theory that I was just a pawn. And that infuriated me even more.

'Water under the bridge …' Puja said. Our dinner was over; lamb chops, grilled with a homemade spice rub, served with mushrooms in a white wine sauce. Exceptionally tasty! Puja and Ranjit have always been exceptional hosts; they love their food. Food is one of the … sometimes I don't even know where I am going with a sentence, analogies don't come to my mind. Maybe I will fail at misdirection when I perform next. Have I lost my touch?

Back to the point, Puja was spot-on in a way. Was there any use in waking up sleeping stray dogs now?

No, you might say.

I say yes. I want to. I will.

'I need to sort out this mental turmoil,' I said.

'How?'

'I have an idea, but I'll need your help.'

'Anything,' Ranjit said.

'As long as it is legit,' Puja added, and then put in another qualifier immediately. 'Or fun.'

'Fun, surely.'

'So I take it that it's not legit then?'

'Two negatives make a positive, don't they?' I asked.

'What do you mean?'

'What I have in mind isn't *strictly* legit, so anyone claiming to be virtuous shouldn't be in attendance.'

'Please elaborate while I fix us another drink,' Ranjit said and walked away.

When he returned, I told them how cheated and used and frustrated and disgusted I felt. I played on their emotions: how badly their friend had been treated at the hands of a conniving businessman whom Ranjit had once thought of as respectable. Oh, I can act; I can be a drama queen when I want to be. I told them about how rigorous my imprisonment was. It's called rehearsed authenticity; I've practised it – you guessed it – in front of a mirror more than a hazaar times, except this time it was for the greater good, and not to swindle my friends. My only friends. I needed to give a flawless performance.

'You're crazy,' Ranjit exclaimed, walking away to the bar, fetching the bottle of Jack Daniels and calling out to the maid to get some cans of Diet Coke. He was definitely interested. He hadn't shunned me. Not yet.

'It can work.' Puja.

'No way, and it may not be worth it.' Ranjit.

'It will be totally worth it, I'm in.'

'What do you think is your role in it?'

'The whole production and direction.'

'Two against one, Ranjit.' I added.

Puja winked as though some deal was getting sealed. Perhaps it was.

'I have to think.' Ranjit.

'About?' Me.

'It will cost.' Ranjit.

'We know.' Puja.

'And there will either be big returns or no returns.' Ranjit.

'You get the first cut. Even if you take the entire winnings, I won't complain.' I offered.

'I won't rob you, but yes, I might borrow some of your share and invest in your name.' Ranjit.

'Of course.'

'Worst case—' Ranjit.

'There is no worst case if we play our cards right.' Me.

'I think so, too. Only losers plan for the worst case.' Puja. Yes, she sounded a bit high.

'Really, have you both applied to become motivational gurus?' Ranjit.

'Maybe. You in or out?' Puja.

'Oh. Em. Gee. Give me time to think.' Ranjit.

'And let me plan every detail.' Me.

We left it at that for the day. It was midnight, and we were all over our limits. Any decision we made might not have been balanced. Oh, the irony – what part of the plan was rational anyway?

'Stay here tonight,' Puja said.

I didn't argue.

We finished our drinks. Ranjit yawned and retired for the day, but Puja said she couldn't sleep. She was as riled up as me, and wanted to stay up to fine-tune our plan further. *Our plan.* I could see her pupils were dilated with excitement. But we needed a lot more intel.

And lots of money – which, between us, we had.

TWELVE

'Can't Get You Out of My Head' – Kylie Minogue

DDLJ

'*HUM SHAREEF KYA HUE … POORI DUNIYA HI BADMASH ban gayi.*' Remember the dialogue? It was said by Shah Rukh Khan in a film called *Dilwale* which, unfortunately, didn't do so well at the box office. It was meant to be another blockbuster with SRK and Kajol after DDLJ. *Dilwale Dulhania Le Jayenge.* I guess you know by now that I go off on a tangent sometimes – that I misdirect – but if you've stayed with me, please indulge me long enough to tell you why I got reminded of this dialogue. For once, it isn't misdirection.

Then again, it might be.

It's not funny how quickly things can change. Since I started my research, after that night at Puja and Ranjit's, I've become aware that in the last six months or so – since I've been out of the circuit – a few casino-like operations have started in Mumbai.

Unlicensed, of course.

All functioning very much under the radar. I'm fairly certain the cops in the city are aware, but they are getting paid a substantial amount to look the other way. I wouldn't put it past them.

Do you think *Chamiya* bars – where girls dance to Bollywood tunes and men shower them with cash – are licensed? No, but they thrive all over the city. In empty car parks and abandoned factories, behind warehouses and real bars – but you can only find them if you're looking for them. Your average Bhola Nath *jee* doesn't just stumble across them.

The police overlook these bars. There are bigger criminals to catch, and more serious crimes to investigate than to go around arresting small players like dancing girls or the club owners and patrons. Maybe that is the axiom the Mumbai Police follows.

These unlicensed casino-like places are still only a few. Unlike a Chamiya bar, the money that changes hands in these casinos is mind-numbing and unbelievable. Crores. With that kind of money comes protection. The police cut will also be big, which explains why they look the other way. It all makes sense.

Moreover, the people or groups running such enterprises don't fit the Bhola Nath profile. They are gangs, mafia organisations, the *bhai*-world people who control the police through the politicians. Very likely, they operate with the blessings of someone high up the ladder. The constable you see in the streets hardly has any power, except taking a hundred-rupee note off a traffic rule-breaking motorcyclist. He might hang around such prospering illegal businesses and score a free drink or two at the end of the shift, but that's about it. It's always a *bada*-sahib somewhere who's the puppeteer, pulling strings, making a killing, taking kickbacks. We all know. We all ignore it. Crime is only illegal if the criminal gets caught. Sacred cows can graze in peace. This world is built on hypocrisy. Capisce?

It merely took me a week to contact my old sources and get them to do a thorough recce to establish that there are only three such casinos in operation today. Blessed by different *bhais.* No one knows the name of the owners. The manager would rather die than reveal them.

It all started with one outfit in Dadar. As soon as one mushroomed, three other followed. Copycats. One closed after just a month of operation. The three that remain – in Dadar, Bandra and Versova – are thriving now. They are not open 24/7; they are not open 365 days either – this isn't Las Vegas. They're not that blatant. They assemble once, maybe twice a month. I'm informed women play too, which was a welcome surprise. I'm not a misogynist like Zara pointed out when she kicked me out of her life, but I found it hard to imagine women wanting to come and bet and gamble at seedy joints. I rapidly realized that these places are anything but. They pretend to be extremely professional outfits. Classy joints. They have croupiers, Eastern European barmaids in skimpy outfits, jukeboxes, the whole works – a mock Vegas. Like cheer girls at IPL matches; a leaf from the book of basketball league matches in the US. I mean, honestly, since when did cricket need cheer girls?

Well, if punters have to deposit crores in cash upon entry into a mock casino, the decor and the operation better live up to the clientele. That's only fair, I suppose.

I can't wait to see one.

But.

Entry is by invitation only. Understandable. If only a select group of people know about something like this, it's easier to contain it. The owners want to keep it simple, but that makes it challenging for me.

I can't just walk in. I need to know someone who's a member, who will introduce me, vet me and vouch for me. Those are the rules. After all, ten to twenty-five crores can be won or lost in a single night. Oh, and there's one other piece of information I've picked up. Since these three casinos are run by three different organisations, the patrons generally subscribe to only one of them. They don't mix. Doesn't surprise me one bit, if I am honest. What amazes me is that there are so many high rollers in Mumbai that they can feed three such places, since each of these casinos has six to seven tables and each table has a minimum of four to five players. Like I said, a lot has changed in the few months I've been out of the loop. See I wasn't pointing you in the wrong direction this time. So please let me say it again: *'Hum shareef kya hue … poori duniya hi badmash ban gayi.'*

Time to get back into the circuit.

You might say I'm planning to infiltrate the wrong place. I'll be recognized and rejected the moment I step into one of those casinos.

But what if you are wrong?

What if no one sees me?

You can't stop what you cannot see, can you?

I'm confident I'll win big this time. I'm confident I can play the part of a puppeteer.

Confidence. Yes, that's the name of the game.

♠

'That is all good, but I thought we were just having fun the other night, I didn't think you were serious, Dimpy,' Ranjit told me – yes, he still calls me by that name sometimes, although not in public – on the phone when I called to update him with my research. His words flattened my spirit like a bottle of cola losing its fizz. I couldn't believe I had gotten carried away and spent two weeks of my life investigating. Maybe I could sell my market research to some company or a doctoral student for their thesis if I could find one. What was I thinking?

'But …' I said, not being someone who gives up, 'hear me out.'

'Go on, tell me,' he said. I could sense his lack of interest through the line.

'Not on the phone,' I told him. Telephonic conversations are not conducive to such clandestine plans. How do you know who is on the other side along with the person you're talking to? Even if you're talking to your best friend, you have no idea who else is in the room with them. For all you know, what you plan to say might not be something your friend thinks is important – Ranjit was already dismissing my plan as a fantasy – and doesn't care who listens in. You might end up revealing your million-dollar idea to a third person.

'It's not like the olden days, there are no wires someone can tap into,' Ranjit mocked me. I could visualize his face as he did that, I've known him long enough. I was sure he was rolling his eyes.

I realized talking to Ranjit was futile. The only way to convince him was to get Puja on my side. I felt a sudden pang of anxiety: what if Puja was as dismissive of my plan as Ranjit? She seemed interested two weeks ago, but so did Ranjit. We hadn't spoken since that day. What if the other night, at their fancy penthouse, they saw my entire plan as a drunken man's revenge fantasy drama script? Well, I can't lie to you, it did begin as a revenge scheme to get back at Anand Kumar and Roshan, but the more I thought about it, the more I realized how devious my plan was. If I got Ranjit and Puja on my side, it could succeed. The inverse was also true. Without their help, my plan was a deflated balloon. 'You must be busy now, I'll come over in the evening,' I told him before disconnecting the call.

There was only one way to find out if Puja was still interested. I called her.

'Where have you been for the last two weeks, I called you twice.'

'No …' I put my iPhone on speaker and looked at my missed calls. 'Did you leave a message?'

'No, I thought you'd call me back when you saw a missed call.'

'When did you call?' I was still scrolling on the screen. Then it struck me: 'Have you blocked your caller ID?'

'Not me, I don't even know how to do that. But – hang on a minute – Ranjit used my phone the other day to call someone when his phone was out of juice so he might have … sorry. Now I know why you didn't call back. My mistake. How do I switch that back on?'

I walked her through the steps to change the settings.

'Anyway, even if I didn't call, where have you been? AWOL for over two weeks?'

'I was reconnoitring the market—'

'What happened to our cunning plan?'

I could kiss her. If she was asking about that plan, it meant she hadn't given up on it like Ranjit had. I had an ally. 'You didn't let me finish; I've been reconnoitring the market for just that.'

'Oh good! I wondered if all that we spoke about the other night was just talk. When are we meeting to discuss it further?'

'I just spoke to Ranjit, and he dismissed the whole thing saying it's unreal and not something he thinks is worth taking forward.'

'Is he crazy? I mean, it has been a long time since I've gotten so excited about something, and he thinks it is unrealistic? Why don't you come over today and we can convince him together.'

Just what I was thinking, I could have said, but I didn't. 'When?'

'Anytime. He should be back by seven, but why don't you come over now – let's discuss what you've found out and make a firm business proposal for Ranjit. That's the only way he'll understand. He is, after all, a businessman.'

'Makes sense.'

'See you soon … we'll order biryani for dinner.'

It's nearly noon now. Rajkumari Zeenat has returned from her stroll or her late-morning hunt, and is looking at me as if I was supposed to have completed the household chores and kept her meal ready: *what do you mean my lasagna isn't ready yet, servant boy?* In the few months she has been with me – and despite her crafty tactics – I have started appreciating her company. I love her.

'Chicken or fish?'

Don't care, servant boy, just put it on my plate quickly. She brings out her tongue and licks her nose and lips. Her whiskers are wet too, shining and twitching. I should go serve my mistress and head into the shower.

I know Her Royal Highness will be gone by the time I come out of the bathroom. I am blessed to receive such love and loyalty in return, you see.

On the way to Puja's place, I thought about it all once again. Ranjit had been dismissive of the plan. Puja might not buy it either; maybe she'd change her mind after she heard about my research. But surely, a rejection was better than not having tried. If both of my friends felt I was flogging a dead horse, so to speak, then I would quit. It was not worth losing friends over this. Nothing ever is.

THIRTEEN

'That's What Friends Are For…' – Dionne Warwick Elton John, Gladys Knight & Stevie Wonder

PUJA WAS WEARING A SHORT WHITE LINEN DRESS THAT WAS quite sheer, but she was not conscious that the outline and fabric of what she was wearing underneath was visible. Well, I was in my white linen trousers and a white round-neck T-shirt, too. It's just March, but the temperature in Mumbai is already nearing 30 degrees. Puja had the central air-conditioning switched on and I could feel the difference, coming in from the outside. We looked like a coordinated couple but believe me, it was nothing like that. Although I couldn't help looking at the legs that had attracted me to her in the first place when I was in school, remember? I could see the goosebumps on her legs. She's still as gorgeous, maybe even more now. Less cheesy, more classy.

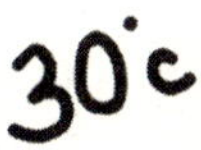

'Come on in,' she said, giving me a tight embrace.

'How have you been?' I couldn't think of anything else to ask.

'Bored,' she said closing the door behind me, 'I wish Ranjit didn't spend so much time at work. A girl needs company … but he's so involved in this business, building and construction, that he hardly has any time for his poor wife. Do I sound like a whining woman?'

'Not at all. I mean he needs to pay attention to his gorgeous wife.'

'Thanks.'

We walked into the living room – it is an open plan kitchen, dining and living space, must be around 2,000 square feet. Their house is a duplex, with three bedrooms, three baths and a dressing room on the upper floor. It's luxurious, and it evokes envy.

'I've ordered lamb biryani for dinner later, but what do you want for lunch?'

'Anything.'

'That's not on the menu. How about grilled cheese sandwiches?'

'Fine by me.'

She called her maid, Radha, and asked her to make cheese-and-tomato sandwiches. I wanted to tell her to skip the tomatoes; they steam up in grilled sandwiches and scathe my tongue every time, but I didn't say anything. Mr Nice Guy, always an accommodating guest.

Radha returned with two glasses of water.

'Coke or beer?' Puja asked.

'Beer, please.'

Puja asked her to pull out two Kingfishers from the refrigerator.

'So what have you found out regarding our secret operation?'

I told her. Three known dens. Run by not-so-fine gentlemen or groups. I told her about the number of tables, the professional set-ups, the amount of money involved. The locations, the staff, right down to the last detail I had discovered.

'How do we get into one of them?'

The beers arrived then. We waited until Radha was gone.

'*We?* Hold on. You are certainly not going in. Even *my* presence would raise eyebrows. We have to find someone else to get us pictures of these places to know what they look like, so we can plan around the same.'

'What do you mean? The other day when we spoke about this, my understanding was that the only chance our plan might succeed was if you fronted it. I'm not so sure Ranjit, or even I will be interested if you are not going in. What am I missing?' Puja made a valid point, but not one I hadn't thought through.

'If anyone sees me there, it's over. Anand Kumar and Roshan Godara will recognize me and will most certainly refuse to play. Worst case, they'll tell the others about me. That's a risk we can't afford to take. We will only get one chance at this, so unfortunately, I get to direct but not act in our home production.'

'What are you thinking?'

'We'll need to hire women and men and train them.'

'And you'll give away your secrets?'

'If we succeed, I won't be playing cards at casinos ever again, and if I lose no one will let me play with them, so it doesn't matter.'

'So why don't you train me? You just said some women play high stakes too at these places.'

'Yeah, but the whole operation is clandestine; our plan only works if no one knows about it. Nobody should be able to trace it back to you, me or Ranjit later.'

We chatted all afternoon. I made notes on paper; a to-do list for us, the number of people required, a timetable for us to organize everything; while Puja ran numbers in an Excel sheet on her iPad, a kind of estimate to present a comprehensive plan to the boss later in the evening. We both knew we couldn't run this con without Ranjit. He was the key; we needed his buy-in. He had to be a hundred per cent convinced that we could pull this off, and willing to stick his neck out to win. He's a friend, so I would try my best to ensure he did not take the fall, but we all know things can go wrong despite the best of intentions. 'Everyone has a plan until they get punched in the face', those are Mike Tyson's words not mine. Despite his certified dumb wittedness with a disgusting record to back it, the words still make a lot of sense. Sometimes gems like these come from the mouths of people you least expect, don't they?

Sorry, I've drifted off the script yet again …

What I mean to say is, hand on heart, I will sacrifice myself if I must, before I let anything terrible happen to Puja and Ranjit. They are more than friends now; they're my family, my only family – but how do I know if sacrificing myself will be enough to save them? If things get out of control, everyone might have to face the consequences. But I believe there is a less than one per cent chance of failure, and if at any point we feel unprepared or uncomfortable, we will abandon it. We might lose some money in the preparations, but that's okay. People lose money on the best of investments, too. Haven't you read the warning every investment bank rolls out in small print – sometimes so small you can't read it without a magnifying glass? Investors should remember that the value of an investment and the income received from an investment can go down as well as up, and they may not get back the amount they invested … blah, blah, blah!

♦

Ranjit was late, but the lamb biryani was on the dot. Coincidentally, both arrived at the same time. 8 p.m.

'You're late.' I heard Puja say to Ranjit, who had already, it seemed, paid the delivery guy and was carrying the package.

'I'm sorry, baby.'

'Hi, Ranjit.'

'Hey, Dimpy. I didn't know you're here.'

'He's been here since the afternoon. We've had a few beers – you have a lot of catching up to do.'

'Something's brewing, I guess.' Ranjit.

'Already brewed.' Puja.

'What is it?' Ranjit.

'Our plan, the plan we spoke about.' Me.

'The one you dismissed this morning.' Puja.

'I didn't dismiss it. I just said there are a lot of holes in it.' Ranjit.

'Not anymore.' Puja.

'What do you mean?' Ranjit.

Radha came and collected Ranjit's bag, and took it upstairs to the third bedroom, which is a kind of study/office.

'We spent the entire afternoon working out every detail for you.' Puja.

'And?' Ranjit asked.

'I think we have the final draft for you to see and give us your approval, my dear husband.'

I had begun to feel like a spectator at my own game, but I let the feeling pass. Puja was doing a far better job than I ever could. She knew Ranjit better than me; she knew how to tackle him better than me. Sometimes thou should acknowledge that thy team member's particular strength is superior to thine own. Sachin Tendulkar never challenged Anil Kumble on bowling, not that I know of. It would have been unintelligent of him if he even tried.

Moreover, watching Puja assured me that I had a strong ally in her. Ranjit was sure to be persuaded as long as he couldn't turn Puja against the idea by poking holes in all that we had discussed and worked on all afternoon. I glanced at Ranjit's face. He was studying the Excel sheet intently while Puja provided explanations, but his serious mien suggested he was far from being completely indoctrinated. Maybe a few questions still swam in his businessman brain. I needed to intervene and put his mind to rest before he discarded the entire thing altogether, but without making it obvious.

'Can I have another beer?' I asked. Sometimes it is good to lighten the atmosphere. It helps in getting your point across.

'Sorry, I forgot to offer.' Puja looked at me. I winked. She got the message. If nothing else, a little more alcohol would help Ranjit loosen up. She called out for Radha and asked her to get three beers. I'd honestly lost count of how many I'd already consumed, but I thanked Radha when she brought me another glass. Ranjit raised his glass and said cheers!

'What happens if the plan boomerangs?' Ranjit asked; he had left the iPad on the table in favour of the yellow notepad I had been writing on. I guess the estimate we put together had done its job. I repeated that any one of us – if we sensed any danger, right up to an hour before we started – could pull the plug. Whatever money is spent until then would be split two ways.

'What happens afterwards?'

'None of us will be in the picture. No one will ever know who was involved, who was behind the whole thing. If it backfires and someone has to take the fall, I'll do it.' Mr Sacrificial Lamb.

Ranjit looked at me. He knew me as well as I knew him. I guess he was mentally working out if I could be trusted. Yes, we'd been friends since school. But me not ratting out their assignations in his bedroom, or them smoking in their school days were a far cry from taking the fall for this. If the plan goes badly, we are not looking at jail time – no one at an illegal casino will seek help from the law; they won't make a police complaint. If they are fleeced of crores, they will simply spend some more money and hire a hitman or something. Break our legs. Ranjit's concern was genuine. I am single, with no established business in the city as such. He has Puja and his company to run. He can't up and leave Mumbai overnight if shit hits the fan.

If Ranjit didn't support us, Puja and I could do rat shit. I wish I could share the plan for you to appreciate, but at the moment it's best that I only share the details on a need-to-know basis. What if someone gets a hold of this diary before the con?

Ranjit shot off another set of questions. I responded to all of them one by one, providing him with as much detail as possible. Three beers later, he picked up the iPad again, looked at the Excel sheet and said: 'This estimate requires some fine-tuning.'

'Are you in?' Puja.

'There are still some risks, so let's look at mitigating them first.' Ranjit.

'Agreed.' I was ecstatic, but I didn't want my over-enthusiasm to show.

'And … as you said,' Ranjit looked at me, 'if any of us feel we shouldn't go ahead until the last minute, we abandon it and never talk about it again. If one of us drops out, the other two won't go ahead. And we remain friends. Promise me you guys won't go ahead without me.'

'Certainly not.' Puja.

She gave a kiss to him and a hug to me.

'No way.' I knew for certain that this was unachievable without Ranjit, so it wasn't a difficult promise to make.

FOURTEEN

'The Winner Takes It All' – ABBA

HAVE YOU EVER SEEN A CAT WALKING? I MEAN, HAVE YOU REALLY, *really* observed their walk? It's a majestic movement. With absolute precision Zeenat puts her hind paws in almost the exact spot where she placed her forepaws. I believe all felines do that to minimize their tracks and keep the noise down. The walk is termed 'direct registering'. Fashion models walking the ramps are taught to walk on an imaginary line on the ground to ape a cat's walk. Why am I telling you this? Because I just noticed Zeenat walk into my bedroom.

I get a lick across my ear. God knows what she has consumed outside – she could do with brushing her teeth, maybe even a strong mouthwash. I suppose she feels the same way about me.

After Ranjit agreed to go ahead with our plan last night, the three of us popped open a bottle of champagne and celebrated as though we had already won the jackpot. This was followed by some rum and cola before we sat down to eat the lamb biryani around midnight, the taste of which still lingers in my mouth. Puja and I were completely over the top – we had been sipping beers since late afternoon. Ranjit called an Uber and put me in the car. I must have come home around two in the morning, and I don't remember brushing my teeth. I just stripped and crashed. I can see yesterday's clothes in a pile next to my bed. Zeenat isn't one of those flatmates who do your washing once in a while!

Sometimes, late at night, I wonder how my life might have been if I hadn't split up with Zara. If I had told her the truth, right from the beginning. Though what is the point of such deliberations when it is an impossibility now? Would we have worked if I, like her, was a decent office-going person, in a regular nine-to-five job – a real job with a templated role and a defined pension? Thoughts are just that: thoughts, and they continue so on and so forth and so very forth! But it inevitably dawns on me that I couldn't live the life of a public-sector employee. Stable income and a decent pension are fine, but are we humans given life just to work for survival, deleting all the fun we've ever imagined? The answer is an emphatic *no*. No one – and I mean *no one* – should sacrifice all that they love in life, for just one aspect of life. Or love. Be it a partner, a car or any other riches. Don't get me wrong, I loved Zara. Still love her. But I wasn't willing to give it all up then, and I am not now either. I emphatically stand by my decision – I won't stop living my life for anyone. This is who I am. A scheming, conniving gambler, you might say. That I lie and deceive to make a living with no job – I mean, the way the world defines a job. But my love was pure.

I can admit that I lied to her about who I was, and I can appreciate that it upset her so much that she called it quits. But I was otherwise honest in my relationship. I know what you're thinking: how can someone lie about their true identity and expect the other person to ever trust them again? What else could that person be lying about or concealing or not telling you? I guess if I were put in her position, I'd do the same thing. It's rational thinking, of course. But that doesn't help the fact that I still miss her. I'm not a bad man. I hate self-pity, so I won't dwell on this any longer. But the truth is, I miss her; I miss the companionship, the love and the sex. There, I admit it!

♣

There are three essential steps in the plot we gave a face-lift to last night.

One is to procure as many details about the casinos as possible; most crucially, on the people they employ and who amongst them would be willing to switch sides and be our eyes and ears. We need to identify them early to get more info. One defector per casino is enough to start with. Even if they don't have all the data and facts we need, we can direct them to dig up what's needed. It's easy when you are on the inside.

Two, we need to hire people and train them. I need to find the right men and women who I will then train over the next four to five months. Like I've said before, winning at cards cannot be left to chance. Getting lucky is good, but luck cannot be part of the strategy. Remember, to win crores we have to spend a few lakhs. I call that an investment. And I have to invest time, too. So hiring will commence soon, in case anyone wants to apply. Watch this space!

Three, we need to establish who these high-net worth punters are. I know a few: Anand Kumar, Roshan Godara, Jinendrabhai Patel and a few others I've played with in the past. But we need to quickly ascertain who we want in attendance on the night we hit the casino and send feelers out to these individuals. Feelers only – inviting them directly is out of the question since we will be operating in the background. We know these players don't patronize all three casinos, but we have to direct them all to one place for one grand night for maximum impact. This game we are playing isn't something you can pull off more than once. The night we are thinking of will involve big buy-ins, big stakes and big winnings – for us. We are talking forty to fifty *khokas*. A *khoka* means a crore, in case you don't know. A lakh is called a *peti*. These codes were once used in the underworld, but after they were worn out by Bollywood, I'm told the underworld has changed to new lingo inspired by the IPL. By the way, the code for the police is 'umpire', and not *pandu* anymore … but please let us stick to the point here before I start rambling or you will accuse me of misdirecting by diversion again.

You might wonder why I am going ahead with such a risky plan when I can just roll through life on my savings, do something else and move to a different city. Let me ask you a question: has your ego ever been bludgeoned? Not just hurt, but *clubbed*? If you were asked to just sit, lick your wounds and move on, would you? Well, some might, some won't. I most certainly, cannot and will not rest until I've avenged my humiliation and defeat.

Plus, there's one thing that you must not forget. I. Am. A. Gambler.

FIFTEEN

'Arre Deewano Mujhe Pehchano'
– *Don* 1978, OST

I'M DEEP SINGH SODHI. A CUT-SURD. MONA-SIKH. I AM neither young nor middle-aged, but somewhere in between. My ancestors – grandfather and his two younger brothers, to be precise – emigrated to India in 1946, just before the Partition, and established themselves as fruit and nut traders, later growing the business to become one of the biggest wholesale merchants in India. What do you mean you haven't heard of *Badam Seth,* aka the Almond King? Well, that was my grandfather.

In case I've piqued your interest, I must tell you I'm an exporter of dried fruits and nuts myself, and we supply to wholesalers in New York, London, Tokyo and Prague. Why Prague, you ask? Well, it just makes the whole thing sound more realistic if you throw an unusual name in the mix, since the names of the other three cities sound hackneyed. You can think of it as a kind of misdirection. See, Prague is what you're thinking about now; not me, my business or its authenticity.

My job, ladies and gentlemen, is therefore done.

I was never a gym-going guy. I used to play squash to stay fit but ended up pulling a hamstring. My doctor has told me to stay off the squash court for some time; ergo, the gym is my only way to exercise. But only for a short while, until I can return to competitive sports. I have no intention of burning calories on a treadmill forever. With my work not being strictly nine-to-five – I'm always coordinating with the international offices I just told you about – it suits me to join this gym in Cuffe Parade rather than one near my home, which, incidentally, is on Pedder Road.

For those of you who haven't realized it, this is my fourth avatar. You see, Rahul Mahapatra has to be buried since his name is in the police records now.

Yes, Deep Singh Sodhi is single and ready to mingle. Another cheesy one from me? Both Hollywood and Bollywood might have subliminally worked on your mind and given you a false impression over the years: that the hero always gets the girl. Not true.

There's another reason why I am at this gym, which I shall tell you later.

SIXTEEN

'I Still Haven't Found What I'm Looking For' – Scarlett Johansson & Bono

ON MONDAY MORNING, I WENT ON A TOUR OF THE CUFFE Parade gym I'm now a member of. It was more glamorous than I had envisaged, and its members seemed a little pretentious. They appeared more interested in showing off than actually working out. Doesn't bother me. There was a lot of Lycra and flesh on display, as you can imagine. Women in short bicycling shorts and men in skintight T-shirts to display their six-packs – or eight-packs. Some had sleeveless vests on, and I could see bulging veins throbbing on top of their biceps or triceps or whatever. Others wore shorts that revealed their toned thighs, which, I'm certain, women find highly attractive. I might be considered a good-looking guy, but in that gym, I felt like a poodle after a wash. Fit, yes, but not in any way muscled. At best, I'm two-pack – there's no such thing as two-packs, I guess.

But I'm not interested in looking like the Hulk, in any event.

I was going to the gym for a specific purpose. I was there to follow someone in secret and later, when the time was right, woo her and plant a seed in her. In her *mind*, you pervert, what were you thinking?

One glance around the gym and it was evident that the

crowd hadn't set the bar too high for me. Of course, there were fitter bodies, gorgeous faces, bare legs and scantily clad torsos – and all of them could shame me on a cross-trainer or a treadmill – but that was hardly my intention for being there. My motivation was entirely different and what made me happy was that the coast looked clear. Most of the men and women at the gym were in their early twenties, eyeing each other, passing smiles, ogling at each other's bodies, maybe even arranging dates or humping like bunnies. While there was some interaction between the older crowd, little transpired between different age groups. Some older men could not help rubbernecking and salivating at younger women; I worried one of them might get a sprain in the neck. But there weren't many younger men interested in the older women, leaving the goalpost forsaken for a new player.

And you know that a new player had just walked in and taken a stance. Deep Singh Sodhi was looking for a particular woman in the gym.

♠

At 8:30 a.m. the next day, I was at Churchgate Station, Mumbai: the world's busiest railway station. It's not unusual for a carriage of a Mumbai local train, designed for two hundred people, to carry eight hundred. Packed like sardines. If you do the math, on a typical local train with nine carriages, you're talking approximately 7,000 people rushing out at the same time. That is if you're lucky and only one train has arrived at the platform in the same hour. The crowd is enormous: officegoers from CEOs to peons, local hawkers who serve the morning chai and omelettes; men, women and even children. People rushing, jostling, bumping towards the exit at full speed, like the world might end – or perhaps their careers – if they are delayed by two minutes. I promised myself that that was the first and last time I would take the local train. I must find another way to commute.

Two hours later, at the gym, I saw the familiar white Volvo XC60; worth sixty lakh rupees on the road, far more than anything my father earned in his entire lifetime working at Raja Cycle Store.

Jasmine Kumar entered the gym. Gorgeous and tall with straight, shoulder-length dark hair with auburn highlights, tied in a ponytail that swayed as she walked.

Anand Kumar's wife, ladies and gentlemen – the one I had surveilled earlier, the one whose moral compass doesn't exactly point north; the one who is known to sleep around in response to her husband's malady of not being able to contain his dick. Perhaps as some kind of … act of vengeance? I don't know and I don't care. I'm not in this for sex. It might happen; and if it does, I will endure. I am more than willing to be seduced if some part of what I whisper to her travels into her husband's ears. Believe me, it will happen. It will happen because women and men cheating on their spouses tend to talk more than usual. They talk excessively, they talk nonsense and they try to fit in some truth in it to make it sound believable. I've told you all about Ardh-satya before. Mix fifty per cent truth in a bowl of lies and it becomes far more believable than a flagrant lie. Trust me, I have experience.

Like I've said, this isn't about sex at all. This is about screwing Anand Kumar, and if I have to start with his wife, so be it.

I am younger than her by almost a decade. She's forty-two now, but she doesn't look it. Straight spine, shoulders held high; dressed in a sports bra and shorts that looked like the small nylon ones we wore at school in kindergarten. She is desirable. I hadn't expected her to be so attractive, but seeing Jasmine had stirred my insides.

I may lose my resolve but what's the harm? I'm single. And if she is a libertine, it's no bother. Jasmine likes to interact with younger men while her husband gallivants with younger women – we know that, don't we?

As I watched her enter the gym, I passed her a smile. She returned my politeness. She smelled like she had taken a bath in Kenzo. It was surprising that there wasn't a queue of men waiting to take her out on a date. I guess ageism exists in every field. Why should extramarital affairs be any different?

I couldn't just turn around and follow her. At best it would have been amateurish, worst case she might have thought I was keen. Yes, yes, I know what you're thinking … I *am* excited and eager, but she doesn't need to know that. Right after her arrival, she went in for a workout; one I guessed would take ninety minutes if she took a shower too. Since I was already there, and had paid the membership fee, I decided to go for a dip in the pool and jacuzzi in the meantime.

Jasmine seems to be committed to her exercise regime. Post my workout and a spa treatment – two hours later – I was sat at the little café inside the gym, sipping on a strong Americano. There was still no sign of her. She must have been pumping the metal hard. Eventually, she made an entrance. Hair wet, red-eyed. It looked like she had had a dip in the pool after the gym. Shit! I should have waited in the pool, maybe timed my swimming a bit better. Well, there's always tomorrow.

As she passed my table, we exchanged smiles again. I finished the rest of my coffee in one sip, loudly said 'bye' to the barista and walked out. I was at the gym for exercise, and a coffee, and quickly had to rush for a meeting right after.

I'm a busy man.

SEVENTEEN

'What a Wonderful World' – Sam Cooke

HOW GOOD WERE YOU AT BIOLOGY IN SCHOOL? IS IT BIOLOGY or Zoology? Doesn't matter what it is labelled, just listen carefully to what I have to say. Chromosomes determine sex in mammals. That's a fact. Females have two X chromosomes while males have one X and one Y, and that's why men are fickle-minded. I made that up. The sex of a child depends on the male, not the female, so stop blaming women for not delivering the child of your desired gender, you male morons. That's a fact, too.

But why am I giving you a lesson in chromosomes?

Well, since I cannot go into the casino to play with Anand Kumar, Roshan Godara and the like, someone else has to stand in for me. Whether the operation succeeds or fails, or who takes the fall, is immaterial. I will fleece people of crores in a single night, and regardless of you might think of me, I do not want to betray the people who help me do it, even if they have shown that they are morally flexible by joining me in the long con I've planned.

Hence, I will not reveal their names in my diary. Instead, I will use XX for girls and XY for boys, as per the crash course you've just received an A+ on, in Zoology. Or is it Biology?

The recruitment was done through a third party – we had

originally thought that Ranjit could do it in-house, but that would have been a bit careless. What if one of the candidates ratted us out before, during or after the event? And you know what they say: if you've already thought about it, there's a good chance it might happen. But let's stick to the point.

We finalized eight candidates in March. We only need three, or maybe four, but it's always best to have a few extras. Some might fail the intense training, some might develop cold feet at the last minute, someone might fall sick on the day, who knows? Our time frame for training is six months – until Diwali – which means a maximum payout of approximately fifteen lakhs. It is a minuscule amount in the scheme of things. And the entire fifteen lakhs will be paid only if all eight survive the six months of severe training and turn out to be as deft-handed as they've proclaimed on their résumés. Don't be shocked when I tell you everybody lies on their résumé. You don't have to believe me, just look it up on LinkedIn. Everyone is doing their boss's job.

Where was I? Oh yes, those selected for the night will get a share of the jackpot, too. Not to mention that every single one of them will learn the tricks of the trade from the master himself. Yours truly, by the way.

Another group of people will be hired, but they don't need to be trained. To avoid bleeding cash, they will be brought on closer to the date and provided with the requisite props and costumes. More on that later.

I have rented a two-bed furnished flat in Versova on a six-month, short lease for another four lakhs upfront. I guess I should come clean to you. When I say *I* rented the place, it was via a shell corporation we created – Ranjit and I – and put some cash into. Truth is, it's not even a registered company, but who checks? You call yourself 'Art Lovers Private Limited', design an arty logo, print some stationery and most individuals and small-time traders will lap up the misrepresentation. All you need to do then is find people and small enough firms who are happy to accept cash because the last thing you want is a banking trail. We've also bought burner phones, on a pay-as-you-go basis. We'll discard them as and when required. It is impossible for me to write down every detail, but I don't want you think I haven't thought of all this. Certain things might not be recorded here, but they're certainly not missed. Remember, if you've thought of a loophole, I've already spotted and mitigated the risk even if I don't mention it explicitly.

If one of the recruits changes sides or takes a French leave, we've ensured that they should have no idea how and where to lead people to me before the event.

Just one more thing – *ah! Here she comes, to take her crown* – sorry, my own little Miss Sarajevo aka Zeenat has arrived. One might be forgiven for believing that U2 wrote these lyrics with her in mind. The expression on her face says it all: *why isn't my meal ready, you lazy pleb?*

EIGHTEEN

'Raju Ban Gaya Gentleman' – Eponymous OST

I WANT TO BE A MICHAEL. FOR NO APPARENT OR RATIONAL reason, I just want to. Michael Jackson, Michael Jordan, Michael Phelps, even Michelangelo or George Michael will do.

In the end, I choose Michael Ferreira – the first Indian to win the World Open Billiards Championship, who went on to set an amateur world record way back in the seventies. The name might ring a bell or two for oldies like Roshan Godara and Anand Kumar, but the people I'll be dealing with in this role will be completely clueless. And even if one of them knows the name, it doesn't worry me at all. There can be more than one Michael Ferreira. It's not so uncommon a name in Mumbai and Goa. I'm aware there is a DCP Ferreira in Mumbai Police. If she is related to the legendary Michael in any way, I don't know it.

I have a French goatee – fake, of course. Artistic, all-black, thick-rimmed glasses. And a wig that makes me look ten years older.

I live in Versova.

Also on Pedder Road.

I'm back to a dual existence again.

Rahul Mahapatra and Saurabh Mathur are out.

Deep Singh Sodhi and Michael Ferreira are in. Michael is a backstage acting coach who has taught some big names in the industry today. Of course, he doesn't get credit as the film stars don't want to admit they ever took classes.

I still don't have a car. However, given my distaste for public transport – my journey during the rush hour the other day was horrible – we have, through our shell company account, hired a Land Rover, with a chauffeur in livery, for the next six months. Estimated cost: one lakh a month plus fuel. Paid in cash.

Game on!

NINETEEN

'That's Not My Name' – The Tings Tings

नाम गुम जायेगा

WHILE I HAVE PROMISED MYSELF NEVER TO USE THEIR NAMES in the diary, it is paramount to document all the recruits, don't you think? I'll be discreet. Remember, this is for me to distinguish them. Besides, how else will I explain who's in and who's out to Puja and Ranjit? A lot will need to be recorded in my memory, since I don't want to give any details that might reveal their identities.

I hope you still remember the little Biology lesson you received an A+ grade for.

The girls:

XX1 is twenty-eight and 5'5", with shoulder-length straight hair and dark Americano-coloured eyes. She always wears ripped, distressed jeans. Sometimes they are so ripped they might as well be shorts.

XX2 is twenty-five and 5'7", but she has a mature demeanour. She can easily pass as someone a lot older, which is good. One of our selection criteria was that, if we put make-up and clothes on the candidates, they should look the part. Of someone who – age no bar – can confidently walk into a casino and not break a sweat if they lose a few crores. The jury is out on XX2. Her demeanour might be a façade. I can't take the risk, but I'm not deciding her fate now.

XX3 is thirty-seven and 5'8". She's got the style, the panache. What exactly was Ranjit's brief to the agency? Are tall women his guilty pleasure? I'll ask Puja the next time I see her. That reminds me, Puja has already spoken to an agency via a third party – always keep others at an arm's length – that will provide training on etiquette, clothes and makeup for black-tie events when the time comes.

XX4 is thirty-two and 5'6", and for one moment, I thought she was Jasmine's younger sister. The resemblance is striking and with a little grooming, she could be playing at Anand Kumar's table. This is a stroke of luck. I'll need to focus on her. In the next few weeks, I should learn more about Jasmine, which will help me shape XX4 to look and behave more like her.

The boys:

XY1 puts me off right away. He's got a roving eye and a suspicious disposition. In short, he is everything I don't want in the team. He is bossy, boisterous and seems to have an attention-seeking disorder of some kind. He asks too many questions, and curiosity isn't always a good thing. I have a sense that he's that one rotten apple that can spoil the whole barrel, and so he becomes the first casualty. I call the agency and ask them to let him know. I am positive that, for now, seven candidates are enough to proceed with. If we need to hire more people, we'll take that call later.

XY2 is thirty-five and 6'. Suave, sophisticated. Good-looking in a Greek-god way. He seems like he's a villain who's just walked out an old, black-and-white Alfred Hitchcock film. He exudes confidence without making any effort. He underplays himself.

XY3 is thirty-five and 6', too. He's got a poker face through and through. It appears that he was given a lifetime dosage of Botox at birth; no booster shots required. I can imagine him in a suit, sipping a Cognac, cutting cards with élan.

XY4 is forty-three and 5'5". Short, balding, but he has a *khandani* – born into old money – look about him. Which I know is true. He comes from a wealthy background but somehow lost the riches.

The seven candidates are struggling extras. None of them have been able to break into the glitzy world of cinema, not even on television or in a web series. The brief was clear: no recognizable faces. They have been told they were hired to participate in a reality show on TV, six months from now, provided they pass the strict training. There is a grand prize to be won, and the venue and other details will be shared when the time is right. The money we've offered is big enough for them to sign a confidentiality clause. There's nothing a struggling artist fears more than a legal battle; it can sink their career before it's even begun.

You might think I'm cunning, sending them into the lion's den without them knowing. And you'd be wrong. You have to appreciate that we cannot tell everyone everything. The fewer the people who know the plan, the higher the probability of its success. Eventually, we will outline most things in detail, but only to the finalists whom we eventually select. The others get their salaries until the time we think they are no good at picking up what I teach them. Fair and square?

♥

What's wrong with me? Am I losing my touch? Is the stress of it all getting to me?

For the second time in a row, I had mistimed my visit to the gym – 'Fitiful'. Its owners have been creative to the point of being useless; Fitiful is supposed to be a portmanteau of 'fitness' and 'beautiful' but, in my humble opinion, if you have to separate the constituents to explain what you mean, it's pointless. I am in no mood at the moment to dwell on things unrelated.

Today was my second attempt to catch up with Jasmine, and I failed yet again. I saw her sashaying down the corridor, which meant she was late for her exercises. Last time, she went into the gym around 11 a.m. and returned past 1 p.m. Today, I was there at 12:45 p.m. and she had just arrived, so I assumed she'd be out around 3 p.m. Instead of spending two hours at the gym again, I walked out to grab a bite of *vada pav*. I hadn't eaten one in ages. I asked the driver to take me around to Colaba, behind the Taj Hotel. Once there, I asked him to park, and took a stroll down memory lane.

When Zara and I were together, her office was in Cuffe Parade and hence, I got to know the area well. Or rather, I should say she showed me around. I'm one of those creatures who wouldn't venture out of my flat if I didn't have company or a specific reason to. I'd rather chill at home with a beer, mainlining hazaar web series or films. For days on end. I have no appetite for the so-called touristy things. Nada.

I wolfed down two vada pavs at a speed that would shame Zeenat. I love the red garlic chutney powder they prepare, but let's keep to the point here.

I was back at the gym one hour and forty-five minutes later; Jasmine's car was still in the parking lot. I picked up a coffee and took a table at the cafe, watching the door from where she would exit the gym/pool/showers.

'Is it okay if I sit here?' I hadn't seen her approach, but I realized a girl was standing near me. Before I knew it, she had pulled up a chair.

No, I wanted to say but instead I had smiled, nodded and uttered: 'Of course.' Courtesy had demanded it. Moreover, she was gorgeous, like everyone else in the gym. Approximately my age. In shorts and a cropped T-shirt, revealing her thin midriff. Waif. Pierced belly button. Damp hair. Carrying an expensive, stylish gym bag with a logo I didn't recognize. I bet like all men and women her age, she too posted glamorous pictures on Instagram thrice a day in various outfits. Hell, she could have been one of those Instagram influencers with millions of followers, for all I knew. Anyone can be a celebrity these days. Under normal circumstances, I'd have been chuffed to have someone like her consider sitting with me when there were empty tables in the cafe. But in the current situation, I was anything but. I wasn't there to let someone chat me up. Or seek a date. I didn't want Jasmine, if she walked out right now, to think I was with another woman. I winced at the thought.

'I haven't seen you around before.' The girl had firmly settled down on the chair opposite me, now.

Do you interview everyone you see the first time around? I wanted to ask. I wanted to be alone when Jasmine turned up. Instead, the words that I heard coming out of my mouth were: 'How do you know?'

'We keep an eye out for freshers.' She smiled. 'You look worried. Oh my god, are you waiting for someone?'

I didn't know how to respond to that. If I said yes, I could anticipate her next question: *who*? If I said no, she'd probably call the waiter and ask for a drink.

'A call.' I eyed my phone at the table between us. 'I'm waiting for an important call.'

'Girlfriend?'

Why do some people think they need to know everything? 'No, a business call, actually.'

'I'm Rima Bedi,' she said.

'Deep Singh.' And just then, I saw the door fling open and

Jasmine walk out. 'My apologies, but you'll have to excuse me, Rima, I need to make that call.' I got up and walked away before she could respond.

I was just around the corner, pretending I was absorbed in conversation on the iPhone, when I saw Jasmine walk to her car. Unfortunately, I had lost another opportunity. I carried on with the pretend conversation on the phone before returning to Rima and my coffee, hoping to make the most of the situation.

Unfortunately, Rima had left the table.

TWENTY

'Farebi …' – *Neeyat* OST

'LOOKING UP IS LOOKING NORTH. ENGLAND IS LOCATED to the north of India. England had a Queen for the longest time, which means if you look up towards the ceiling, your partner at the table should grasp that you have a Queen in the cards you've been dealt,' I explained to my newbie students in the first session. 'Likewise, if you look east, you're looking towards Japan, and Japan has a King.'

N=Q
E=K

These are simple things that any beginner must learn. On the night of the con, to win big, our team members will have to partner up. And partners need to understand each other without exchanging information – well, at least not explicitly.

'Look tense like you're introspecting, then twirl either of your eyebrows, and you indicate to your partner that you've got a Jack because, if you look at my sketch, you'll see it looks like a face. And since the King and Queen have already been allocated other gestures, the only other picture-face card is Jack. The reason I'm explaining the rationale behind these is that it will work as a kind of mnemonic rather than you having to commit everything to memory.'

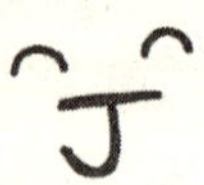

'You mean like we did when we appeared for college exams?'

'Yes.' I explained to them that when they were at the table on that final day, even a microscopic flash of hesitation would render their efforts futile. A *tell* in poker is defined by a player's change in expression or mien – even as small as an ant's testis – that can give away their own assessment of the cards they hold in their hands, which is enough for the opponents to move in for the kill. All poker players are known to constantly look for such tells. And my trainees will be playing in the big leagues for the first time, so they'll need to learn how to evaluate their opponents, look for tells and signs. 'Be under no illusion – the other players *will* be monitoring you at all times since they'll be playing with you for the first time, looking at your eyes, focusing on your countenance. If you start fidgeting or sweating, they'll know you're lying and then it'll be game over. And God forbid if they catch you cheating …'

'Are these universal signs?' asked XX2.

So far, I have been unerring in my initial assessment of the candidates. Did she take me to be a moron? If these were universal codes, how did she think we would get away with using them at a table full of professional card players?

'No,' I told her. 'I've devised them specifically for our purposes. There are no universal cyphers as such – what would be the point otherwise?'

She nodded.

'But how do we know which suit it is?' That was a smart question; anyone with half a functioning brain should have asked it. I was so glad it was XX4, the Jasmine lookalike. I told you I want her on Anand's table on *the* day. She already looked ready for prime time, if you ask me.

I'm sure *you* know that the cards you've been dealt are valuable – or not – based on two criteria: the suit (spades, clubs, diamonds and hearts) and the number or picture on the face of the card.

'I'm glad you asked,' I smiled at XX4. 'We shall cover that in the subsequent sessions. Let's park it for now, if that's okay?'

A few of them nodded.

So far so good. After finishing with the numbers, I moved on to the next few signs and gestures.

'In the event the croupier has dealt a good hand to the person on your right and you know it, call out "correct", but use it in a sentence that makes sense in some context.' I could see that they wanted to know why. I didn't wait for the question. 'The synonym for correct is right, and we are talking about the person on your right. Makes sense?'

Nods and yeses.

'Consequently, calling out the converse – "false" – is a hint about the person on your left. But be warned: using the word false in a sentence on a poker table can raise eyebrows and make others wonder if something is fishy.'

Fishy reminded me of fish, and fish reminded me of Zeenat. I wasn't sure whether I had left some food for her, having been with my students all morning. I know she doesn't go hungry if I don't feed her but I have become fond of her now, and feel I must serve her.

'I think the legs of my chair are a bit wonky, kind of faulty.'

'Bingo.' I responded. It was XY2, my darling diary, it was XY2. He had used the word "faulty" instead of false but communicated the same message. 'Bravo!' I looked around and said to all, 'Innovate and improvise, just like this – the essence is to deliver the correct *message*.'

Everyone looked towards their right.

Message received, loud and clear.

'Thank you, Mr Ferreira.'

'Remember there are three mantras: speed, precision, misdirection. Keep these three in mind while performing any trick. I shall tell you more as we progress. I think this is enough for today.' We had time so why cram it all in one day? They needed to go home, think, digest, practise.

To prevent you from thinking I'm barking mad or careless for not giving my pupils a signal for Ace, you're mistaken. The truth is quite the opposite, as a matter of fact. Call me paranoid, but it would be reckless of me to write down every code or signal that I tell my disciples in this journal. However, just to put your mind at ease – and to prove that I have thought of everything – I will tell you this. The way to signal an ace in hand is actually quite simple; you don't even have to open your mouth. Depending on the game being played at the table you might have three or five or whatever number of cards in your hand. Have a look at them, then place them back on the table, but make sure you do not keep them in a deck. Spread them a bit and while you are at it, place one a little differently than the others. One means an ace. One lone card indicates an Ace. Capisce?

♦

I am back at Pedder Road. Zeenat is missing. Maybe she's arranged a sleepover with some friend or managed to raid a restaurant's kitchen. She's left me no note. I have a feeling that even if I give her a smartphone, she won't text to let me know she won't be coming home. She's an alpha female; she loves her independence.

'I think we should let XX2 go.' I called Ranjit, after dinner, and told him about the events of the day.

'Why not try her for a few more days?'

'Okay, but not for long. If we have to let her go, the less she knows about our plan the better.'

'Fair point.'

I knew I would oust XX2 later in the week. Six people are enough when you only need two or three players on the final day. So despite Ranjit's disagreement with my advice, I called XX2 and let her know that the training was suspended until further notice. I doubt she'll call others to check – they don't seem so pally with each other – but if she does and finds out I've singled her out, so be it. She should get the hint. In a couple of days, I'm going to ring Ranjit again and lean on him to call the agency to let XX2 know she's been dropped. We cannot afford to take risks here.

♣

Boris. No last name, no middle name. I'm a betting man and I'm willing to wager every last rupee I have that Boris isn't his real name either.

He is built like a small mountain, with curly, jet-black hair, a round face the size of a basketball and, perhaps to make the surface area appear smaller, he has a goatee like me. Only mine – Michael Ferreira's – is fake. He is forever dressed in black, with dark faux Ray-Bans. It is March but he does not remove his pleather jacket, even when he is indoors. He is the manager at one of the casinos I described earlier. His moral compass points towards Antarctica, and he is the least apologetic about it. *They hire me for a night every month or two, so I have to make money elsewhere – and it's not like I'm robbing a house of priests,* he told me at our second meeting.

He seems oblivious to the danger of being disloyal to the people who own these clubs, and the penalty if he is caught. Or perhaps he doesn't care – maybe he suffers from Reverse Napoleon Complex as many large men often do, I'm not making this up.

It doesn't bother me, as long as I stay in the clear and no one sees us together. As the manager at one of the casinos, he has a wealth of information: security cameras, the employees, their uniforms, roles and responsibilities, the dos and don'ts, availability of other services, customer check-ins at the start, kinds of chips, playing cards, etc. Someone once told me "etc" stands for 'end of thinking capacity', and not et cetera. Whatever version you believe, it still carries the same meaning. The best part of the English language—

No meandering. Back to Boris.

Yeah, Boris is paid well by us. He's on a monthly retainer of sorts. His only task is to take photographs of the casino when it's in action, so we can truly appreciate the scene. This also captures some of the patrons. I've seen Anand Kumar and Roshan Godara in the pictures, sitting at the table, a drink beside them. It is apparent that there is some sort of chemistry between them, suggesting they are a team – maybe they're swindling others, maybe it's plain camaraderie – it is hard to tell. But if I had any doubts they were in cahoots, the images confirm my suspicions. After eliminating me from the scene, it seems they nicked some of my ideas and have been screwing other players. I have to admit, for a minute I was so enraged I got up and went to the washroom.

Boris isn't a threat to Michael Ferreira, unless we are spotted together by someone who knows both of us and puts two and two together. Boris has no clue who our targets are. He cannot go into his club and announce that one Mr Michael Ferreira is digging up info. He'll be the one in the shithole for passing on the gen, not me. If someone tries to locate me in Versova, they won't find anything. I have cameras that will inform me of any intruders in my absence. And when the dust finally settles, all that anyone who comes looking for me will ever find is, well … dust!

In any event, targeting the club where Boris works is out of the question. We need to target another site where he can lead the operations. He has no other role to play. Once we pay him, he's off. We meet at my Versova residence since I can't afford to meet Boris at my Pedder Road flat. You might have guessed that loyalty isn't his strongest suit. If he can drop a dime on his employers … well, two-timing isn't a one-way street. You get the point.

Maybe he will never tell anyone about me, but it never hurt anyone to be careful. There's no such thing as being *too careful,* is there? Regardless, Boris has turned out to be a good resource. He is a fountain of intel, and nuggets of information spout out of his mouth like one, too.

Today, he pulled out a piece of paper and laid it in front of me. He had sketched the floor plan of the club he works at, and his little schematic will be of great help to us. Whatever is missing can be filled in later with the photographs he's already provided.

Wow!

All I can say is wow! I'm not kidding, look at the image on the facing page.

Standard casino interiors. No clocks, no windows; never let the patrons know how long they've been inside. Serve them good-quality booze, and plenty of it, at prices below what high-end restaurants and bars charge – get them drunk. Hire attractive staff and put lots of skin and muscle on display, both female and male. Let the patrons feast their eyes, too. Distract them.

Boris explained that there was a lot of security inside and outside the place, which didn't surprise me. There were myriads of personnel inside the premises that doubled up as eyes and ears for the owners. All things considered, it was a very straightforward operation. You came in, left your coat in the cloakroom, verified your identity at the reception, went through another security check before arriving at the vaults: A or B. There, you were supposed to exchange your cash for chips before moving to the club area. Boris told me that irrespective of the time of night, he was always on his feet, moving around. There are five tables in the casino – sources in other casinos have confirmed that they have as many tables as well. Five is the maximum number of tables any one of them has, but on some nights, they add or remove a table depending on the crowd. There was seating in the corners for people taking a break or just hanging around, like in a club. Boris confirmed what patrons didn't know: that one of these four sofas was reserved for casino personnel to watch the tables. Tables numbered ① to ④ were for a maximum of four people, and the players on these two tables dealt the cards themselves. The cards were provided by the club. Outside cards weren't permissible for obvious reasons. Table ⑤ was the largest one. It had five seats. It was the one with a croupier and was considered the 'professional' table. It was on this table that the highest stakes were played. That is the table I want Anand Kumar and Roshan Godara at, and I think I know how. But I am seriously lagging on that. Correction: I haven't got started on that.

Boris also told me there is a concealed door behind the bar; a kind of secret exit in case of an emergency. They've done dry runs. Provided everyone follows the rules, around fifty people can be evacuated in under three minutes. The patrons would be disgorged into the night. In case there was a raid by the authorities, the place would be vacant by the time the police entered the main hall. Yes, there'd be cards and counters on the tables, and drinks scattered around, but there would be nothing else to go on.

The money lockers are emptied within the first ten minutes of all the guests arriving and paying. The money leaves the premises, and a van returns later to bring it all back, minus the casino's share of ten per cent. In case of emergency evacuation, the wins and losses are forgone and the money would be delivered back to the players as soon as the heat cooled off, within forty-eight hours. Of course, such an emergency had never occurred, but those were the rules.

The illegitimacy of the casinos' existence meant that there was no car park outside. Patrons were asked to take cabs to the place, or park in other lanes in the area. They were encouraged to carpool whenever they could. Too many strange cars in the locality could raise concern.

They've thought of everything.

I locked up some time after Boris left. I didn't want him to suspect the Versova flat is not my permanent and only residence. Nor did I want him to see my car and driver. As I was driven back to Pedder Road, I made a promise to myself that I would meet Jasmine the next day. Come. What. May.

TWENTY

'Cold Little Heart' – *Big Little Lies* OST

ARE YOU PAYING ATTENTION? ARE YOU *REALLY* PAYING ATTENTION? I ask because this is a crucial part. If you were, you should have realized that I've repeated entry number twenty. Ironically, while I'm asking you to be watchful, I have made a mistake. But here's a lesson: everyone makes mistakes – you'll be hard-pressed to find someone who can say they've never made a mistake in their lives. It's an impossible feat. And while we all make mistakes, victory comes to those who recover quickly and make it good in an instant.

On Saturday, contrary to my promise to myself the day before, I saw little point in going to Fitiful. When Anand Kumar is at home over the weekends, I know Jasmine usually skips the gym. So, as scheduled, I arrived in Versova in the evening for a class with my students. All except XX2.

And it is during the class that I made an error.

'Michael,' XX1 called me, and I ignored her. Not because I am hard of hearing, or she was far away, or I was being smug. It was a genuine mistake, a slip. I haven't practised enough to respond to my new moniker. If you open a can and pull out a new name every time you switch identities, there is a high probability of getting caught out when people start addressing you by that name, especially at first. Your synapses don't flutter subconsciously like they do when someone calls your name. In my case, I doubt that I'll even react to my birth name now. But it's practice. They say it takes over 3,000 repetitions to teach a dog to react to a single command.

If you read fiction or watch films, you'll note that the people who use aliases always make up names using their original initials. *J*aideep *B*iswas becomes *J*ayant *B*adola. JB remains JB and works like a mnemonic, a trigger. The more adventurous ones reverse the initials – *B*ipin *J*ain. But I'm sure you can appreciate my plight: there is a limit to the names I can come up with using D and R from *D*impy *R*aja. I've lived several lives over the years, and I've learnt to cope with such faux pas by developing the skills to overcome them. The first rule is to think on your feet. Whenever possible, bring levity to the situation. And before I get accused of segueing and making this a *gyan*-session I must tell you how I reacted.

'My apologies,' I said, after she repeated my name. 'I thought you were asking me if I came here on a cycle.' Remember the hazaar rhyming jokes in the villain Ajit's dialogues of yesteryear: *Michael on cycle, Mona and Sona*?

She smiled.

There you go.

But I needed to be more careful.

In that day's session, I took the group through the basic gestures and signs to communicate the suits. I'll give you one example. If a player at the table appreciates the casino without mentioning the word 'club' – *the drinks at this place are brilliant; the service at this casino is amazing* – you guessed it, the suit they are talking about is Clubs. I'm sure you can figure out that Diamonds and Hearts aren't difficult to communicate either. Foot tapping is Spades because that's where spades are used: on the ground.

I let them absorb this before we broke for the weekend. I told them that more rigorous training would start soon.

♠

'I swear I'll dump him and come live with you,' Puja told me, when I called up to whine that Ranjit hadn't moved an inch on the arrangements yet. While nothing could possibly make me happier than to see Ranjit fail in this instance – and to have Puja live with me – a man can only dream.

When we started planning this long con, our roles were clearly outlined and I started on the tasks allocated to me immediately. Hired a flat in Versova and began training the eight women and men as soon as they were recruited. I know Puja has been doing her bit with costumes and make-up artists and the other responsibilities she was assigned – you will see her work later, I won't tell you about it yet. Ranjit was indirectly involved in the recruitment process, but his job is far from over. None of this can succeed if he doesn't take his job seriously. When I had spoken to him in the afternoon, he had sounded distracted and gave me some baloney about why he hadn't started on his part. *I'm waiting for this or that* – without elaborating on either *this* or *that*. I know he's busy since he has a large business to manage, but still. I worry if he's having second thoughts – it's best to know and address them now.

'Is he even serious?' I asked her.

'No sex for him until he starts giving me a daily report from today.' Whatever you might say about Ranjit, Puja sounded as serious about this as me. Which gave me much-needed confidence.

Thank you very much, Puja. How I'd love for you to be mine is a story for another day. I'm sure she knows I love her. Have loved her since school and her short-skirt days. Water under the bridge now, isn't it?

Anyway, after the short call with Ranjit, I had started to wonder if my fantasy was just that: a fantasy. But Puja helped get my spark back. I am confident that she'll drill some sense into her husband. I want Ranjit to believe in the idea, I don't want him to say *yes* as a compromise. Compromises can be unpleasant since neither party is wholly satisfied; everyone merely settles for them, and that typically results in people putting in sub-optimal effort. In my mind, it's a lose-lose situation. We cannot afford that.

♥

Monday.

It was time to get into rigorous training, as I mentioned before. To explain and get my students working on the Hofzinser spread. It's just one of the ways to cull cards. I'm aware that you might not even know what *culling cards* means. Culling cards is nothing more than controlling cards. You decide where a particular card ends up in the deck when you shuffle the pack before dealing. You can cull a single card, or multiple. However, for beginners, I recommend you go with just one card initially. Of course, you can learn the skill from tutorials on YouTube too, but it's not the same. The video will tell you the technique, but you need someone to teach you the finer points, like Madari Baba honed my skills aeons ago. And then you have to practise it a hazaar times in front of mirrors, and then some more, to be deft at it; to become competent enough to carry it out with your eyes closed.

'You take the deck.' I looked at my students and all of them appeared alert, concentrating, their eyes curious. Like Zeenat looking at a pigeon – zeroed in on the target, which was my hands at that moment.

'I'll choose a card,' I continued and pulled out the ace of spades, 'This is the chosen one.' Then … I spread the deck, randomly put the card back into it and closed the spread into a neat pack again.

I could sense their excitement. They were looking at me, eyes wide. And they'd missed the sleight of hand.

'Where do you think the ace of spades is in the deck now?'

They had no clue.

'The card is at the bottom of the pack.' I turned the pack around and showed it to them.

They were bewitched. I could see their faces forming a *how*. How did it happen so quickly? All I did was place the card in the middle of the pack and close the spread, right?

Blank looks.

'This is one of the most basic versions of the trick, but it is extremely powerful. When I place the chosen card on the top of the half-pack in my left hand …' I repeated it slowly for them to see, 'and then close the spread with the cards in my right hand, I align the lower-most card with the chosen one – the bottom-most card in the right hand aligns with the topmost card in the left.' I stopped and showed it to them. Their eyes were even wider now. 'Now, as I close the spread, I pull the ace of spades out until it's free from the deck and resting on the little finger of my right hand. I spread the half-pack in my left hand so that in one swift motion, I can slip the chosen one to the bottom of the pack before I close the spread. Easy-peasy lemon squeezy.'

My students or disciples – whatever you might call them – were still entranced. 'And …' I elaborated further, 'you can perform the same trick and place the chosen card on the top, depending on the game, the circumstances and where you want the chosen card to be in the pack.'

Their eyes were still curious, still wondering. They still had no clue how it had happened before their eyes.

I repeated the sequence, and this time the ace of spades ended up right on top of the pack.

'You can go to YouTube and search for "culling cards", but I strongly advise you not to, since you might be surprised how many variations there are, and it will only confuse you. I want you to practise the Hofzinser Spread,' I warned them. 'We do not have the time to learn all the tricks. You need to focus on the important ones and practise until you can do them in your sleep.'

I gave them the usual spiel on putting mirrors around, practising until their hands hurt and running through it a hazaar times, then repeating it hazaar more times when they thought they were adept.

I then gave them a lesson on misdirection, and how distracting the audience is one of the key tools all cardsharps use.

'You divert the audience's attention by drawing their eyes or brains away from what you're about to do … it is your job to make them focus their eyes elsewhere or to channel their minds into thinking something different. Misdirection, precision, speed – you master these three, you're the king of the table. By Wednesday, when we regroup, I want all of you to show me how smooth you are in culling cards. Practise both, placing the card at the bottom and on top.'

I could see them whispering to each other as they packed up for the day and left. I knew I'd given them limited time to practise. Such skills take a long time to develop to a pro level. A few will fall flat on Wednesday, but that will – what do they say? Separate the grain from the chaff.

21

'Help' – The Beatles

TWENTY-ONE. YOU MUST KNOW TWENTY-ONE IS A SIGNIFICANT number for card players. It's Blackjack, which is also called twenty-one. Therefore, I decided to write the entry number differently. Capisce?

My doorbell rang as soon as I stepped out of the shower that evening. I wasn't expecting anyone. I wrapped a towel around myself, rushed to the door and looked through the peephole. It was Puja and Ranjit.

'Oh, hi you,' I said. 'What a nice surprise.'

'Thanks for the naked welcome.' Ranjit gestured at my exposed torso. 'Do you want to take off the towel, too?' Mr Comic Ranjit.

'Yeah, no hugs for me, please. You guys can go ahead and hug,' Puja said.

'Give me a minute.' I ushered them inside and retreated into the bedroom to dry myself and dress up.

Hate at first sight. I bet you haven't heard that one before. Well, hate is as strong an emotion as love. There are several similarities and although I'd very much like to tell you about a few, I am conscious that you'll accuse me of digressing yet again. The reason I mention it is that in the brief three or four minutes it took to don a T-shirt and jeans, Princess Zeenat had left the bed and made herself comfortable on the sofa facing Puja. And it was evident from her body language that she didn't like another woman in the household one bit. No sir.

'How did this stray cat get into your flat?' Puja looked at Zeenat with disgust. The feeling was mutual.

'Oh, she's Zeenat.' In that instant, it occurred to me that I had never mentioned getting adopted by Zeenat to Puja and Ranjit. Since our Saharanpur days, I was typically the one to visit them. On the few occasions that they had dropped by through the years – when Zara was with me – Zeenat wasn't in my life, and I had never felt the need to update them about my bachelor life with a cat.

'Zeenat? So you know her name?'

'Yeah, I named her.'

'When did this happen?'

I explained the entire sequence of events. How she had appeared in the flat one day, after I got out of the slammer, and how she'd been my flatmate since then.

'Have you taken her to a vet? She might be diseased,' Puja said. Zeenat, like she was following our conversation, looked at me.

'No, she's not,' I said protectively. Zeenat seemed to sense Puja's distaste because she jumped into my lap. I never knew she was so territorial that she would be offended to have someone else in the flat. I had never seen this side of her.

Maybe she loves me as much as I love her.

Offhandedly, I noticed that Ranjit had put on some weight. Either that or he had pulled out a five-year-old pair of jeans. A little tummy was hanging over his belt. Puja looked fantastic as usual. She still carried the girl-next-door charm, the same one she had exuded in her short uniform back then. Maybe it's just me; I still remember her as she used to be in those days. Some memories remain etched in your mind. Or perhaps they make you want to stay in a time bubble forever.

While I admired Puja in her skintight jeans, it became obvious to me that Ranjit was a tad distracted. As I tried to find the words to ask, he erupted all of a sudden. 'I think the two of you need to wake up from your pipe dream and face the truth. The plan – your plan,' he looked straight at me, 'as it stands now, has more holes than a worn-out sieve, my friend. And we will all end up in trouble if we go forward.'

I wondered where this was coming from. Just a few days back, I had called and spoken to Puja, and she had assured me she'd bring Ranjit in line. Something hadn't worked. She had clearly failed to convince Ranjit because he still seemed to have reservations. No, not doubts … he seemed to believe that the entire plan was outrageous, a *khayali pilau.* He had bought into it wholeheartedly a month ago and even started work on it by getting a third party to help us with the recruitment. He was the one who had organized the money for my limo service, and to pay Boris for information. What had gone wrong after that?

Whatever it was, it had to end. We were either going forward or dropping it just then. We needed to get all our ducks in a row, or we would get nowhere.

'What's troubling you, Ranjit?' I asked.

'Everything, if I'm being honest. I think we have no chance of getting away with it.'

'*I* think we have—'

'It's easy for you to say. You'll happily leave town if something goes wrong. I have to stay here, live in this city, run my business. What if something goes wrong … anything – where does that leave Puja and me? We will be behind bars regretting we ever thought we'd get away with something as far-fetched as this.' Ranjit sounded abrasive, like he'd all but given up.

'He's been in this foul mood ever since we last spoke; scared, worried and drinking excessively,' Puja interjected.

'So let's drop it,' I said, and I was serious. 'Nothing in this world is more important to me than you two, and if you guys aren't convinced or it's stressing you out, giving you sleepless nights, there is little point in progressing with it. Now, what can I get you to drink?'

'Anything strong.' Ranjit.

'Is whisky strong enough for you?'

'Yes, straight please.'

'I'd like a bite, too.' Puja.

'And I can order some food. What do you fancy?' Me.

'What are the options?' Puja.

'Chinese, tandoori, grilled seafood, pizza.' Me.

'Let's do Chinese. Spicy, please.' Ranjit.

'Egg-fried rice, spicy noodles and sweet-chilli chicken.' Puja.

'Okay,' I said, getting up to find my phone and make a drink for Ranjit. I pulled two bottles of beer out of the refrigerator for Puja and me. I called and ordered food, and was told it would take up to forty-five minutes. Fine by us, we weren't going anywhere. When I returned, I noticed that Zeenat had forsaken her post and left the flat. I made a mental note to leave out some leftover chicken for her when she returned.

'I am not saying we abandon the plan totally,' Ranjit started after a sip.

'Please elaborate.' Honestly, I was in no mood to swing between yeses and nos. He needed to decide what he wanted to do and then stick to it. I did not want to spend time convincing him, since it hadn't worked so far. So I just looked at him, waiting for him to carry on. The silence hung in the room like smoke for a while before he took another sip and opened his mouth.

'The devil lies in the detail.'

Wiser words had never been spoken. But as a rule, I hate clichés delivered in a passive-aggressive tone to make the other person feel like a complete idiot.

Yes, if you took the reference and slant away, what Ranjit had said was true – when had any plan succeeded without attention to detail? But when he said those words, he sounded phoney, like he was reciting someone else's words. Which he was. But I could sense he had something on his mind. I know him. He's one of those guys who generally come straight to the point.

'And what do you think we've missed?' Puja.

Ranjit looked at both of us. 'I can't pinpoint one thing, but it all sounds too ambitious. Can I have another drink please?'

I brought the bottle of Macallan into the living room and poured him one. Puja and I were merely halfway through our bottles of Kingfisher.

Over the next forty minutes, until dinner arrived, Ranjit threw twenty random questions at us regarding our plan, which Puja and I responded to. It was apparent he hadn't sighted any fractures in the plan, he was simply scared. Fear of failure and what-ifs had engulfed him. And I could appreciate his perspective. He didn't point out again, but the elephant was still in the room. If something did go wrong, I could leave town – which I was planning to do anyway – but where did that leave him?

He trusts me; he knows I'll keep my promise and ensure their safety, but who is to know what might happen if things go wrong? No army strategy, they say, stays the same once the first bullet is fired. It is a case study in continuous improvisation. Yes, we are capable people, but this might have enormous repercussions. We could lose everything or go to prison. Worse, we could all end up dead.

Ranjit had his sixth drink with dinner, and it was clear that there was little point in discussing anything that night. For one, arguing with someone under the influence is pointless. Secondly, even if I managed to convince him that I had thought everything through, it was of no consequence. I had, twice before, done just that, but he had changed his mind later.

'No worries, my friend,' I assured him when he requested one for the road. 'Maybe you have a point, maybe it is an unreasonable expectation on my part. I got influenced by my desire to get back at Roshan Godara—'

'*Shhh!* Let's talk tomorrow,' Puja said, and got up. Ranjit followed. I saw them to the door.

◆

I woke up to the doorbell. Rubbing my eyes, I looked at my 6:29
iPhone on the side table. It was not even six-bloody-thirty in the morning and someone was at my door?

Unbelievable! You may call me a hermit, but I don't entertain too many people at my flat. Who did my visitor expect to see? Rahul? Saurabh? Deep? Michael? Dimpy? It would be challenging for me to establish who was on the other side of the door before I got there, and it would probably be too late by then. But this was the third time, in less than twelve hours, that someone had rung my doorbell. You might think I've miscalculated – that it's only rung twice. I seldom make errors in counting. Think again!

Still in bed, I wondered if someone had confused my flat for someone else's. I did not have a nameplate on my door – again, which name would I put there? I noticed Zeenat still hadn't returned since she had left the evening before. Whenever she returns late at night or in the wee hours of the morning, she usually jumps on the bed and makes herself cosy. And before you jump to any conclusions, I must tell you that she's hygienically conscientious – not once has she returned with a dingleberry, mind you. Perhaps she had gotten a hump because of Puja. Silly cat.

The bell chimed again. Then there was a knock on the door, too. Someone had come looking for me. I got up, threw on a T-shirt over my boxers and sauntered to the entrance.

My visitor was smart – they had sensed I was on the other side of the door, despite my attempts to tiptoe to see who it was before deciding whether to open the door or not. They called out to me.

'Open the door, Saurabh … or Rahul.'

Saurabh? Rahul? I knew that voice.

I wanted to say I was neither of them now, but when I looked through the peephole to confirm who it was, I couldn't believe it.

Ah, but before I open the door in my story, let me check if you've figured out when the doorbell rang for the third time. I bet you forgot the consider that the bell was also pressed by the guy who came to deliver Chinese food last night.

TWENTY-TWO

'Mein Yahaan Hoon Yahan ...'
– *Veer-Zaara* OST

YOU WILL SOON FIGURE OUT WHY THE SONG IN THIS ENTRY IS from this particular film. Honestly, I wanted to call it Veer-Zara but ...

I ran my fingers through my hair to comb the unruly, bedraggled curls before I opened the door.

Standing there, in faded blue jeans and a white cotton shirt with the sleeves rolled up to the elbows – looking resplendent like a freshly bloomed daisy – was the love of my life. Zara Khan.

'Zara, what a lovely surprise,' I said and opened my arms. To my astonishment, she came straight into them. She clung to me and buried her face into my chest instead of kissing me. I heard her soft cries before I felt the tears wetting my T-shirt. 'What's wrong?'

She didn't respond. Instead, she clung to me even harder. I could feel her tremble, sob. If she carried on weeping, I knew there would soon be a river running down my T-shirt. She opened her mouth, but no words came out. She wanted to say something – I could hear her throat constricting. I was left wondering whether this was some kind of reconciliation. Did she regret dumping me, had she come back to apologize? Was that it?

No. It had to be more than that. As far as I knew, she was justified in tossing me out of her life; I was a prick. Still am, in that sense. If anything, I had only added more layers to my lie, created more personas.

'What is it, Zara?'

More sobbing. I could feel her heart beating harder, throbbing like a coiled spring aching to break loose. Fear? Anxiety? Love? Remorse?

I held her, made her walk with me and sit on the sofa. 'Breathe in, breathe out … calm down, Zara. Tell me what's wrong.'

She looked at me, grabbed my neck, pulled me close and kissed me. Not a peck, a kiss. A deep, lovers-reunited kind of kiss. Lips and tongues were involved. I tasted her salty tears. Our hands found each other's bodies, the exploration started all over again.

'Make love to me.' Those were her first words.

I always followed her orders, and I wasn't going to start disobeying her now, was I?

We kissed again.

Still intertwined, we started to remove each other's clothes while moving towards the bedroom at the same time. Multitasking for me can be a real struggle, I have to admit. But I succeeded on this occasion. By the time we were in the bedroom, we were down to our underwear. We got rid of them ourselves and tumbled into bed.

♣

I can't say I was sated afterwards, though it would have to do. I had a lot of questions for Zara, but she beat me to it.

'So … who did I just make love to now – Rahul Mahapatra or Saurabh Mathur?'

'Neither,' I said without hesitation. Having lost her once, I wasn't ever going to lie again and risk losing her forever.

She turned on her side, rested her head on her arm and looked at me, startled.

I smiled at her, but I could sense she wasn't amused. Involuntarily, my hand caressed my face to check whether I was wearing the faux beard.

'Deep Singh Sodhi.'

She closed her eyes, opened them, rolled them. 'Would it be too much to ask which one of these is your real name, the name that your parents gave you at birth?'

'None of the above.'

She didn't speak, just stared at me.

'My parents named me Dimpy Raja.'

'So you have four names now—'

'Five, actually. I am also Michael Ferreira now.'

'Do you realize why I need to ask these questions?'

I nodded. I knew.

'So tell me all about yourself.'

'It's a long story.'

'I don't have any clothes on, so you can safely assume that I am not going anywhere.'

'Let's get something to eat first, please. I'm famished.'

She nodded this time.

'And neither of us should put on any clothes,' I added.

'Not even underwear?'

'No.'

'So, we're playing naked chef now?'

'Yep.'

'Don't deep-fry anything …' She laughed and got up.

We moved to the kitchen. I glanced at her nude body from time to time as I chopped onions and green chillies for omelettes while she grated the cheese.

'Don't cut your finger off looking at me, Dimpy Raja. You've seen my body enough times; there's no need to steal glances. Now, tell me about yourself. And, please, *please*, don't give me any baloney this time.' I understood the underlying message in her tone. The time for being nebulous was over. It was best to come clean.

So I told her everything. I told her about my journey from Saharanpur to Mumbai, from Dimpy to Rahul to Saurabh. I told her about the various trades and professions I've dabbled in, that the only close friends I have had are Ranjit and Puja. I told her I fell in love with her when I first saw her.

I also told her she resembled Puja, and left it at that.

'She's so much better than me,' she corrected me, half-heartedly, I knew. Even the best of us like to fish.

'No way.'

'Of course she's better.'

'Anyway, that's not the point.'

'I love you, Dimpy.'

'I love you too.'

Then, I told her my real vocation. The one I love. And the reason why I was playing Deep Singh and Michael at the moment. She gasped at the plan – no surprises there. If I told *you* what the real plan is, you might roll on the floor laughing. It took me several sessions to convince Ranjit to join hands with me, and I'm still not one hundred per cent certain if he is going to go through with it. I could see the excitement in Zara's eyes. Whether or not you believed in the feasibility of the long con I've schemed, it sure sounded thrilling, even to me. However, there was a flip side, and it would have been unfair of me to conceal the same.

So, finally, I told her about my three-month incarceration. There was silence in the room for a few seconds.

'What's the likelihood that you will succeed in a plan as audacious as this?'

'Honestly, I think—'

'Whenever someone utters the word "honestly", I think they're lying through their teeth.'

'Well,' I started again, 'if the probability was any less than fifty per cent, I wouldn't have started working on it. We have already started spending money on it. If you trust me, we have over a ninety per cent chance of success.'

'Are you kidding me?' she turned towards me; her pupils enlarged.

'I kid you not, my love, I don't.'

I told her we would be creating a fantasy for people to believe in, and that was never easy. Obviously, if we didn't tilt the game, there would have been a fifty per cent chance our targets could walk away with everything. But we were training people to skew those odds in our favour. 'You can't depend on luck in cards. That's for suckers,' I explained.

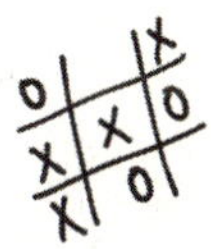

'I want in.'

'What?'

'Do you think only you can amaze me?'

'I didn't say that.' I started whisking the eggs. The cheddar was grated, the onions and green chillies were in the pan. I fried them a little, took them out and kept them on the side, to be used later as a stuffing in the omelettes. My naked co-chef had put the coffee in the French press. I finally gathered enough courage to ask what I had been meaning to since Zara had walked in two hours ago. 'So … have you forgiven me for my little folly then?'

'Little folly? You call getting me in the sack with you without telling me your true name and profession a *little folly*?'

I had started on the wrong foot, it seemed.

'I know what you really want to ask,' she continued with a smile.

'What?'

'Why have I returned?'

'Not really … I mean, I'd like to know what changed your mind but—'

'Stop being polite, Dimpy. If we want this relationship to move ahead, we have to promise to tell each other the truth—'

'The truth, the whole truth and nothing but the truth, I promise.'

'And no lying by omission either.'

'Sure thing. So what made you change your mind and come back to me?'

'I went through the whole gamut of emotions – hurt, anger, depression. Acceptance came when I realized that I still loved you.'

'And …' I mixed some milk into the eggs since I had no cream. Added salt and black pepper and put them in the pan.

'I quit my job.'

'Why?' I wasn't sure whether to express my surprise or not.

'I wasn't getting anywhere. It was a small boutique firm and it recently got sold to J. Patel & Brothers, a chauvinist family business. Misogynistic, really, the way they side-tracked the three women who worked there. It was either sleep with them or find another job.' Her eyes moistened as she narrated her exit from the job she had so loved when I knew her earlier. I can only imagine how heart-wrenching it must be, seeing the detritus of something you've worked all your life towards.

'I'm very sorry.' I left everything and took her in my arms. Not such a good idea, considering we were both stark naked.

'Can I share a secret?'

'I thought we were past that point,' I responded.

'I never liked working nine-to-five. After the initial excitement, it was a brain-numbing repetition of never-ending mundane tasks, like someone had glued five Mondays together, week after week.'

So the truth was that we had both lied. I did, and you know that, through my diary. But she, too, had pretended to be someone who loved their job and career, honesty and straightforwardness. The only difference was that my offence – concealing my true identity – was far bigger. And that I had been caught out. However, I'm glad all that pretence is now behind us, and we can build a life together. A future.

'It's okay. I remember our long conversations when we were together,' she mused, 'You always said there is no good or bad way of making money – everyone is out to swindle someone else. So yes, I have called it quits in the world of banking and finance. I want to do what you do. Will you teach me?'

'What about your family?'

'They've cut ties with me.'

'What? Why?'

'I'm nearing thirty, and not willing to get married to the guy they want me to, back in Hyderabad, so they've all but disowned me. Mum called me to say that my dad was livid. I was given twenty-four hours to pack up my stuff and get down to Hyderabad or …'

'Or what?'

'Or they'd disinherit me, but I decided to stay put. And here I am, an abandoned woman. I was left to reflect on everything – my past, my family, my job, my career, meeting you – and I realized I was happiest when I was with you.'

Our eyes moistened again.

'I love you, Zara.' I switched off the flame. Took the pan off the stove.

'I love you too, Dimpy.'

'Omelettes are ready,' I announced.

As if on cue, the bread popped out of the toaster.

'Are we supposed to eat bare-assed too?'

'Yes ma'am.' I didn't ask her anything more. I could see that she had gone through a lot in the past few months. So had I. And we both had become aware we needed each other more than anything else.

'So were you planning to befriend Jasmine and sleep with her?'

Jealousy is a sign of love, isn't it?

'I love you.'

'That is hardly the answer to my question.'

I knew hers was a trick question. I would be damned if I said yes, damned if I lied.

'It's okay if you were considering it, as I was not in your life then. But if we are together, that is not an option anymore.' I liked the way she said it with a straight face. No ambiguity whatsoever.

I nodded my acquiescence.

♠

We made love again, and it was a *lot* better. The first time that morning, I performed like I had been challenged to break Usain Bolt's world record of 9.58 seconds. I sure did break the record, which, in the context of lovemaking, was a disaster. I was badly out of practice. Out of control. The second time, we went slow, in a far more enjoyable rhythm. We rediscovered each other's bodies; the curves and nooks that we had longed for, our shared ecstasies and joys, the mutual pleasures that only lovers know about. We orgasmed together. Correction:

both of us orgasmed. She had been polite enough not to point out my inadequacy and bad bedside manners during our first session. The second time around, I could sense her delight, as she dug her nails into my back when I came. I stayed inside her until I slipped out due to anatomical reasons.

We made love two more times that day.

But here's the thing. You can't make up for months of lovemaking in a day irrespective of how desirous you feel. The biology of your body cannot support it. The performance dwindles. So here's the accompanying life lesson: if you love someone, don't let them walk away for any reason. Anything you can earn or spend, buy or sell, win or lose cannot be more important than you and your love. Remember your grammar? *Karta ne karm ko karan se sampradhan ke liye* … Always remember you are the noun, and the noun leads the verb. If you don't recognize what I'm referring to, pick up a copy of Wren & Martin and brush up your grammar. Grammar, as you should know, is the backbone of any language … oh, here I go on a tangent again. But don't complain; you just got some great advice for free.

As I lay in bed, listening to Zara's soft snoring and watching her breathe, her body rising and falling, my mind went back to Zeenat. Where was she? Why hadn't she returned? Had she abandoned me?

No sooner did the thought of Zeenat desert my mind, another anxiety took over. Could I trust Zara with the biggest gamble of my life? The answer, to me, was a resounding yes. However, I needed to talk to Puja and Ranjit. I knew they would likely agree, but I didn't want to presume. I also had to talk to Zara when she woke up … but before I knew it, I had fallen asleep, too.

TWENTY-THREE

'White Wedding' – Billy Idol

WE GOT TO THE BHATIA RESIDENCE AT 7:15 P.M. I HAD SPOKEN TO Zara when she had woken up, and she had shared my opinion that we should talk to Puja and Ranjit before injecting her into the plan. Besides, it had been a while and she wanted to see them, too. Her walking out of my life meant that she had lost touch with them abruptly. We decided to keep it a surprise for them; I just told them I had something important to discuss.

Zara stood to the side as I rang the bell. We didn't want either of them to see her through the Judas hole. There is a reason it is named after Judas – I bet you don't know why, do you?

'Hey, buddy … what the f—wow Zara, what a pleasant surprise!' Ranjit looked shocked and rightly so. He stepped inside to let her in, and embraced her. 'So lovely to see you again. I hope this idiot,' he pointed at me – *moi, un idiot?* – 'doesn't do anything stupid to annoy you again. PUJA … look who's here!'

'Zara!' Puja seemed even more excited; she had yelled louder than Ranjit upon seeing her.

The exhilaration subsided after a few minutes of kissing, hugging and some tears of joy. The pleasantries over, a bottle of champagne was popped open and it felt like we were back where we had left off months ago. We updated the Bhatias about Zara having quit her day job, about the fraught relationship with her family and her wish to join our little caper.

Puja held Zara's hand to give her some kind of comfort. 'We are a family, too,' she murmured, and I knew she meant it.

'These Patel brothers who took over the firm you worked in, is one of them referred to as JP?' Ranjit asked.

'Yes, do you know him?' Zara.

'Not really, but I've heard of him. However, your man here knows him well.' Ranjit.

'Me?'

'JP is Jinendrabhai Patel, your erstwhile partner.' Ranjit.

'You're joking.' Me.

'Nope.'

We matched a few more notes and it turned out Ranjit was correct. That added another opponent to our list – another mark. It shouldn't have shocked me, since I always knew that Jinendrabhai, for all his money and pomposity, was an uncouth guy. The way he leered at women; the words that were there at tip of his tongue, unspoken; his gruff manners; his arrogance and rudeness when he was with someone less moneyed than him. 'He should be taught a lesson, too. That gives us three principal targets now: Roshan Godara, Anand Kumar and Jinendrabhai Patel,' I said.

'I hope you guys are together for good now.' Puja.

'I hope so, too.' Zara.

Puja picked up the remote and put on some music, dimmed the lights. 'Have you guys thought of getting married?'

I replied, 'I have to admit, the thought *has* crossed my mind. Maybe in a while—'

'Why in a while, why not soon?' Puja.

'*Nek karya mein vilambh kyon?*' Ranjit.

'Meaning?' Me.

'Why delay something good?' Ranjit translated, like I was asking for a literal meaning. Everyone's a comedian, I've told you so.

'Thank you very much, but I'm sure you know that I understand Hindi perfectly well. I asked because—'

'I know, I know.' Ranjit placated me with raised hands. He looked at Puja who seemed to catch some cue which I missed.

'Let's get you married.' Puja.

'When?' Me.

'Now.' Puja.

'How?' Me.

'What do you mean how?' Puja.

'We need time—'

'Time for what?' Ranjit.

The Bhatias were ganging up on me while Zara mutely watched.

'We can get you married here and now.'

'But …' I looked at Zara again, but she seemed to be enjoying this.

'We don't even have appropriate clothes on,' I protested.

'Clothes don't make a wedding.' How profound of Ranjit. 'You only get into your wedding clothes to get out of them when you start screwing.' How crass of him, too, in the same breath.

'Hold on.' Me.

'How else do you think you two will get married? You're of different faiths. You'll need to get married twice. Once in a temple in the presence of a pundit, once in a mosque where an imam can bless the ceremony. The only other way is to have a registered marriage or a ceremony in the presence of your friends, Las Vegas style.' Puja.

'We've made no preparations.' Zara finally broke her silence.

'I've got rings for you,' Puja said. 'In fact, I always thought I'd present these rings to Dimpy whenever he got married.'

Puja went into her room and brought back two rings. Plain gold bands. Just like that, we exchanged rings and got married. We decided to formalize it in court later, when we could arrange a date with a registrar.

'I now pronounce you wife and boy.' Puja.

Ranjit raised a toast, 'You may now do nookie with the bride. I mean, you must have already done that a few times since you reunited this morning. I bet your nuts are dry now, like ball bearings without any grease left.' The grossness of Ranjit's jokes is usually directly proportional to the amount of alcohol he has consumed. Don't mind him.

'You're incorrigible.' Puja.

The music was still playing in the background as she led us to the guest bedroom, and I faintly heard Neil Young telling someone that he was still in love with her on this harvest moon.

Harvest moon refers to the full moon that appears closest to the autumn equinox, but you know what? I do not have the time or the inclination at the moment to tell you about it. I'm in a rush, as you might have guessed, to spend time with my new bride.

♥

Monday morning.

I couldn't go to Fitiful. The day's planned activities had to take a back seat. With Mrs Zara joining our team, we needed some rules of engagement.

The four of us agreed on the following points:

1. She needs a new name, a new identity. She was rechristened as *Chikki Singh.*
2. We will need to work on a narrative for when – not if – someone asks for her background.
3. Chikki Singh does not travel with me in my hired car. There is no need for the driver to know who she is. Chikki still owns the black BMW X3 that we travelled to Lonavala in, so commuting independently shouldn't be an issue.
4. As a matter of fact, we will not meet anyone as a pair unless required. The two of us together will be a hazaar times more conspicuous than either one of us individually. People tend to remember couples more than individuals, no question about that.
5. Chikki Singh is to join the disciples in training with cards. She will be dropped after only a few sessions, but she must work her way into the group to give us an early warning if any of our recruits is a turncoat, or if there is any other cause for concern.
6. My plan to offer my body as a *plaything* to Jasmine is off the table.
7. Chikki is to become a member at Fitiful, too. Since I am no longer operating alone, we need to work on Jasmine as a team.
8. She is to assist Puja with the make-up artists and costume designers for the big night.
9. At all times, whether acting alone or alongside Puja, Chikki needs to stay at arm's length from any vendors and third parties.
10. Like all of us, Chikki will not be attending the big night in person.

There were other rules and restrictions put in place – the dos and do nots – but I don't intend to write everything down. After a sumptuous and productive brunch, we travelled to Chikki's place, packed up some essentials and returned to Pedder Road.

We haven't vacated her flat since she needs to give a three-month notice to her landlady. Might as well retain possession of the place when we are still paying rent. Who knows, we might need it for something.

TWENTY-FOUR

'Intro' – The XX

ZARA HAS NEVER OPERATED UNDER MULTIPLE PERSONALITIES, so giving her two IDs might be tricky. Nevertheless, she has to get used to managing two separate lives simultaneously.

Ladies and gentlemen, I present Chikki Singh:

She's from Ajmer – a town in Rajasthan that is recognizable enough, but too small for a coincidental fellow-towner to bump into her in Mumbai. She moved to the city recently, as an aspiring model-actor, and has joined the gym to keep herself fit and toned. Chikki Singh and Deep Singh Sodhi don't know each other yet. Watch this space!

Simultaneously, she's been recruited to train for the reality show we are preparing. Chikki Singh is the new XX2, a replacement for the earlier one who got fired by Michael Ferreira when she failed to meet the strict standards set by yours truly. But these two personas will have separate audiences. Two birds, one stone – ever heard of that one?

I can only hope you are keeping up with *my* multiple personalities.

TWENTY-FIVE

'Love Me Like You Do' – Ellie Goulding

IT WAS AROUND 4:30 P.M. BY THE TIME WE FINISHED MOVING Chikki's stuff. I had to empty more than half my wardrobe to accommodate her clothes; I can be a gentleman sometimes. Tired and sweaty, we made love standing in the shower. It was a first time for me and though I am not going to go into details, it was amazing. I totally recommend it. You should try it if you haven't. Well, let's move on to more pertinent things, shall we now? There's lots to discuss.

60 HOURS

By Tuesday morning, Zeenat had been missing for almost sixty hours, and that was a matter of concern. She'd never been away for so long since I've known her. Where was she? Did she get so upset seeing Puja at my flat? If that was the case, how would she accept Chikki? In the months I had known Zeenat, I never for once imagined she'd be the jealous type. Then again, she was living with a recluse so what could she have had to be jealous of?

'Zeenat is missing,' I said, as I brought coffee into the bedroom.

'Who's Zeenat?' Chikki asked.

I told her.

'So you adopted a stray cat?'

'I didn't; she adopted me, and please don't refer to her as a stray.'

'Sentimental, are we?'

'Not sentimental, but I have to admit that I am attached. I didn't anticipate this when she first dropped by, but we've been housemates for months now.'

'Come here, let me give you a cuddle.' I put the coffee down and we embraced. She continued, 'Can we not file a report with the police?'

'I don't think the police will be interested in finding her. They will see her as just another stray that's wandered off, much like you did, moments ago.'

'Has she disappeared on you like this before?'

'A couple of times, but on those occasions, she just went missing for a day or two at most. I don't think she liked Puja the other evening.'

'Oh, so she's a possessive pussycat?'

'Well, I never saw this aspect of her personality before – I'm just guessing.'

'If that is so, and she comes in now with me starkers in your bed, will we have to fight each other to ascertain which one of us is your Queen of Hearts?' I could see that Chikki was immensely enjoying the conversation. I guess I looked like a child who had lost his pet, or perhaps a lost pet looking for his mistress.

'Anyway, let's have coffee and get to work. Zeenat will return when she does. I'll tell the building watchman to keep an eye out.' I said that but I am still worried.

I hope and pray she's safe. I hope she loves me as much as I adore her.

♦

'Jinendrabhai Patel,' I began after our morning coffee, 'does he recognize you?'

'What do you mean?'

'I know he and his brothers have taken over the company you used to work for. But did he attend office regularly, and did you guys interact?'

'He came to work two or three times a week, but yes he knows me, recognizes me,' she pointed at her face, 'I was high up in the food chain in the company, remember?'

'I wasn't saying you weren't, big cheese. What about your car?'

'No, we never made out in my car, if that's what you mean.' She winked.

Chikki, ladies and gentleman, was the new stand-up comedy queen. I guess Ranjit's depraved sense of humour had rubbed off on her. We shared a laugh.

'It just struck me that if he recognizes your black Beamer, it will be stupid to drive around in it. In case anyone remembers the girl who drove a black BMW, it won't take long to connect the car to you, and then us,' I explained. Isn't there an adage: if anything *can* go wrong, it *will*? If you've already spotted a weak link in the chain, why not change it?

'I doubt JP or his brothers will recognize my car but yes, some ex-colleagues might. Also, it's likely on the office building's car park CCTV. We had cameras at the entrance and exit.'

'Then we need to dispose of the car. If you lose money, I'll make that good—'

'Dimpy, I know we got married impromptu, without discussing a few basic rules, but we need to talk.'

God, that sounded a bit too serious for early in the morning.

'We can't have *yeh-tera, yeh-mera* in our marriage. I'm glad you didn't start writing a prenup at Puja's place on Sunday evening—'

'Is that even legal in India?' I wisecracked.

'It might be, it might not be, but that's not the point I'm making. If we start our marriage with who pays for what and who makes good a loss on the sale of an old car, we aren't going to go far.'

'We won't go far without the car anyway, ha-ha.' I could sense Chikki was not at all amused at my joke.

'I'm serious. It's not yours or mine, it's *ours*. You don't expect me to pay you rent living here, do you?'

I shook my head.

'We are a unit now.'

'Point taken,' I concurred.

'But yes … we should sell the car and buy another one.'

'I don't think we should buy a car and register it in either of our names. We'll hire another one for you.'

'But won't we need to show an ID to hire one?'

I told her about Art Lovers Private Limited.

'You're smarter than you look,' she smiled.

'I try to underplay my cards.' A nifty response, wasn't it?

'Touché!' she blew a kiss to me. 'But no driver, please. If we have two cars, both with drivers, we can't travel together in either.'

'Yeah, that makes sense. You're as smart as you look.'

She ignored this rejoinder. Bah!

'So, what's the plan for the day?'

'We need to find a new way to meet Jasmine—'

'By *new way*, I'm guessing you mean you no longer have to sleep with her.'

'You guessed correctly.'

'Hang on a minute … if we are enticing Jasmine because

she will lead us to Anand Kumar, how can we be sure that he will bring Roshan Godara along?'

'They are proverbial birds of a feather that flock to casinos and gambling dens together. We need Jasmine to trust us enough to pass on our information to her philandering husband. Once Anand Kumar buys it, Roshan will tag along, believe me. But not Jinendrabhai. We need to think about how to get him there separately.'

'We'll think of something, but for now, let's get ready to see Jasmine at Fitiful.'

'Tackle one bird at a time, I like that. Do you want to shower first, or should I?'

'Why don't we take a shower together, my new husband?'

Do animals have instincts like we see in books and films? More specifically, do cats have a sixth sense? Are they telepathic? I ask because when we came out of the shower in our birthday suits, guess who was sitting on the bed?

Her Royal Highness Zeenat. The prodigal princess had returned.

You can't imagine how happy it made me feel. Ecstatic. A deep kind of relief. I wanted to pick her up and hug her. 'What are you looking at, pussycat?' I asked her mockingly.

'Your mouse.' Chikki points at my … you know! What was the matter with Chikki today? She was making too many below-the-belt jibes.

'Cheeky.'

'No, I'm Chikki – and what about you, mister with the little mouse?'

Zeenat seemed to appreciate Chikki embarrassing me. In a

flash, she jumped from the bed and I watched, bewildered, as she headed over to Chikki instead of me.

'*What?*'

'She prefers my smooth leg to your hairy one.'

So she'd abandoned me for a new friend? Or was she trying to make me feel envious now, punishing me for making her jealous of Puja the other day? Were cats capable of that level of emotional intelligence or was it only in my mind? I didn't care. I was delighted, joyous even, that unlike her apparent dislike for Puja, Zeenat fancied Chikki.

She rushed back into the shower, put on a robe and picked Zeenat up. 'I'm Chikki. You must be hungry, Zeenat.'

She purred.

'She's always hungry.'

Countess Zeenat gave me a *shut-up-page-boy* look, her whiskers twitching at the mention of food.

'You get ready, I'll feed my baby first. Where's her food kept?'

'Why don't you ask your baby?'

'Come on, don't be a jerk or I'll tell her to grab your mouse.'

I realized I was still in the buff.

'It's in the kitchen, the last cabinet on the right.'

I let the girls head to the kitchen and went to my wardrobe looking for something to cover my *mouse* before they got back. Best to keep it secure – the cats in my flat had doubled now. Why risk it?

TWENTY-SIX

'Tune Abhi Dekha Nahin …'
– *Do Aur Do Paanch* OST

OUR STRATEGY IS STILL TO ENTICE JASMINE, BUT SOME LATERAL thinking is required now. That I no longer have to bed her – as though that was ever going to happen – is evident.

'What a relief!' I assured Chikki, but I'm sure she could tell I was being sarcastic. She believed me as much as a frog believed an alligator.

However, the whole shenanigan of befriending Jasmine has actually become a lot simpler now that Chikki and I are a team because she is privy to things I am not and has access to areas I don't. For instance, she can go into the women's locker rooms and get closer to Jasmine. Far less superficial than having to hang around the coffee shop waiting for an opportunity. She would just be seen as a new girl at the gym trying to be friendly with another member.

The plan is for Chikki to confide in Jasmine. *Have you seen that handsome guy? I have the hots for him. He's the reason I've taken the membership.* Oh, and by the way, the handsome guy Chikki is referring to is none other than yours truly.

We intend to make Jasmine believe Chikki needs help. That she is *truly, deeply, madly* in love with me, but isn't ready to make the first move. Thus, she will recruit Jasmine to set up a date for Chikki and me.

See, we're improvising. Improvisation – the word comes from the world of art, when actors or musicians are asked to perform extempore. On your feet, on the spot – but I have no intention of digressing at this pertinent moment in the narrative, so please don't distract me. If you want to know more about improvisation, check the dictionary. Don't bother me, please.

If Chikki confides in Jasmine, it is only a matter of time before the other woman does the same. We know about Jasmine's indiscretions, so keeping Chikki's flat for the next three months might come in handy should she want a place to take a guy for a nookie. It's only fair that friends help each other out in such situations. You scratch my back and all that.

♠

Chikki dropped me off half a kilometre away from Fitiful and drove ahead alone, so that we could arrive separately, but within five minutes of each other. As I walked in, I spotted the familiar white Volvo XC60. Jasmine was in that day. I went to the lockers, changed and headed to the gym. I cycled and rowed for forty-odd minutes until my breath was ragged. Note to self: I need to get fit. I looked around but could see neither Jasmine nor Chikki.

Where were they?

I used the treadmill for another five minutes, took a shower, went swimming for thirty-five minutes and then sat on one of the tables by the poolside. There was a slight smell of chlorine in the air but nothing so strong that it couldn't be endured. I ordered an egg-and-mayo sandwich and a pot of coffee. I knew

I had to linger for a while – though I wasn't sure how long – so I picked up one of those health magazines that are only ever bought by gyms, full of pictures of naked torsos to make you go green with envy. I guess that is the whole point of them. And to sell protein supplements. I should have ordered a protein shake rather than coffee to look the part. No sweat; if I had to wait longer, I would order that next.

Would Chikki be able to befriend Jasmine on her first day at the gym?

Maybe.

Maybe not.

Didn't matter. A few days more couldn't hurt.

I have to admit I was flummoxed when I saw Chikki and Jasmine walking out of the showers together; beaming, sharing a joke. Friends already? I did a double take.

I have to admit, it does scare me shitless: who is Chikki? Until a few days ago, she was someone I knew, who dumped me since I wasn't morally fit to be her boyfriend. Now she's become some sort of a swindler? It seems like a rather quick transformation for someone I knew as a corporate big cheese when we dated the first time around. I know I married her, and the thought shouldn't cross my mind, but what if she swindles me too?

Had she told me the truth? The whole truth? Maybe the name JP had slipped out of her mouth. Maybe she hadn't expected Ranjit to know JP was, in fact, Jinendrabhai. What if Jinendrabhai and she were in cahoots?

My thoughts abruptly came to a halt when I heard a sweet, plummy voice ask: 'Excuse me, do you mind if we sit with you?'

I looked up. It was Jasmine, with Chikki in tow. They weren't in the pool so why were they in swimwear? Maybe they had gone to the sauna and decided to come out before they changed. It's not like I was complaining. Both women wore wraparound shades. Up close, Jasmine looked every bit as stunning and glam as her profile photo on Facebook, if not better.

It wasn't difficult to find her on social media despite the fact that she used her maiden name: Jasmine Nanavati. Yes, I've stalked her online, though I suppose the politically correct word is 'research'. Her profile is not locked. Alpha female. She has bikinis in every colour of the rainbow and then some. I can confirm that she takes every opportunity to flaunt her toned body. She's got long legs. Her nails are always done. She's got two tattoos on her gorgeous self but only one is visible – three stars on the inside of her right wrist – while the other one is a heart on the small of her back. She likes a good G&T. Anand Kumar does not feature in any of her photos, nor does she mention him in her posts. Her relationship status is blank – it's for you to interpret. Her wedding band is off in all her pictures – but someone with a keen eye can see the untanned band on her finger, betraying that she usually wears a ring.

She wasn't wearing one when she addressed me. My eyes rested on her bosom longer than I wanted. Her breathing made it rise and fall. Chikki noticed, rolled her eyes.

There were other empty tables around the pool, so it wasn't merely about finding a place to sit. I'd been struggling for more than a week, and Chikki had built Rome in a day. She'd done it within ninety minutes, actually.

'Of course not, it will be my pleasure.' The words flew out of my mouth like flowers. I'm using a metaphor incorrectly, but you get the point.

The girls took a seat. Jasmine sat on my left facing the pool, Chikki opposite me. The waiter came running before we could introduce ourselves.

'I'll have a strawberry protein shake, with a generous portion of peanut butter please.' Jasmine.

'Make that two.' Chikki.

How lovely – two friends with similar taste. I wanted to laugh, but I knew better.

'Make that three, please.' Me.

'Sorry, we didn't introduce ourselves. I'm Jasmine and this is my friend Chikki.'

'Hi, I'm Deep Singh, so nice to make your acquaintance.' I am an exporter; I speak to people around the world. I have impeccable manners, okay?

'Are you new to the gym?' Jasmine.

'Yes, but I've been around for a few weeks.' I was devastated. I'd seen her, passed her a smile that she'd returned a couple of times at least and she did not even recognize me. That was hardly a morale boost for handsome me, was it?

'Chikki is new here, too. She joined today.' Jasmine.

My bride coyly nodded. God, she is a consummate actor. If she's taking me for a ride, there is no hope in hell for me. Note to self: I need to watch out, if only for a while. *The devil lies in the detail.* I think it is said that since God is kind, he overlooks some things – but the devil spares nothing.

My mind went into overdrive again.

Has she been lying to me?

Why would she lie?

Why did anyone lie?

I can't believe *I* am asking this. Me? The irony is worth pointing out.

Can I really believe her?

Can I take her at face value?

Then again, if I can't trust Chikki, who can I trust?

Am I just paranoid?

These bizarre thoughts, that Chikki – my Zara – could cheat me had never bothered me before. But … I've never had so much at stake before this. Questions, questions and more questions erupted. I have to do something about this before I develop actual paranoia.

Our protein shakes arrived and that halted my wild and baseless pondering. 'So I assume the two of you know each other from before?' I asked.

'Why would you assume that?' Jasmine. She was taking the lead in the conversation.

'Well, Chikki, as you say, has joined this gym just today, but it appears to me that you two are old friends – I decided to play Sherlock.' Me.

'Well, for one, neither of us is old …' Jasmine.

Everyone I meet seems to be a stand-up comedian these days.

'… and two, you're wrong. We met earlier today and became friends.'

'Wow, really?'

'You don't seem convinced.' Chikki.

'It hardly matters whether I'm convinced or not. Now, the three of us should be friends.' Me.

Jasmine winked at Chikki while I sat there. *I'm not blind*, I wanted to tell her, but instead acted like I hadn't noticed.

'That's what we came here for.'

I pretended to look surprised.

'Chikki is single, are you?' Jasmine.

'I am, are you?' Me.

'Chikki thinks you are dating material.' Jasmine completely ignored my question.

'What?' I reacted like it was the most shocking thing I had heard in a long time.

'Why, do you like Jasmine more?' Cheeky Chikki!

'Oh, I didn't say that.'

'So I'm not worth your time then?' Jasmine.

The women seemed to enjoy ragging me.

'I'm happy to date both of you.'

'A throuple. Why not! But Chikki has to agree. You're her find.' Jasmine.

I looked at Chikki.

'I was only joking. Chikki is my new BFF. I won't steal away her boyfriend.'

'Boyfriend?' I feigned surprise again.

We all laughed. Friends like us crack jokes at each other's expense all the time.

'So, what do you do, Deep?' Chikki asked me.

I presented the narrative for Deep Singh Sodhi. Cut-surd from Delhi, exporter, traveller, workaholic, single, remember?

'What about you?' Chikki asked Jasmine.

'I was born and raised in Mumbai, very much a local lass. I married early. We own a lot of petrol and service stations across Mumbai. A few car dealerships now, too. Our house is in Cuffe Parade; you guys must visit us sometime. Where do you live?'

'Pedder Road, but I work here,' I clarified, as part of my Deep Singh brief.

'What about you?' Jasmine asked Chikki.

Chikki Singh eloquently presented herself as a new arrival from Ajmer. No hesitation, no temporizing. Impressive.

'So, both of you share the surname Singh?'

I wanted to educate her that Singh is not a surname but, like Kumar, a middle name. People may or may not put their surnames after it. But the last thing I wanted to do was piss Jasmine off with the fountain of trivia I carried. No going off track here.

'I moved to Mumbai a couple of months back to try to get into the glamorous world of modelling.' Chikki.

'Oh, you certainly have the face and body for it. Let's see you in a bikini next time.' Jasmine.

Ooh-la-la!

We sat for an hour, asking questions, getting to know each other better before we exchanged phone numbers. We decided to catch up two or three times a week at the gym. Then the three of us shook hands and split. The girls chose to give the pool a miss and went in to change, and I walked out. At the time of writing this, I'm sat waiting for Chikki's call at a cafe a kilometre away.

TWENTY-SEVEN

'Suspicion' – Elvis Presley

BACK AT HOME, I PULLED OUT TWO BEERS, OPENING AND passing one to Chikki.

'Let's take them to bed.'

'Really?'

'You must be horny, the way you were staring at Jasmine.'

'I. Was. Not.'

'Oh please, the way you were looking at her tits—'

'It's not what you're thinking.'

'And what do you think that is?'

This discussion could only go one way. Down. I realized I should stop digging myself further into a hole.

'My eyes wandered off for a moment, I'm sorry,' I surrendered, with a mock-slap to the forehead.

Chikki burst out laughing. 'I was just kidding! Look at you, all red in the face. I'm not a jealous wife, in case you thought so. And to be fair, she is gorgeous.'

We were on an even keel on that point. No arguments.

'How did you manage to become friends so quickly and convince her to come talk to me?' I asked.

'Remember when we first met, you told me about Mandrake?'

'The magician, yes.'

'Well, magicians don't reveal how they do their tricks.'

'Touché! Well, we've made friends with Jasmine, so let's try to see her as often as we can. If I can't make it for some reason, you should still go ahead.'

'Let's play it by ear.'

'And buy yourself a string bikini,' I teased her.

'Why? I'll take all my kit off for her to assess me. She might want more than a visual inspection.'

Cheeky Chikki!

♥

Chikki's gone to the salon for some beauty treatments. She said she'll also swing by her flat to pick up some things. Three hours minimum. My anxiety is getting the better of me once again. I realize this cannot go on. I can't keep suspecting my wife of being involved in some kind of conspiracy to bring down my friends and me. Not in the least when I am plotting the biggest gamble of my life. Not when we plan to push all our chips to the centre of the table, put all our faith in the last card drawn – even if we are controlling the cards. If someone knows about our plan and wants to sabotage it, it will be easy.

दो जिस्म, एक जान

The truth is that one should never suspect one's spouse or there is no relationship. We are supposed to be *do jism, ek jaan*, after all. Two bodies with a single soul. Until death do us part … okay, back to the point that's been bothering me.

I called Ranjit.

'I know how it sounds, but my suspicion is getting the better of me.'

'Ordinarily, I'd shun you since I know you're a nutter. But a lot is riding on this, so we better check. I'll ask someone to dig into her past, maybe follow her – but I'll keep it separate to the nth degree so it can never be traced back to us, in case she finds out. Give me a week, in the meantime carry on as usual.'

There are hundreds of private investigators in Mumbai, I know. Ninety-five per cent of them specialize in finding evidence against cheating partners, nothing more.

'Of course. And one more thing,' I said.

'What?'

'Not a word to Puja.'

'Are you crazy? Not at all.'

'How're things at your end?'

'A friend of a friend is coming over from New York, so I've asked him to bring some camera glasses.'

'What are camera glasses?'

'Glasses with a camera, simple. These are glasses a person can wear, with a spy camera that can record high-definition video onto a 128 GB micro SD card.'

'How much can it record on 128 gigs?

'I'd say it should be around forty-fifty minutes per GB so a single card can store a lot.'

'But we'll only get access to the videos after the event.' I couldn't see the point.

'I'm sure there is a way to connect it to some wireless transmitter, so that it can relay the images to us in real-time. The more closely we can watch and observe, the more we can guide the team inside.'

'Brilliant, Ranjit.' This tilted the balance further in our favour. It also meant that Ranjit was now totally in, if he'd started thinking about the scheme without us having to cajole him. 'How's everything else?'

'Progressing. One more thing. We should recruit more people through Boris – we need the staff on our side on the day.'

'Of course. Why don't I speak to Boris, since we need to approach people like him who don't have a strict moral code? I bet he knows his colleagues better than us.'

'Yeah, that makes sense. Let me know how it goes.'

'Will do. Let's catch up over the weekend.'

'Ciao.'

Sorted. Ranjit would make a few discreet enquiries, and we'd know if there is any reason to mistrust Chikki. One thing I've learned in gambling is to take the guesswork out. Guesswork leads to surprises. Surprises are only good for birthdays and Christmas.

Always take the guesswork out of any scenario, plan, game, life.

You would be forgiven for thinking that I'm a two-faced bastard who mistrusts his wife, considering I've just asked my friend to spy on her. Believe me, it is necessary – if not for me, for my friends. I cannot put Puja and Ranjit in any kind of danger. I promise if you were in my place you'd do the same. I understand if some of you still think I'm pathetic, asking Ranjit to spy on Chikki, but history is awash with betrayals.

Vibhishana betrayed his brother, Ravana.

Aurangzeb deposed his ill father, made him a captive and got two of his brothers killed.

Jesus was betrayed by Judas.

Lady Macbeth incited her husband to kill the king.

Those of you who still want to argue the point should ponder why a word like familicide exists in the dictionary.

Anyway, it can't hurt to be conscientious. To err on the side of caution. There is no such thing as too much carefulness. If you think it's weird, think about how weird it is for *me*. I can't trust my soulmate. The question you should be asking is what happens if – God forbid! – I come to know Chikki *is* conspiring against me. How will I live with myself?

The sooner we can clear Chikki of this suspicion, the better it will be for my well-being. The uneasiness is percolating into my brain 24/7, consuming me. Whether I acknowledge it or not, the truth is that it is causing distraction when I need to focus on far more important things right now.

◆

Not long after my call with Ranjit, I heard conversation in the corridor and opened the door. Chikki was talking to Mrs Daswani – the neighbour who had told her about me being Rahul, not Saurabh, or the other way around, I couldn't even remember.

'I'm so happy that you two sorted out your differences. I always knew there was some misunderstanding. How can one person have two names?' She saw me and said hello.

Well, you're talking to Zara and Chikki, and five of me now, I wanted to quip, but I smiled and said hello back.

'You two should come over for dinner sometime, I'll talk to my husband and let you know the date.'

'Thank you.'

As Chikki shut the door, she said, 'Thank God, you came out at the right time – she was almost interrogating me and I was worried. I'm surprised she still remembers my name.'

I turned around and kissed her on the forehead.

We embraced. I felt her warm breath on my neck as she buried her face into me. Her perfume filled my nostrils. God, I love Chikki.

I know what you might be thinking.

If Chikki is an infiltrator or if she has any malicious

intent, we are doomed, since she already knows too much for this arrangement to go ahead. And you would be correct in thinking so. But if we come to know something like that, it is still not too late. We'll cancel the whole gig and say we were just kidding. She won't accept it, but if we find out she is a turncoat then we won't care whether she believes it or not. Because the relationship is doomed, the marriage is off.

Yes, it will mean a lot of effort and preparation has gone to waste, but we'll walk away from it all, cut our losses and live another day. I'll feel betrayed and humiliated too, but I will be okay. It is the stupid ones, not the wise or brave, who walk into a lion's den knowing the beast is inside, waiting for dinner. However, if you still decide to march in, may I suggest showing some courtesy to the king of the jungle by carrying some plates, forks and knives, please? Maybe serviettes, too?

TWENTY-EIGHT

'The Gambler' – Kenny Rogers

CARD TRICKS CAN BE PERFORMED FOR PURE ENTERTAINMENT. You know I used to do that in my previous life as Saurabh Mathur. However, when cardsharps or cardsharks do them, they are referred to as card mechanics. This word is used for people who cheat at cards. Why have these terms come up? We are back to seven card mechanics in training now.

I walked in to find all my students waiting to show me what they had practised over the past few days. Next, I had to take them through the hazaar tricks possible. A bit of theory, an introduction. I didn't intend to teach them all the tricks. There was just not enough time for them to learn and practise. I'm sure you'll agree that it is far better they know a few tricks that they can carry out deftly than knowing lots and performing them all clumsily.

However, I still had to inform my students about other tricks. They need to know so they are wise enough to spot a pattern if it emerges; so they can keep an eye out should one of their opponents turn out to be a card mechanic. It isn't implausible that there are others out there. It is better to be suspicious than gullible. To pretend that no other cardshark might turn up on the planned night could lead to disastrous consequences. No one has taken an oath to play fair. There is a lot of money riding on this play date. If you don't prepare, you are not prepared – it is a simple fact of life. It would be presumptuous to think we are the only ones warming up for the game. Ever heard the proverb: *Chaubey jee chale Chabbe jee bann ne, Dubey jee bann ke laute* – go for wool and come home shorn?

Not being able to perform a trick does not, in my opinion, mean that you can't catch someone else perpetrating it in your presence.

But first, I introduced the new XX2 to the group. I told them that the previous one had been excluded since the selectors (not me) decided that she did not have the aptitude for the job. As per the rules, I did not divulge any names. This XX2 would be dropped soon enough, but first Chikki needs to assimilate into the group and find out if they have exchanged names and addresses. Not that it matters if they get pally or make whoopee as long as they don't meet in public places. The plan for the big night is that they will enter the casino as strangers. If anyone sees them together and recognizes them, it will pose a problem. I know the odds are low, but we have to control all we can.

After the introduction, I asked the team to show me how well they could cull cards, now that they'd had sufficient time to practise.

XX2 – as you know – was new, so she got to watch.

XX3, the tallest girl in the group, volunteered to go first. She got full marks for her enthusiasm. She was wearing a white rib-knit T-shirt and those ripped jeans that have become fashionable these days. She let the new girl on the block select a random card from the deck. A three of clubs. As she fanned the cards exactly like I had demonstrated and closed the spread, I caught sight of her little finger supporting the chosen card before she slipped it to the bottom of the pack. But my assessment at this stage was unfair – I had taught her how to carry out the trick and I was looking for her to make that move, so it was obvious I'd see it. Others might have spotted it too, since they were looking at her with their eyes peeled, but they waited for me to deliver my verdict.

I showed my approval with applause.

'Didn't you see me slipping the card to the bottom?' XX3 asked.

'I did, but that's irrelevant. You have a way with cards. The fluidity of your fingers, the nimbleness. I give you full marks for precision, but you need to go at a hundred kilometres per hour – currently you performed at fifty. Speed reduces visibility – the faster you perform the lesser the chances that someone can spot your play, so you need to practise a lot more.'

She seemed happy with the feedback.

'But a very good first attempt. Who wants to go next?'

XX4, the Jasmine lookalike. She had practised too, I could make out. She wasn't as confident as XX3, but a lot quicker.

All six participants performed for me, twice. If I were to rate them solely based on the day's performances, I'd say XX3, the six-footer XX4, the debonair XY2 and the *khandani*-looking guy XY4 showed potential. Which is okay by me. I might not even need all four of them on the final day. I need two, maybe three out of six. I made a note to myself to discuss this with the other three partners later. Chikki will, of course, not be going in. Not because she won't be as good after training – in fact, I could teach her 24/7 – but as per the Ten Commandments, we weren't going to send her in. With Jinendrabhai Patel identified as one of the marks, it was out of the question.

'Well done, guys, I'm really proud of you all,' I commended them. 'Today, I will demonstrate a new trick, and you'll get more homework. When we meet next, you should be able to cull the cards ten times better and faster than what you did today – German precision at lightning speed.'

They looked mortified. Did they think we had hired them for an easy job?

'Now, today I'll teach you false shuffle.'

They nodded. I guess the name was self-explanatory.

'False shuffling is controlling the cards, putting them in the place that you want to be. In continuation of what I taught the other day – and which most of you have demonstrated that you have learnt – what do you do after you've chosen a card, culled and brought it to the bottom? There is little point in that if it moves when you shuffle again, right?'

Some nodded, some looked confused.

'Let me elaborate. You cull the card and bring it to the position of your choice – the bottom, in this case – and then shuffle the pack. Your chosen card should remain at the bottom or else the culling is rendered pointless.'

Nods this time. They got it.

'I'll teach you one of the simplest methods to false shuffle. Don't get me wrong, it might be simple but it's every bit as effective. The essence, as always, is—'

'Speed, precision and misdirection.' XY4.

Do you see how intelligent my protégés have become?

'Bravo!' I complimented him and picked up a pack of cards. 'Let's suppose you spot a card – let's say …' I picked a random card, and it was seven of diamonds, 'this one, or any particular one that you want to control. You need to hold the pack in your left hand if you're right-handed and in the right if you're a lefty – in your offhand.'

I saw everyone looking at each other.

'Anyone left-handed?'

Nope.

'Okay, so everyone holds them in their left hand.' I raised my hand and held the cards in the position, ready to shuffle. I placed the seven of diamonds at the bottom of the pack and showed it to them. Then I shuffled the cards in what seemed to be the normal way, although it was anything but. I carried out the shuffle at a fairly high speed. Imperceptible to them, I was holding the bottom card tightly, almost clenching it.

'As you watch this, remember you can do it too – practice makes a person?'

'Perfect.'

I had misdirected them, and in that time, shuffled quickly, slipped the topmost card on top of the seven of diamonds and held the two even tighter. Why? Because gripping two cards is simpler and safer than one. Then, holding the two bottom cards, I genuinely shuffled the rest without moving those two. No one saw that. They knew what was going to happen, but they still couldn't spot it.

'Here we are,' I said and upturned the pack. The seven of diamonds was still there.

'I know what you did.' XX3.

'You do?'

'You misdirected us for a second asking that question in between, making us focus elsewhere, didn't you?'

'Misdirection. It works every time. You expected it, but you were still hoodwinked for a second. Trust me, a cardsharp merely needs a millisecond of diversion. You see with your eyes, but you process what you see with your brain. If you succeed in engaging your opponent's brain elsewhere, you will win.'

I showed them the trick again, slowly this time. I stopped at the precise point I had asked them the inane question. I slowed down further and let them watch as I slipped the top card to the bottom. Then I gave the pack a shuffle without moving them.

'Got it.' XX3.

I watched them fumble for the next hour until it was time to pack up.

'You need to practise these two tricks in tandem. First, cull a particular card, place it at the bottom and then give it an intense shuffle. The chosen card should remain where you've placed it. Practise in front of mirrors, like I've told you before.'

'When do we meet next?'

'Monday will be good – you get four days in between. Will that be enough?'

Nods.

'Once you've mastered this, I'll teach you the bottom deal.' Self-explanatory again. You dealt a card or cards from the bottom of the pack.

They left; Chikki included. I waited twenty minutes, looking out in case someone was still around; although I'm sure if someone was, Chikki would have called or texted me. Still, better safe than sorry and all that. Then I was driven home in luxury.

TWENTY-NINE

'Who's Foolin' Who' – Bobby Womack

'ARE YOU FREE NOW?' RANJIT ASKED.

'Nope, but I'm not expensive either.' I told you, I can be funny too when I want.

'Hilarious.' He told me to come into his office. It was Friday, and we had a double date in the evening anyway, but Ranjit wanted to see me alone to discuss some plans. What could be so urgent that it couldn't wait until the evening? Moreover, he made it apparent that I was to see him alone, not with Chikki. His invitation sounded conspiratorial, if not ominous.

'I'll come by,' I said. I'd have to think of some way later.

♣

'What will I talk to Jasmine about?' Chikki wondered when I told her that I needed to catch up with Ranjit at his office. I didn't give her a reason why I wasn't inviting her to come along, and she didn't ask either. Good.

'Oh, you can't be short of topics to discuss. Talk like close friends when they want to get to know each other better. Films, books, travel, music, work, your pasts, future ideas ... with some references to her sex life, her husband, other men, ambition. Just don't talk about gambling or anything, not yet.'

'And what is it that Ranjit wants to discuss that can't wait until the evening?'

'I don't know. He says it's a lot of papers to carry home. Besides, he doesn't want to ruin the evening talking about our plans, which I totally agree with. Once we start discussing this we hardly move on to other things.'

Of course it was a lie. I knew Ranjit wanted to see me alone. The anxiety was killing me. I couldn't wait for Chikki to leave so I could make my way to his office.

♠

'Nothing,' he said, after we had dispensed with good mornings and asked someone to send coffees in. 'Chikki's clean.'

'Your James Bond hasn't discovered anything incriminating?'

'He's found nothing. He's been following her around whenever she goes out of your flat. She hasn't met anyone, forget Jinendrabhai Patel or his brethren.' He passed me two A4 sheets of handwritten notes outlining Chikki's movements. Her journey to the beauty salon wasn't mentioned since the surveillance was put up after that.

'What about her phone?'

'You want me to tap her phone? Who do you think I am, the flipping FBI?'

'You're right, that would be going too far. I think we should call this off.'

'You're convinced she's with us, then?'

'Yes. In any case, if she decides to betray us, she can do it just as easily over the phone.'

'You have a point.'

'I've spent some time thinking about it. Even if she warns JP and he passes on the info to Anand and Roshan, what's the worst that can happen? They simply won't turn up at the party. They won't call the police or put out an advertisement in the papers. Though it will be heartbreaking since we'll have spent a fortune planning it – all our time and money and expectations.'

'Hmm ...'

'I'm happy to drop the surveillance if you are.'

'Your call, buddy.'

'I feel I am being dishonest, having my wife followed. Don't you?'

'I can appreciate how you feel. I will ask them to call it off right away. We still have time – she's not Charles Sobhraj, she won't be able to sustain a lie for very long while she's living with you.'

'You're correct.'

'I always am,' said Mr Smarty Pants. 'Also, I have to show you something.' He unlocked the bottom drawer and pulled out a fancy flat box. The spy camera glasses. 'When we meet in the evening, we can tell the wives that we had to take a look at these and hence I *had* to see you today.'

I nodded. Good thinking, in case we got asked.

He opened the box. They were basic clear glasses, with a slightly thicker arm that had space for a micro SD card. There was a small button on the inside – invisible when worn – and the camera was hi-def.

'Brilliant stuff. How many have you got?'

'A baker's dozen.'

'And who will wear these?'

'All staff inside the casino – as long as they are as unethical as Boris and switch sides for a day – maybe one of the players, too. I've been careful to order a mix. Some dark glasses, like the security guys wear to conceal who they are looking at. Some clear ones that might look like someone's prescription spectacles. Different shapes, of course, so they don't look like some kind of uniform. Imagine thirteen people wearing the same pair of glasses.'

I was thrilled. Ranjit *was* truly on board now. No turning back, no more cold feet. And my gut told me Chikki was with us, too – only time would tell. Puja had always been as enthusiastic as me. We would be the Awesome Foursome.

We chatted for another hour. Ranjit made a few calls to check on things, called off the spying on Chikki. Remember, he wasn't dealing with any of this directly. He had to call people who in turn called other people to pass on his questions and instructions. There were at least three or four degrees of separation. The confirmations started coming in by lunch.

'Done for today,' he said. 'Now let me focus on some real work.'

'I'll let you carry on. See you this evening.'

THIRTY

'Sinnerman' – Nina Simone/Sofi Tukker

END OF APRIL. WE WERE AT MY VERSOVA FLAT, ME AND MY students. Another one of them hadn't made the cut – she was all over the place, her hand-eye coordination was poor, her speed could shame a snail – so we simply removed her from the group.

Wink, wink, it was Chikki, who had done her job. She had mingled with the others and found they weren't meeting each other outside of the classes. She tried to change that by asking them to go out for drinks. XX3 complained to me, and Chikki was asked to leave.

Ranjit had done thorough background checks to see if any of them had connections with our marks: Roshan Godara, Anand Kumar or Jinendrabhai Patel. Nothing there either.

Six remained now. And I had convinced Ranjit that all six must stay until the end. Why? Because we had changed from our earlier plan of sending three into the casino to planting all six inside on the night. I'll divulge more when the time comes.

I had decided not to teach them a single new thing until they all excelled in culling and shuffling, as it would cause unnecessary confusion. But all six students amazed me that day. They were quick, precise. They even talked to me while they carried out both the manoeuvres. I watched them from various angles but couldn't fault any of them.

'You have impressed me, beaten all my expectations by a huge margin, I have to admit,' I commended them.

I could see they were delighted.

'What do you think is the next logical step – after you've culled the card or the cards you want, moved them to the bottom and maintained their position after shuffling?'

'We need to deal that card to someone?' XX4.

'Correct. Today I shall show you how to bottom deal.'

No explanations required there.

'You've culled and brought the card to the bottom. You've shuffled it, but there is a chance someone might want to cut the cards … in which case, you will need to cull again to bring it back to the bottom. Then you deal normally to everyone at the table, but slip the bottom card or cards to your partner.'

I told them never to deal themselves a winning hand. As a precaution, I avoided mentioning terms like 'prestige' and 'flourish' in their presence. These were terms that magicians used. And magicians are the arch-enemies of gamblers. It is for the best that these women and men don't exhibit any traits or even speak jargon that remotely resembles that of magicians. No one should suspect anything. Any dispute on the night will not go to a court of law. The other punters won't seek evidence. One doubt and they'll simply get up and leave the casino. They'll want their money back right away. No, we can't afford that.

'What if there's a dealer? Won't these exercises that we've learnt and practised be rendered pointless?' XX4, the Jasmine lookalike, asked.

XX4's question wasn't ill-judged; she made a valid point. We had realized this recently, and one of the reasons I was meeting Boris again later that afternoon was to sort out this dilemma. He had already helped us by giving me pictures of the casino, drawing out the layout and giving me names and contacts of certain members of his team who were willing to, let's just say, *cooperate* with us on the big night.

'Of course, there will be dealers at some or all tables, and for that reason, not all of you will play at the main table the entire time. Some of you will start at other tables and gradually move to Table Number One; others will start at the high-rollers table, lose a few hands, have a drink and downgrade to the low-stake ones. We'll decide who plays at what tables, when and for how long, when we get closer to the date.'

Smiles. Nods.

Note to self: speak to Boris about what amount deposited at the door entitles people to Table Number One.

♥

'*Marwaoge kya* sir?' Boris shrieked like I'd just given him an electric shock.

'No Boris, I don't want to get you killed, but why do you say that?'

'A pay-off to the dealer? No way a dealer will take a backhander and work for you or me or anyone else—'

'There's a price for everything ... what if we *incentivize* them enough?'

'Dealers are the closest to the owners, think of them as the owners' eyes and extended arms – and I don't need to remind you what sort of people own these places. We can be your eyes and ears, but the dealer has to actively play against the house to be working for you. If the owners come to know, they might lose a limb or life, or limb before life, who knows?'

'How many dealers are there in the place you work?'

'Just two – both are women who the owners trust more than anyone else out there. They aren't both present every night there's a game, but having two ensures there's a backup in case one of them can't make it.

'However,' Boris continued, 'there was one instance when they had to bring a replacement in, since neither of the usual ones could make it for some reason.'

Why hadn't I thought of this before?

'Who was that?'

'Some girl, but I don't know her name or contact details.'

'How about not having any dealers on the night?'

'It has happened before but how will you ensure both the girls and the replacement don't turn up? Are you planning to kidnap them?' He smirked. Smart-ass.

Oh Lord, please forgive him for he doth not know what ye have planned!

I ignored his jibe. 'Will the punters be willing to play without a dealer at the high-stakes table?'

'Yes, because many the players want a friendly atmosphere, and prefer to deal themselves – it has happened before.'

Bingo!

An idea was forming in my brain. Two, as a matter of fact. We could play without croupiers – to me, the word 'dealer' sounds like a dope dealer, so I'd rather use the correct word for *card* dealer – or we could plant our own. This little gen has opened a lot of new possibilities.

After Boris left, I made another note; this one to discuss the croupier conundrum with the others.

THIRTY-ONE

'Ab Ke Saawan' – Shubha Mudgal

THE MONTH OF MAY, WE QUICKLY REALIZED, IS A TOTAL washout. The Mumbai monsoon has arrived two weeks earlier this year due to some westerly winds. It rains nonstop for days, there are storms daily and the local train network has come to a standstill, bringing the city to a grinding halt. The train tracks flood and the road traffic in the already congested city increases tenfold – I exaggerate but you get the point. Car owners and hawkers stuck in the potholes created by the washing away of tarmac, abandon their vehicles and wares and go home. They will return to claim their belongings or insurance when the water recedes. Until then, there will be utter chaos.

The trouble isn't two or three wet days; from experience, I know the true challenge is the havoc left behind, the aftermath. I haven't met any of my six students since imparting to them the knowledge of bottom-dealing. The work Ranjit has been assigned has ceased too. No one is willing to step out of their homes as two dilapidated buildings have already fallen, killing fifty people. God bless their souls.

We had given ourselves six months when we started. The target, I told you earlier, was Diwali, which falls in late October this year. If we write off a month, it's not good news.

Things are not all dismal though.

Let's look at the brighter side of things.

The honeymoon Chikki and I couldn't have is happening at our home. A textbook honeymoon. The bed and us. No distractions, no going out, no work. However, Zeenat has taken the executive decision to spend more time with us. Mademoiselle doesn't like to get her paws wet. Initially, it felt awkward, even embarrassing to make love with her present in the room. She looked at us like we were true descendants of apes – jumping and rolling in the bed, and everywhere else around the house. She even visited the bed sometimes, to check out our moans and groans while we were in the act. But after a few instances, she gave us a pass, started being coy; like a mother-in-law, she left us on our own. Or maybe the room smelled of sex. *Tacky, primal beings*, I'm sure she'll be telling her friends when she meets them again after the rainy season.

Fortunately, the neighbourhood shops are open. Beer, wine, milk, coffee, bread ... the essentials are being delivered at home. Our meals are hardly a bother with so many restaurants providing room service.

It is a setback, but all isn't lost. Even if the weather stays as wild as it has been until mid-June, we still have enough time left to pick things up where we left off and run with them.

Ranjit, Puja, Chikki and I FaceTimed every other day for a week.

I call my six students to check whether they are still practising. They promise they are. Why shouldn't they? They are still getting paid. I do one-to-one sessions with each of the six on FaceTime to see how they're progressing, correcting them if required, but they seem to be working hard. All good.

Chikki has only met Jasmine a couple of times since we sat together by the poolside the very first time. Their acquaintance hasn't moved to the next level. Forget getting intimate, it can hardly be termed a friendship at the moment. Right now, our strategy is to ensure that Jasmine feels she is playing a big part in getting us together. We want her to stay in a cloud of self-importance. She will feel vital, believe me, if we make her believe she's doing Chikki a favour. If I've read her correctly, she'll only ask for a favour in return for doing one.

After I encourage Chikki to reach out to her, Jasmine calls twice – which tells me she's warming up. They find enough topics to discuss, and plan to catch up at the gym and go shopping after the rains subside. It seems our plan isn't in a tailspin. Not yet.

THIRTY-TWO

'Holiday' – Madonna

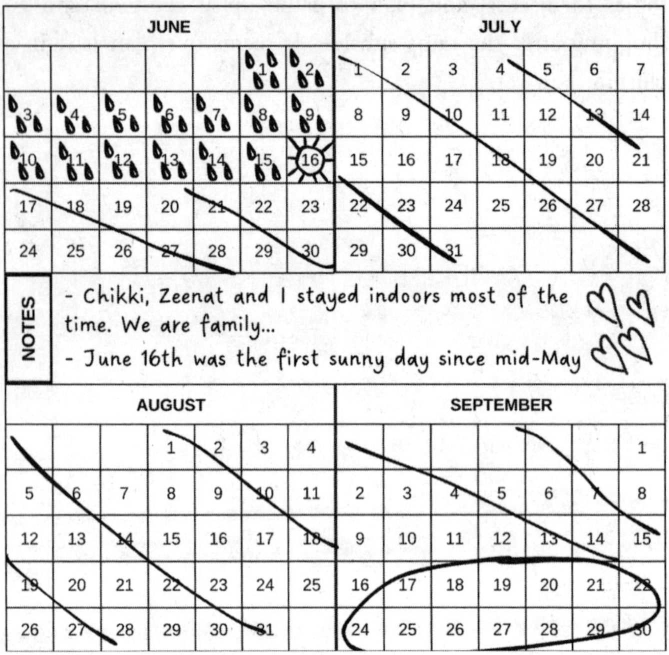

ALTHOUGH THE CALENDAR SHOULD BE SELF-EXPLANATORY, I still feel the need to explain. After the monsoons came uninvited, we spent the remainder of May and the first half of June locked in, honeymooning. The subsequent months –

July to September – were uneventful. When I say uneventful, I mean monotonous, more-of-the-same, a repeat of activities in the months preceding them. However, I think it is my duty … now, now, now, duty is such an interesting word that I cannot go past it without digressing. *Duty* is what one expects of others. As the saying goes, duty is beauty. I can go on, but I'm sure you get the point I'm trying to make.

I have a responsibility – a kind of moral obligation at the very least – to summarize what we've achieved in these past three and a half months. Ergo, I have made a bulleted summary for anyone who gets hold of my diary, and has enough patience and interest remaining to indulge me:

- The training of my students continued as per schedule. I coached them and made them practise various skills to perfection. You are aware of the bottom deal, but there are other ways to cull and deal cards: second-card deal, Greek deal and several other variations on the same theme. By mid-September they were proficient in all the moves – read: sleight of hand – that I had taught them, and I am confident they are well-equipped to go on the 'reality TV show' we've been preparing them for.
- Besides the coaching on cardsharping mechanics, I've also indulged in training them how to keep a poker face. Their demeanour shouldn't give away their purpose. You might think this is obvious, but a methodical approach to maintain a straight face is required when you're at the table with professional card players. We are talking several crores being at stake, mind you.
- As we've made progress in planning out our long con, Ranjit has gotten extremely serious. In fact, Puja, Chikki and I were surprised to find him taking the lead. He called upon me to report how I was doing with

the training of the candidates, instead of me calling to check how he was handling his tasks. Crazy, isn't it?

- Puja and Chikki continued to be on the dot. They have – with several degrees of separation, as Ranjit – organized the costumes, the make-up and etiquette lessons for our six candidates, individually. They are ready, and can't wait to get to the casino for the *reality show*!
- We changed Chikki's car for the reasons I mentioned earlier. We bought a used white Maruti Ignis – less conspicuous than a Beamer.
- We cancelled my rented car since I had no use for it for an entire month. The new car we hired in June came from a different rental company: a top-end Toyota Innova Crysta. It feels a little odd after the Land Rover, but that's okay.
- Chikki aka Zara and I copulated like bunnies, but I don't think you want to hear all about our sex life anymore, do you?
- Chikki and Jasmine have become close friends. They go gymming together, shopping together, discuss sex and morals. Jasmine is sure she was instrumental in introducing us. As I had predicted, she wanted to be sure she'd done a favour before asking for one. And she soon did. She asked for keys to Chikki's flat as she had begun to have regular afternoon rendezvous with a hunk at the gym. She admitted to Chikki that she loved the company and that her husband was interested in other – younger – women. She knew he couldn't keep his tool in his pants, and she had to get some too, elsewhere.
- I met Jasmine too, along with Chikki, to express my gratitude for introducing me to the girl of my dreams. Over the course of several conversations back in August,

I had slipped in that I loved cards. She said her husband was a compulsive gambler too. We left it at that.

- Chikki and Jasmine later spoke about cards and gambling and casinos. Jasmine disclosed that the nights her husband went out gambling were the best for her since she could have some *real* fun. She confessed that she had spent one of those nights with two men at the same time, and quite enjoyed the experience – don't ask me how or what. Like I always say: to each his own, whatever floats your boat …
- As a corollary to the discussion about Anand Kumar's gambling addiction and Jasmine's out-of-jail pass for steamy sex, she asked Chikki to let her know about any big events on the gambling calendar so Jasmine could plan her fun. She also showed interest in using Chikki's flat for the same. That works for us, since we decided to extend the lease on Chikki's flat for two months after Jasmine decided to start frequenting it. A last-minute short-term extension cost a lot more than normal rent, but it will be worth it.
- Zeenat – and yes, this is extremely important – my lovely moggy returned injured one day. I think she got mauled by other animals – dogs, bigger cats, we don't know – but Chikki and I had to rush her to a vet, and she was kept in intensive care for two days, which I wasn't aware existed for animals. We almost lost her. I hate to admit it, but I cried. Despite her irritating habits and couldn't care-less attitude towards me, she is my child, my responsibility, my duty – you see, duty is important. She needed a surgery. We spayed her – I guess she was attracting a lot of tomcats and the fight had been instigated for that reason, or so the vet assumed.

The slow-going holiday period – if you could call that one – is over. We are now about a month away from the big night. We knew from the start that it would be a twisting path, one that we needed to tread cautiously, but a month taken off the schedule means we have to accelerate as well.

Isn't it only the intrepid ones, the most determined ones, that succeed in the end? Enough said, there's still lots to do. Despite the bravado I'm projecting on the surface, I have to admit I'm pretty vulnerable underneath. Shit scared, as they call it. Chikki tells me it will all be fine; that if anyone can do it, I can. Don't we all believe we can do the impossible because people who love us think that we are capable? A kind of believe-in-each-other cycle, perhaps.

THIRTY-THREE

'Kabhi Tumne Kisi Ko Phansa …'
– *Jwalamukhi* OST

FOMO: FEAR OF MISSING OUT. UNLIKE OUR ANCESTORS, WHO went hunting to survive, and experienced real and palpable fear at every step, ours is imaginary. Picture yourself being in the jungle and coming across a lion. That is genuine fear. Tangible. Your skin will tingle, you'll get gooseflesh, your body will respond to the danger at hand. Fight or flight. If you're not careful, you might soil your pants. Unless you're quick enough, you might end up being the lion's dinner. However, in the privileged sections of the modern world that we inhabit now, there is hardly any mortal danger of that nature. What people fear more is missing out … missing out on gossip, missing out on information, missing out on opportunities to make money, missing out on events – especially if they know someone who can profit from what they've missed.

#FOMO

I know for certain FOMO will work in our favour. If we pass on information to Anand Kumar, via Jasmine, about an extravagant night with super high stakes at a casino in the city, he will come. If said night is at a casino he frequents, he might come alone. If we call him to another site, he will certainly cross-check with Roshan Godara. It does not matter if Roshan is a regular at that particular casino or not, as the two of them will likely decide to come together. There's safety in numbers – I know, I know it's a cliché. But however much you roll your eyes, the thing about clichés is that they are true. Overused expressions, but true nevertheless.

♦

I had taken a day off work – *wink, wink* – and I was at Fitiful with Chikki at nine-thirty in the morning. She was in the gym, attending a yoga class we knew Jasmine was at, too. I was in the pool doing laps. We had decided that we could not lose any more time. As I told you earlier, we had been passing hints to Jasmine about the upcoming event at a casino. She had confirmed Anand Kumar was a keen gambler, but had she spoken to him? Had he shown any interest? We couldn't leave this until the last minute.

As planned, I swam for forty minutes, then occupied a table next to the pool and went to shower and change. When I came out, I could see Jasmine and Chikki in the pool. Chikki was in a bright blue bikini. A word to the wise: no one should make the same mistake twice. If Jasmine didn't like Chikki wearing a swimsuit, so be it. Besides, Chikki looked great in the bikini. Jasmine was wearing an oxblood bikini, and she looked equally gorgeous. They swam while I did the crossword – one that I'd carried from home because it would lead us into conversation. You see, you are only as prepared as you've planned.

They synchronized their exit from the pool and headed towards the changing room. The three of us were together at the table fifteen minutes later.

'Hi.' Jasmine arrived first.

'Hi,' I said with a 440-watt smile on my face, the one I'd learnt from Zeenat.

'You're very absorbed in these papers today ... I thought you were taking a day off,' Chikki started the conversation, pointing at sheets of paper in my hand.

'Oh, this is not business. I'm trying to solve this crossword, but my mind is all over the place and I simply can't find the word I'm looking for.'

'What is it that you're looking for?'

'Five across, a ten-letter word for *someone who likes to take risks.*'

'Hmm ...' Jasmine pursed her lips.

'Adventurer,' Chikki said.

For the unversed, we had found this crossword at home and rehearsed it.

'Wow, I didn't know you were into crosswords, too.' Me.

'How long have you two been together now?' Jasmine.

'A few months.' I looked at Chikki to corroborate.

'Yes.' Chikki.

'How can you possibly know everything about each other? I bet you don't even know where her G-spot is, yet.' Jasmine.

'Maybe I do – I'm quite adventurous.' I couldn't afford to stray from *adventure* or *adventurer* or *adventurous.*

'Oh really?' Jasmine.

'He's over-adventurous if you ask me. He's booked a high-stakes seat at a casino,' Chikki chipped in at the right moment. 'Remember I told you about this upcoming event?'

'Yeah, yes, you did. In fact, I asked Anand, but he wasn't aware of it.'

'Well, does he like cards?' Me.

'He's a compulsive gambler, to tell you the truth. He plays more than he should, but it's his life, his money.'

'Does he play at any of these new establishments that have mushroomed in the last couple of years? Professional, under-the-radar operations?'

'I wouldn't know, but he goes missing with his friends every once in a while. And sometimes when us wives compare notes, they are at no one's place, so we assume they go to some casino or a club.' Jasmine.

'Well, then he must be visiting one of the other ones. But it's okay, I don't think there are enough seats left. The organizers have a small event in mind, and only high rollers are invited as such.' Me.

'He plays big, I know.' Jasmine.

'How big is big?' Chikki asked.

'We are talking about gambling bets, Chikki, so do not insinuate,' Jasmine winks.

'I wasn't.' Chikki. Coy.

'Big means we're talking about someone who has the wherewithal to put a minimum of four to five crores on the line.' Me.

'What? I'm not letting you anywhere near that place.' Chikki. In disbelief.

'I'm committed, Chikki – this is something I always wanted to do, at least once in my lifetime, so please don't stop me.' Me. Pleading.

'Five crores? That's a lot of money – you can buy a two-bedroom flat in Mumbai with that amount.' Jasmine. Surprised.

'You can, but it doesn't pump your adrenaline. And for an *adventurer* like me, that's far more important than adding another asset to my portfolio.' Me. Daredevil.

'Anand would give his right arm to play at such a high-stakes night.' Jasmine.

Bingo!

'If he goes, we can spend some time together, Jasmine.' Chikki. Expectant.

'As much as I love you, if he is out for the night, I'm

not spending time talking; I want to have fun with a hunk.' Jasmine didn't mince words, or bother with euphemisms.

It was my turn to be embarrassed.

'Do you know someone?' Jasmine. Direct.

'Know someone?' Me. Startled.

'Some single bachelor your age, a friend of yours who's willing to take me out.' Jasmine. Serious.

I acted surprised. Jasmine had confided in Chikki, and I was aware she was open about her sex life, but I wasn't going to reveal that I knew about it. She, however, read my mind.

'What are you gaping at? Do you think women do not need sex?' Jasmine. Earnest.

'Oh, that isn't what I was thinking.' Me. Sheepish.

'Ah, so are you making a mental list of hunks you know?' Jasmine winked at Chikki like she'd cracked the joke of the day.

'I'll certainly keep my eyes open.' Me. Yielding.

'Someone like you – young, fit—' Jasmine. Gesticulating.

'But not you.' Chikki. A warning.

'It's not penny-ante stuff … you think your husband will want to play such high stakes?' Me. I wanted to bring the chat back to Anand Kumar.

'If he knows this place is safe—'

'It's as safe or unsafe as any other club he goes to. There are just three or four such places in town that I know of. He might be visiting one or two of them, so there's no harm in trying a third. Maybe he already knows the place. To be honest, I haven't been to this particular one before either.' Me.

'So you've been to some others?' Chikki. Overacting.

'Just once.' Then I silkily slipped in the name of the place – Boris had told me the code name by which it is referred to by its patrons – which Anand Kumar was known to visit on occasion with Roshan Godara.

'And you didn't think you needed to tell me?' Chikki. Steaming up.

'I'm sorry, it was a long time ago … before you were in my life.'

'But—'

'Let it go, girl,' Jasmine to my rescue. 'I bet you haven't told him about all the men you've dated before he came into your life.'

'Hardly any.'

'So where is this big night, again?' Jasmine. Enthusiastic.

'Versova.'

'When?'

'October 26th, it's the Friday before Diwali.' Me, matter-of-factly.

'Good to know in advance, so I can plan,' Jasmine said with a wink.

'But he can't just walk in there.' Me.

'What do you mean?' Jasmine.

'As is the norm – and your husband will know this for sure – these places are by invitation. And on this occasion, only the crème de la crème of card players from Mumbai will be in attendance. If he is interested, I suggest you let Chikki know and I shall speak to someone who's a regular at that club and get passes for him.'

'I'll let *you* know—'

'I'm flying to Prague tomorrow, and then to London for business for two weeks. But I will be in touch with Chikki, so it's best if she's the one you talk to.'

'You're gone for two weeks?' Jasmine asked, then turned to Chikki, 'you better buy a good vibrator and lots of batteries, girl.'

♣

Here's a life lesson for free. Even if you are a grandmaster playing with an amateur, never, *ever* allow two people to play chess with you simultaneously. It will be nearly impossible to win. It's not that two newbies, when together, combine into some kind of mental superpower. Not in the least. However, two people mean two sets of eyes and two brains. Between them, any move you make will get scrutinized twice, from two perspectives. They will consult each other about every move you make, think of the next two moves concurrently and then take a call to make the best move. If that's not enough, two opponents will distract you. It will never be in your favour to play against two people.

Jasmine is an extremely sharp lady, but she is no match for the two of us working in tandem. We never let her segue into anything other than what we set out to talk about, but she can't see through that. Distraction is another form of misdirection. Capisce?

You might be wondering why I told Jasmine I'm travelling for the next two weeks, and you are right in asking that question. I need to be 'away' since Anand Kumar will not sign up for a high stakes night, risking four to five crores, without wanting to see me or talk to me. If he knows it's me who's behind the event or that I'm even remotely connected to the people organizing or working the event, this plan will go kaput.

Put yourself in Anand Kumar's shoes for a second – what would you do? *#FOMO*: you won't want to miss a party where the gambling nobility, the who's who of the card-playing world, are invited. Despite wanting to go, you won't be inclined to unless you know or meet someone who is. But time is running out – if you don't book, you might not get a seat later. The person who knows all about it – who mentioned it to your wife – is travelling for the next two weeks, and you want further details before you take any decision. What's the only alternative you have? Meet his girlfriend who is a friend of your wife's, right?

And here's my ace: Anand Kumar does not know Chikki Singh.

THIRTY-FOUR

'Wicked Game' – Chris Isaak

JASMINE CALLED CHIKKI AT TEN THE NEXT MORNING. OF course I was *supposed* to be on the flight by then.

An aside: in case anyone wants to know, I am flying British Airways BA138 to Heathrow, then to Prague after a two-hour layover. I could fly to Prague directly, but I need to return to London anyway, so this arrangement suits me best. Always keep such details handy – you cannot afford to slip up.

'Has Deep left already?' Jasmine asked.

'Yes, he had a 1:55 a.m. flight this morning; he's flying via London.'

'Oh, I thought he was going this afternoon,' Jasmine sighed.

'What's the matter?' Chikki asked as I stood near her. I had told her not to put her mobile on speakerphone, since Jasmine's voice was audible through the earpiece. Devices these days are so sensitive … but I'll not stray from the dynamics of this call to tell you about modern technology. There's a time and place for everything.

'I told Anand about this big night Deep was describing yesterday, and he got a hard-on the moment he heard about it. He wanted to meet Deep to get more details.'

'He will be available on his mobile after 2:15 p.m. Central

European Time, so maybe they can speak later this evening. You can pass on his number to your husband.'

'I'll do that, but I think he wanted a face-to-face, since the stakes Deep mentioned were quite high.'

'Oh, he can meet me. I promise I won't steal your husband, Jasmine.'

'That's the least of my worries. He likes women your age, but I completely trust you. Though, in case you are turned on by his charm, be my guest and use my bed – I won't mind, and I won't tell Deep either. You're welcome.'

'Thanks, but no thanks.'

'I was only kidding.'

'I know. I'll give you Deep's number. Alternatively, the three of us can catch up; Anand, me and you?'

'Let me check with him.'

Bingo!

♠

Jinendrabhai requires a radically different approach. When I started planning for this, he wasn't on my radar. As you know, he got added later and I have no direct line to him. If I approach him, he will speak to Roshan and reveal that I'm back in the game. Ranjit knows him, so he and Puja can't approach JP either. And there is no chance Chikki can do it, as he might recognize her, too.

Then it dawned on me that I have another ace to throw.

Boris!

Who can be better than Boris to inform Jinendrabhai about the big night? Boris works at the casino that Jinendrabhai frequents. A familiar name; a name that he knows only in that context. If Boris approaches him, there is no reason for Jinendrabhai to suspect anything.

It occurred to me then that Boris is a goose who can lay a few more golden eggs. I called him to the Versova flat for a detailed discussion.

'Sir, the casino you mention, I have no idea – it might belong to a rival group and if the owners of the casino I work in come to know, I'll be fired.'

'Isn't getting fired a far better outcome than being caught working in your owners' casino for a party that isn't organized by them?'

I let this little piece of advice sink into his brain.

'That's true.'

'Where do you come from, Boris?' I asked.

'Why?'

'Just humour me.'

'Bihar.'

Boris from Bihar – have you heard of a more obvious guile? I was correct; Boris isn't his real name. It can't be.

'Okay. If you don't mind me asking, what do you make on average in a year from this casino job and other contracts that you get in Mumbai?'

'Some three to four lakhs, depending on the tips, but why do you ask?'

'What if I offered you six lakhs – half now, half after the job? Take the money and go to someplace safe, wherever you want to, where no one can find you.'

'Six lakh rupees?'

'Yes.'

'For one evening?'

'Yes.'

I was certain that he didn't even make three lakhs per year, but that wasn't worth arguing. Even if he earned that, the money came in on a monthly or fortnightly basis. The thought of six lakh rupees in one go made his eyes widen.

'What do I need to do?'

'Nothing more than you usually do at the casino. Plus, I'd like you to make a few calls for me.'

'Is that all?'

'No. I'll tell you more later. And not a word about this to anyone. We don't want every pedestrian to turn up for the big night.' I instructed him not to invite anyone who regularly played at the Versova casino. I also told him not to call any staff member who usually worked at Versova. We didn't want anyone to make out the discrepancies – there'd be extra people, cameras, a slightly different layout to suit us. Why offer someone a chance to spot anything different?

'Which night?'

'Good man.'

You might be wondering why, if Boris can call up Jinendrabhai, we don't leave it to him to invite Anand Kumar and Roshan Godara, too? There's a reason: it's always better that people – should they talk to each other and compare notes – hear about an event from multiple, disparate sources. Moreover, Boris doesn't know them at all. Getting a call from him will raise their antennas.

THIRTY-FIVE

'Happy' – Pharrell Williams

CHIKKI WAS GETTING READY FOR DINNER WITH JASMINE AND Anand Kumar. She paid special attention to her make-up, hairdo and outfit – a form-fitting black number paired with high heels. I wanted to tag along with her but couldn't. Months of labour and planning would go to waste if Anand Kumar smelled anything foul. No, we couldn't risk that.

At seven, she gave me a kiss and left. They were dining at The Golden Dragon. The very thought of Sichuan and Cantonese cuisine had me salivating, but I had to make do with something from my freezer that night.

Chikki was driving, not taking a cab. She wasn't a big drinker, and driving gave her the perfect reason to not drink at dinner. We wanted Anand Kumar to believe her; we wanted *him* to drink.

Yes, we've thought of everything.

As I pulled out my third beer, I looked into the freezer to find something good to zap in the microwave. Nothing appetizing. My mind was set on Chinese, so I ordered Sichuan chicken and egg fried noodles from the local takeaway.

Chikki returned a little before midnight. The smile on her face told me the dinner had been a success.

Let me give you an abridged version of what Chikki told me.

Anand Kumar was more than happy to meet her, since it gave him confidence in the upcoming event. He hadn't been to the casino in Versova before, but knew about it. 'They're all the same,' he had said. He was almost ecstatic at the high stakes … his exact words were, 'If you don't play high stakes on Diwali, when will you?' He knew the rules regarding the advance payment on entry and acknowledged the four-crore minimum deposit without breaking a sweat. On a big night like this, he sounded confident he'd return with a lot more. He claimed to be good at cards: 'Bring it on, I'm the King of Spades,' he had boasted.

And yes, FOMO had worked. He had spoken with one of his friends, one Mr Roshan Godara – wink, wink – who wanted to come along, so he needed to reserve two seats for the night, if possible. And before you think I'm fleecing innocents, you need to know that Anand Kumar's net worth is over a hundred crores; Roshan and Jinendrabhai are certainly worth more. Four crores isn't going to bankrupt them. And their naked avarice won't allow them to pass on an opportunity to make their four crores into six.

FOMO, you see, works on multiple levels.

'Your friend Anand is a piece of work,' Chikki summarized.

'My friend? You realize he was the one who put me in the slammer?'

'Was he?' she teased me.

'Anyway, you know that means two things, right?' I asked Chikki.

'What?'

'One, we have just banked a minimum of eight crores.'

'And the second thing?'

'I want to make love to you right here, right now.'

'Not in bed?'

'No, and with that dress on.'

'You're becoming a horny old man, Dimpy.'

'Don't call me that.'

'What should I call you then?'

'Call me Deep because I go deep.'

'You're so corny at times Deep-jee, but I love you.'

◆

'Jasmine asked me for the keys to my flat,' Chikki told me as we were in each other's arms post-lovemaking.

'When? Weren't you guys with Anand the whole time?'

'We were, but we had gone to the Ladies'.'

'Oh … I wonder—'

'Wonder what?'

'She meets all these random guys – what if something goes wrong?'

'What can possibly go wrong?'

'I mean, what if the condom breaks when she's with a lover and … you know—'

'She told me she doesn't like men using a condom.'

I was surprised – Chikki saw it in my eyes, methinks.

'She told me she's fixed,' Chikki explained.

'Fixed?'

'Don't tell me you don't know what "fixed" means in this context?'

I wanted to remind Chikki that I came from Saharanpur. The only 'fixed' I had learnt about was when my father repaired punctured bicycle tyres: '*fix kar diya,*' he used to tell his clients when they came to collect their cycles. Chikki could sense my ignorance, or maybe my brain had projected an idiot-metre display onto my forehead.

'Fixed means she's got her tubes tied up; fixed.'

These guys seemed to be living in some parallel universe. I still didn't get it – which tube, which puncture? – but I decided not to probe any further. I was happy in my little bubble.

◆

I met my trainees again. I have to admit that all of them have surpassed my expectations. They have practised the art and become flawless in their execution of the tricks I had taught them. It would be a difficult decision to pick three out of them; who to take and who to leave behind. But cunning as I am, I have a plan for that, too. Remember I once told you that every plan requires improvisation?

My fellow co-conspirators are pleased when I reveal my latest scheme, which seals it. I need to spend some more time with my trainees to make this as yet unscripted change, but I'm not concerned in the least. It's not like I'm asking them to learn something new, or to perform tricks they do not have sufficient time to practise. I'm just changing their roles. Considering they are all competent actors, it should hardly be a bother. If anything, it's Puja and Chikki who have to work twice as hard to get the cosplay right now.

THIRTY-SIX

'The Final Countdown' – Europe

TWO DAYS BEFORE THE BIG NIGHT, WE MOVED IN WITH PUJA and Ranjit. It was time to celebrate us coming so far. Yes, the main event was still a few days away, but we needed a night to celebrate. We wanted to get drunk, chat until late and not get up with hangovers. Amateurs drink the night before the big day, not us. Chikki's flat had been vacated, as had the Versova flat. Packers had now moved on to my Pedder Road home, so we were in Worli, enjoying the view of the Arabian Sea, feeling the salty breeze that made Chikki's hair go curly. I turned and looked at her – she looked gorgeous in the red dress she had on, her hair loosely tied back, an odd wisp escaping her scrunchie. I bent down to kiss her.

'Get a room, you two,' Puja said.

'Why else do you think we are here? It's you guys who are the intruders, not us,' Chikki retorted.

'Yes, and we don't care if it's your flat,' I added, and we all laughed.

Puja had given Radha, the housekeeper, a few days off. We didn't want anyone overhearing even a fraction of our conversations, especially when we got drunk. Not that Radha knew anyone involved but why take a risk, why tempt fate?

We went through the entire plan for the nth time. We

couldn't afford to leave anything to chance. After coming this far, it would be a shame if anything went wrong. It won't just be a waste of money, it'll be such a waste of an opportunity. Chikki and Puja confirmed they'd done their part, and so did I. But while what the three of us had done wasn't simple, it was certainly not of the same magnitude as what Ranjit had accomplished. His contribution had been the most important. He had to work through several layers of detachment – ensuring nothing ever came back to him – and still meet our strict standards. He'd worked late nights, sometimes all night, but he was confident that he'd arranged for everything we wanted, and I trusted him.

'We have twelve confirmed RSVPs,' I told them. Pride in my voice.

There were nine other patrons of such casinos, besides Anand Kumar, Roshan Godara and Jinendrabhai, who had confirmed they'd be attending. Boris had been instrumental in getting these people on board – eight men and one woman. And while one school of thought might have questioned why any other people should be targeted in our con when we only held a grudge against three, the other perspective was that they were all cut from the same cloth. I don't think morals and gambling should ever be put in the same basket.

'How many of your trainees are playing?' Puja asked.

'All six of them will be there.' Ranjit.

After Boris confirmed he'd take care of the staffing for the night, we decided to go through with all six trainees. We need them at specific places in the casino.

♣

We discussed the plans one final time the next day at lunch. Then we stopped.

Whatever will be, will be.

At first, a sinister silence fell over the flat, each of us contemplating the consequences should anything go wrong, or praying for the desired result. At teatime, at Puja's suggestion, we pulled out the Monopoly board, dusted it off and sat down to play. It was, is and will remain one of the greatest board games ever. There is something about it that absorbs you, that takes over your thoughts as you get deeper into it. I hadn't played it since my childhood days with Puja and Ranjit at his house back in Saharanpur. I don't know if Ranjit cheated, snuck some extra currency as he distributed it or modified the rules to suit him (Puja and I never bothered to check them) but he always beat us both. Two decades later, it seems very little has changed. He beat all three of us.

'How do you manage to win every time?' Puja asked, close to five hours after we had started. We'd been playing like kids. The game was still not over, but we decided to pack up.

'He cheats,' I shrugged like it was common knowledge.

'Nope,' Ranjit said, 'I'm lucky.'

'How can you be lucky every single time we've played this?' I argued.

'What can I say? Some of us are born lucky.'

'Oh really?' Puja mocked.

'Oh, yes. And I'll prove it to all of you once again tomorrow.' He winked.

As I said previously, we were all privy to what the others were doing during these last six months or so. But none of us had seen the full scale of Ranjit's accomplishment, although his chunk of work was as crucial as the Jesus nut in a helicopter. Oh, by the way, do you know what that is? Well, I have to explain, even if it means going off on a tangent. In a helicopter, the rotor is attached to the main body using a single nut. If that nut fails, the main body carrying the passengers would detach from the rotor and fall to the ground, and the next person those passengers would see is Jesus.

But we had absolute faith in Ranjit; we trusted him when he told us all was fine, and under control.

Game over, the four of us realized there was still a lot of time before we went to bed, and alcohol wasn't on the menu that day. On my recommendation, we decided to cook aloo parathas together. Sitting around as the freshly fried parathas came off the pan, we all ate in turns – one person rolling the dough, the second frying, while the other two devoured them with dollops of Amul butter, mango pickle and fresh yoghurt.

10:35 p.m. Ranjit pulled out a cigar. Cohiba. Cuban-made. We went over to the balcony and against the background of the calm, almost black Arabian Sea, he lit up. Chikki tried it but she started coughing immediately, so the three of us enjoyed the smoke. It had been ages since the three of us had smoked together, in Saharanpur.

Finally, it was time to say goodnight.

We were ready for the big day. Well, as ready as one can be. Despite months of preparation and training, we knew that we were trying to cross the ocean in a kayak. It could capsize, of course it could, but if you didn't risk it … you'd never know. Would we win or lose? Well, as they say, there is only one way to find out.

The stage is set.

The deck is stacked.

Lights.

Camera.

Action.

PART THREE

'If you must play, decide upon three things at the start: the rules of the game, the stakes and the quitting time.'

CHINESE PROVERB

THIRTY-SEVEN

'Mera Naam Chin Chin Chu' – *Howrah Bridge* OST (Chill Flip Remix)

IT'S TIME TO PROVIDE STAGE NAMES TO THE TRAINEES AND agree on their background stories.

Vinita, aka XX1: She's young and, not to be judgemental, a person of twenty-eight isn't believable as someone willing to gamble with four crore rupees on a single evening. Unless she's out to squander inherited wealth. Therefore, she's assigned as a croupier on Table Two. She'll have to wear the uniform, which is a white-silk top and a black knee-length skirt. Players at the table aren't supposed to have personal conversations with croupiers, so we don't have to worry about explaining where she comes from or where she worked previously.

Amrita Singh, aka XX3: The tall and stylish woman is one of the invited guests. She will wear a navy-coloured slip dress, with subtle makeup to achieve the look of landed gentry. Her backstory is that her grandfather was once a *thakur* in Rajasthan. She's a divorcee, and drinks vodka like a Russian. She'll start at Table One, then move if required.

Rose, aka XX4: The Jasmine lookalike has been christened with the name of a flower to further strengthen the connection. She will be the croupier at Table One for the night. Anand Kumar and Roshan Godara will start at this table. Of course, they might decide to move on to other tables later on, but we want them at Table One to begin with. We're anticipating both Anand and Roshan will see the resemblance to Jasmine, which should subliminally invoke confidence in her as a croupier. Known faces do that. Hopefully that will become a chink in their armour. But we cannot depend on it.

Sid, aka XY2: The suave six-footer is assigned as the croupier for Table Three. His uniform is a white shirt and black trousers.

Sanjay Kamra, aka XY3: The poker-faced gentleman will start at Table Two, and stay there until further instructed. He will intervene if any other team member is in trouble. As per the rules of the night, he is in a black tuxedo. If asked, his family exports dry fruit and nuts from Delhi. We've adopted Deep Singh's background, since there is no chance of an overlap. No one knows Deep Singh or his credentials.

Prem Singhania, aka XY4: His forty-three years have been made-up to look fifty-five – closer to the age group of our three marks. He deals in diamonds, and keeps a low profile for obvious reasons. If asked, he'll give out his card with a PO Box number. He will start at Table Three and move to Table One after a while.

THIRTY-EIGHT

'Nothing Is As It Seems'
– Hidden Citizens, Ruelle

DID YOU NOTICE SOMETHING PECULIAR? ALL OUR PLAYERS will sit to the left of the croupiers. That is, they will be the ones who decide to cut or tap when the dealer asks. Like I've said before, the deck is stacked. There is no way we can lose tonight. But we aren't stupid. We haven't put out nametags or assigned spaces to people. Amrita, Prem and Sanjay will, purely coincidently, arrive first and take their places. Tables are assigned to individuals at the start, so I've marked Anand Kumar, Roshan Godara and Jinendrabhai arbitrarily at their allocated tables. It might be that they won't sit where they are marked in this sketch, although the host that ushers them to the table will make all efforts to seat them there. Either way, everyone's free to move at any point, albeit we have just fifteen seats for fifteen players so it may not be possible at will. A switch can only happen if another player is willing to trade places or if they retire for a while. We'll see how it goes.

THIRTY-NINE

'Everybody Knows' – Leonard Cohen

IT'S FINALLY 7:00 P.M. ON FRIDAY, 26 OCTOBER. THE DAY OF the party in Versova.

Until the 1960s, Versova was glorified by Bollywood movies as a beach that smugglers used to sneak gold into the country. Whether this was true or not, I haven't verified. What I *do* know is that some thirty years ago, Versova was an upcoming locality trying to compete with Bandra. Both are seaside suburbs, although to highlight the difference between the two, Bandra housed established Bollywood actors, while Versova was the residence for upcoming ones. Residents in Versova who made it big moved to Bandra, while the remainders in Versova were joined by newcomers. Thirty years thence, Versova *is* an upcoming suburb trying to compete with Bandra. Certain things never change. Like some might say I haven't stopped divagating.

Rose's makeup and hairdo were fantastic. She looked more like Jasmine than ever, and just as much of a head-turner. She had no idea that she had been made to strongly resemble the wife of one of the quarries at her table. That might've led to a change in her demeanour, which would have compromised the whole point of her being the croupier at Table One. That, and the fact that she and Prem had the deftest hands. Or should I say fingers?

Rose, Vinita and Sid were already set up at their respective tables. All three were wearing glasses – you guessed it, glasses with recording cameras. We couldn't find ones with built-in WiFi, so Ranjit got them modified a bit to fit a micro-SIM that transmitted the images in real time. With this, it didn't matter if I wasn't on the premises as long as there was a mobile signal. If I needed to communicate, I'd call Boris. As the master of ceremonies, he was licensed to walk around with a walkie-talkie plugged into his ear like an American FBI agent. He could pass a slip to the concerned person with the message. It happened all the time – messages to clients and croupiers were passed on silently so that the others weren't disturbed during the play. Boris wore dark glasses, which he never took off. It was part of his job, so that patrons didn't know which way he was looking or who he was eyeing. Only this time, his faux Ray-Bans had been replaced by dark glasses with a camera. And although he moved around casually like he was just taking a stroll, his eyes were constantly assessing risk. He was trained for this.

Moreover, there were other cameras on location. They'd telecast all the action back to us. We – Puja, Chikki and I – sat in front of three computer screens, each divided into four; we were monitoring twelve cameras in all. They had been numbered for reference. We were parked at Puja and Ranjit's flat, while Ranjit was close to the site. I had insisted that I join him there, but he was adamant: 'It will require three people to monitor three computer screens' and I could see his point. Besides, with the clarity of the video surveillance, I couldn't see the point of being close to the scene. Yeah, I was missing the real action, but I had known from the start that I wouldn't be going in.

The sound wasn't great. We could listen to conversations, but there was white noise in the background. However, we watched like hawks. Ranjit was getting the videos too, but since he was organizing other stuff, his attention would be cursory at best.

'Boris,' I said over call, 'camera number three needs to be rotated slightly to the left, say thirty degrees.'

'Hang on a second, Mr Ferreira.'

'Please don't mention my name,' I said. I know it's a fake identity, but Boris didn't. He needed to believe I was Michael Ferreira, and I was trying to conceal that from anyone within earshot.

You've got to live a lie to the fullest.

I could see Boris on the cameras as he got a stool from behind the bar counter, moved around and twisted camera number three. 'Is it okay now?'

'Just a little more to the left … yes, yes. Perfect.'

Between the three of us at Worli, the work was divided methodically. I was monitoring Table One, Chikki was on Table Two and Puja had her eyes set on Table Three.

Calls, if any, would only be made and received by me.

♠

7:25–7:31 p.m.: The first two customers arrived from the front: Amrita and Prem. They arrived separately with a briefcase and a tote bag. If any of the other patrons were in the vicinity, having a look-see, our three plants would look like genuine players arriving with money.

The facade was a good decision. Just as they were depositing the cash – well, that was a sham since it was one person at a time at the counter – two more players arrived. I didn't know these individuals, and neither did I have any interest in them outside of their deposits. Both men in their late forties, both in tuxedos. There was a smile of recognition when they saw the girl at the reception – they'd obviously met her before. They knew Boris too, since he was the one who invited them.

Jinendrabhai arrived soon after. He recognized Boris after he had deposited his four crores. The hostess led him to Table Three, pulled out the seat right opposite Sid – where I had marked him in the sketch – and he took it. A polite gentleman.

Prem was shown to the same table and he sat next to Sid, exchanging a soft *hello* with Jinendrabhai.

'What can I get you to drink?' The hostess asked, her voice audible through Puja's terminal although with a lot of static in the background.

'Vodka on the rocks please, thanks.'

Jinendrabhai asked for Chivas Regal.

Our players had been told to stick to vodka or gin or white rum, and that they would be served one drink. After that, all their drinks would be water or tonic water, and no one should know the difference. They were not meant to get drunk at the table; others were supposed to.

The drinks were free that night. If you made drinks free, the consumption inevitably went up, which suited us. What were a few thousand rupees when we were looking at crores?

There was another reason for making drinks free that night, which I shall tell you later.

8:30 p.m.: The house was full.

We got a text to confirm that every one of the paying players had deposited the minimum opening balance for the night. We had banked forty-eight crores, which, as I told you, was being moved out in gurney bags into a van that would drive away from the venue in approximately ten minutes, if not less, to a destination only four people in this world knew about. You must've guessed the four, so I won't bother telling you. There was nary a chance that anyone else would know where the money went. Ranjit would do a check, then it would be locked up at one of his facilities. Have I mentioned before that I trust Ranjit completely? I've always believed that if you can't trust your childhood – and only – friend, your life is meaningless. Besides, Ranjit loved money as much as I did, and we had agreed that he would keep more than fifty per cent of our profit for his business needs. He had promised to pay me returns from his investments, and I was not concerned.

I was more focused on defeating the ones who had let me down. Or pushed me down when it suited them.

The game was afoot.

FORTY

'Money' – Pink Floyd

AN INTERESTING STATISTIC: ONE IN EVERY TWENTY-SEVEN people on this earth has, at some point in their lives, gambled. The scales might be different, the winnings and losses too, but they've bet at least once in their lifetime.

The house was full. Not even one empty seat. The guests were all men, except one. She was Mrs Goenka. None of us knew her first name. We had no clue where she lived in Mumbai. But we knew she was married to an industrialist who supplied parts to the automobile industry. He had factories all over Maharashtra, mainly Pune, and as such he travelled a lot. She was about forty, attired in a long black dress. Deep décolletage, dark hair, not a single grey showing. Confident. Money, surely, was no problem for her. She could lose over four crores and not blink an eye. It was the cost of entertainment for an evening. Boris told me that she was quite brash, played erratically, guided by emotions rather than reason. Just as most gamblers were. They took rash decisions, on the spot, guided by their gut.

She was on Table One.

I was keenly observing the events at Table One while my co-workers – Chikki and Puja – were equally absorbed in the proceedings at the other two tables. Mrs Goenka decided to take the seat next to Amrita. Subconsciously, she might have felt comfortable sitting next to Amrita, I don't know. That changed the seating positions we had planned, but no harm done. Anand Kumar and Roshan Godara still decided to sit next to each other, which showed they found comfort in keeping each other close. They saw Rose, whispered between themselves, and smiled. I can't be certain, but it appeared they had noticed the resemblance. I messaged Boris to keep an eye out for them, so they did not communicate with each other during the rounds. That could be disastrous for us.

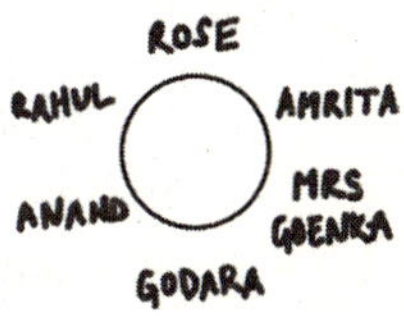

The fifth player on Table One was a young man. He was under thirty for sure. I won't assume he'd inherited wealth, purely based on his age; that would be highly prejudicial. But he looked filthy rich, which was a kind of given if he was at the casino. His name as per Boris's sheet was Rahul Mathur, and he was a distributor of alcoholic beverages across the state of Maharashtra. He was politically connected – surprise, surprise! – and not someone to be messed with. Didn't scare me one bit, though. He sat on Rose's right.

I won't even briefly dwell on the candidates at the other tables. The remaining seven were like extras in a film scene. They needed to be there to make up the background; they were part of the script, but they weren't credited. For us, here and now, they were merely bankers. I just wanted to focus on Table One. Jinendrabhai couldn't win; Sid and Prem would bankrupt him, I had no doubt.

Rose shuffled. I observed closely, as the others did. Nothing untoward: no tics, no sweating. She offered the deck to Amrita, who cut the cards. It was not mandatory, but cutting cards prevented any suspicion amongst the players. In time, when signalled by Rose, Amrita would stop cutting and start tapping, but not yet.

CHIP COLOUR	DENOMINATION
WHITE	10,000
RED	50,000
BLUE	1,00,000
GREEN	2,50,000
ORANGE	5,00,000
BLACK	10,00,000

I could see her hands and it was a neat deal. A card to Amrita, to Mrs Goenka, Roshan Godara, Anand Kumar and Rahul. Then another and another. Three cards each.

'Maximum three rounds blind. Starting bid: ten thousand,' Rose announced.

Out came the chips, worth fifty grand from the first round, and then another fifty. No one had seen the cards. Then Amrita picked hers up. Her eyes went towards the ceiling like she was thinking. Good acting. She threw in two white chips. Double after you'd seen the cards. Mrs Goenka did the same. Another two white chips. The three men played another round of blind and then picked up their cards. No one blinked as a full circle of another twenty grand each accumulated at the table before Mrs Goenka folded.

Anand Kumar asked for a sideshow. According to the rules of the house for the night, you could only do a sideshow with the person on your left. He saw his own friend's cards and folded his. Three players left in the game. Amrita folded.

Her training kicked in: if you're dealt a bad hand, you lose. No choice. But you certainly have a choice to lose with a good hand. Just fold, it's that simple. No one is going to look at your cards and ask you why. Our three actors on the tables had been instructed to do just that. Fold because you *must* lose in the beginning. It doesn't matter what cards you have.

If Godara went bullish in this round – with the two people between him and Amrita now out – he might've asked for a sideshow with her, and the last thing you wanted was to show cards at this stage. It was much better to pack up and let him wonder. That left just Roshan Godara and Rahul in the game. The stakes had risen to a hundred grand when Rahul asked for a show and lost.

Fantastic!

It was best that Anand Kumar and/or Roshan Godara won initially. It would boost their confidence.

As per my estimate, over sixteen lakhs got exchanged over the three tables in the opening games. The stakes always went higher as games progressed, what with the rising confidence and blood alcohol levels. The games on all three tables were to continue without any alterations or trickery for the next three rounds. A few players were beside themselves with joy as they won big. We had to wait a little before my magnificent six started to give a performance. They would be tested, but the rabbit had to stay under the hat for a while longer.

P.S., do you know what P.S. stands for? It comes from Latin *post scriptum*, but the Punjabi P.S. is *pichon soojhi*; both mean the same thing: an afterthought. Now for the afterthought I wanted to tell you about. Remember the statistic I gave you before, that one in twenty-seven people have gambled at some point in their lives? I just made that up.

FORTY-ONE

'The Jack' – AC/DC

JUST THEN, I RECEIVED A WHATSAPP MESSAGE FROM RANJIT.

Money moved.

Yes, I know … WhatsApp claims that their messages are encrypted end-to-end, but we decided to be ambiguous nonetheless.

The money deposited by the punters at arrival had been moved out of the casino premises to the safe place Ranjit had identified. It would be recounted and confirmed.

Three rounds on Table One were over. Table Two was already on the fourth round as Vinita dealt the cards. Table Three was going slow, still playing the third round. A few of them had been dealt a good hand in the second game and it had continued longer, since two of the players didn't want to fold or ask for a show. The excitement in the room was tangible. Electric. I could feel my adrenaline rising despite being nowhere close to the real action.

I quickly glanced at my screen and my fellow eagles' screens, and I could see a lot of chips had moved from their original place. But only the whites, reds and blues so far.

Well, it was time to raise the stakes, don't you think?

'Boris …' I whispered. I knew my message could only be heard through his earpiece, but some of these little devices were extremely sensitive. ‘Get a round of drinks served and ask the croupiers to take the games up a notch.’

‘Roger that.’

I saw him signalling a waitress, asking her to go around the tables to check if people needed repeat orders.

Have you ever noticed that when someone asks you if you’d care for another drink, you inadvertently pick up what remains in your glass and try to finish it off before the next drink arrives? That was happening all over my screen then, and it was good for business.

A little card with a message had been passed to all the croupiers. It simply said *chop chop now* in case it got into unintended hands, a hint to move fast. The dealers knew what it meant.

My eyes were on Rose. I saw her shuffle. Unlike Las Vegas, our croupiers used their hands to shuffle as any card player would. Only in their case, they were *apparently* a neutral party, so the players could place trust in the dealer and the deal. The others on the table watched her too, but not as keenly as I did.

As planned, drinks were replenished – and the people at Rose’s table were no longer watching her. She was quick, but I was on to her, watching her hands. I saw her slipping a card, then another, to the bottom of the pack. She was going for a bottom deal. As AC/DC sing in ‘The Jack’, how was anyone to know that some of the cards were coming from the bottom of the pack? They glanced at her, then picked up their glasses, took a sip, passed smiles to the others at the table. Anand Kumar was looking at Rose’s face like an idiot. Was he thinking of Jasmine, or did he have hots for anyone who resembled his wife, just not her?

Then.

Rose put the deck for Amrita to cut before she dealt. Amrita cut, didn't tap. Rose took the cut cards and placed them at the bottom of the pack. And in that moment, she slipped the last two cards in the half-pack into her hands and smoothly slid them to the bottom of the deck. She was quick, she was good. No one was any the wiser. She started dealing in the same order: Amrita, Mrs Goenka, Roshan, Anand, Rahul. She dealt just two cards each. I could only assume she had dealt both cards from the bottom of the pack to Amrita because she was too quick even for me to spot. Rose was more than good!

'Ladies and Gentlemen, it's Blackjack. All of you have two cards. Blind is 10,000. Blind in each subsequent round doubles, but only three rounds can be played blind. Jack is eleven, Queen is twelve, King is thirteen and Ace is fourteen, not one. You may buy the third card for 50,000, but you are not permitted to discard any. Sideshows are on request only.'

Aha! No wonder Rose had slipped two cards to the bottom. I would bet everything I own that the two cards Amrita had in front of her added up to twenty-one. Rose had modified the rules by allocating numbers to picture cards. In some places, all picture cards – including aces – are counted as eleven, which increases the probability of twenty-one.

All players went blind for the first three rounds. There was three and a half lakh rupees in the middle without anyone looking at their cards yet.

Then I spotted it: Roshan Godara and Anand Kumar, for a fraction of a second, looked at each other. They didn't speak but they certainly exchanged some kind of message non-verbally. Because I could see Anand's right hand – the one with cards – slip under the table. As if on cue, Godara's left hand mirrored the move. Then, as quickly as the hands had slipped down, they were back at the table. They had changed cards, but should that have surprised me?

I ought to have gathered this when they sat next to each other at the table. Yes, it was invisible to the naked eye, but the camera missed nothing, and it never lied. What rattled me was that they had the gall to carry this out in casinos that were run by the vilest of people, the mafia. What if they were caught? I shuddered to think of the awful consequences – too scary to even contemplate – but it was their lives, their risk. I found the manoeuvre quite ridiculous, almost juvenile if you asked me. Another cause of worry was how had they communicated before they choreographed the exchange.

But no, I wasn't calling Boris to let him know. Not yet. No point. We had the recording in case they created a ruckus if they spotted anything from our players.

Everyone had seen their cards now. Amrita didn't buy the third card. No surprises there. Mrs Goenka didn't buy one either. When it was Godara's turn, he folded. I wondered why Roshan Godara was helping Anand Kumar win. The cards could have been exchanged either way, so why had Godara relinquished them in favour of his partner? It was evident that they were in cahoots, so maybe the understanding was that they'd split the winnings. Then it struck me. Anand Kumar might be attempting to impress his wife's lookalike. The alpha male, the victor. Wooing Rose. It wasn't uncommon for men like him to flaunt that they were bright and smart. He was a man of contradictions, this Anand Kumar. He cheated on Jasmine and then flirted with her lookalike. Then again, men like him constantly felt the need to prove themselves.

Anand Kumar pretended to be puzzled when I knew he'd already exchanged a card with his buddy. Perhaps trying to fool everyone, he took a moment to consider whether to buy a card and then declined. Rahul was the only one who moved a red chip to the centre and asked for a hit.

A little clarification might be in order: As Rose explained, in Blackjack the players can either choose to *hit* or *stand.* If they hit, they are dealt another card, and if they stand, they keep the two cards they were initially dealt. *Samjhe kuch?*

Immediately, Rahul's face suggested he was bust with the new card in his hand. He packed up instead of putting in more chips to continue.

Amrita's turn. Her cards were kept on the table. She knew – heck, even I knew – that she had a perfect twenty-one, but she made a point of picking them up to have another look. Then put them back and slid in a blue chip. 100,000, because that's what the stakes were until someone raised them.

Mrs Goenka mirrored Amrita without any acting.

Anand Kumar asked for a sideshow.

Sideshow *on request* – as Rose had mentioned at the time of dealing – meant the person who was asked for a sideshow could decline the request.

Mrs Goenka refused point blank. Anand had to put in his share of chips.

Amrita sat like a statue this time and just threw in another blue chip. Mrs Goenka looked at her cards again. Why did so many people do that? You had two cards; you knew what they were … they couldn't have changed. It was all for the show. She decided to pack up.

Only Anand and Amrita were left in the game now.

Game on, I wanted to say!

Anand doubled the stakes. Amrita matched them.

Back to Anand. He pursed his lips, shook his head and called for a show. I was shocked he did that.

Amrita turned over her first card: Ace.

Anand turned over a Queen.

Amrita had a seven, which made it twenty-one. Blackjack.

Anand had eight; he had fallen short by one. He was one short, and yet he had called for a show. He didn't appear happy, but everyone else had gathered that Anand was a risk-taker. He'd put a lot at stake when his cards didn't total to twenty-one. People like him are all pomp and circumstance. I wouldn't put it past him to have deliberately done this. His betting on a losing hand may give false confidence to others in the subsequent rounds, which he could exploit. Amrita wouldn't fall for that, I knew. In any event, she was supposed to lose the next two games. Winning too many in a row raised eyebrows, which was the last thing we wanted.

I glanced at Table Three. There was a pile of chips in front of Jinendrabhai. I could feel his chest heaving with pride. He was winning. But it didn't bother me one bit. Sid and Prem would make mincemeat of Jinendrabhai before long.

I had no scores to settle with anyone on Table Two. I couldn't care less. Yes, there was a lot of money involved, but we'd win.

Do you want me to write it and give it to you straight? Here it goes: We. Will. Win. Tonight. Come. What. May.

FORTY-TWO

'Red Red Wine' – Neil Diamond

IT WAS FIVE MINUTES PAST TEN. ALCOHOL-FUELLED CONFIDENCE was beginning to show. The background noise between rounds had risen by a few decibels. The night was still young, as they say.

I was focused on Table One again.

It wasn't like we'd been sat there, glued to the screens, since 8 p.m. We had moved around. Stretched our legs. Had a few beers – no harm, since we weren't the ones performing tonight – and nibbled on a snacks zapped in the microwave. We'd received and responded to some WhatsApp messages from Ranjit and, of course, gone to the loo. Want any more details? No? I guessed so.

We took breaks right after Prem, Amrita or Sanjay had a big win, which signified that the croupiers at the tables would not deal them with a winning hand for at least the next couple of rounds. Nothing raised eyebrows more than a streak of winnings. Sure, it happened, but when you were orchestrating it was important not to go overboard. My maths – and the number of chips in front of our players – suggested we were way ahead of the competition at that moment.

Boris moved around and when he was in the vicinity, I could see through the camera in his glasses. I focused on

Anand Kumar, Roshan Godara and Jinendrabhai's faces. They all appeared buoyed up. Ecstatic, yet anxious. They hadn't lost big yet. They suspected nothing. All good, then.

I'd sent a message to Prem through Boris. He needn't move tables now. We'd improvised primarily because no one else had asked for a move, so Prem would need to go around asking if someone else wanted to change. If people hadn't noticed him yet, they would. Why risk it? Also, if players at a particular table had become comfortable with each other it wasn't wise to split them, as a new entrant might change the dynamics. Why fix it when it ain't broke, and all that.

Back at Table One, Rose was dealing again. She was really good. So good even I'd failed to pick up if she had manipulated the cards, but I knew she was up to something since Amrita decided to tap the cards rather than cut them when they were offered. They had definitely communicated with each other – through a wink or a nod or some gesture that I had taught them – but I missed it since my mind was focused elsewhere for a second. That is all the time it takes to miss such manipulations.

Card to Amrita, Mrs Goenka, Roshan Godara – hang on a minute. She deliberately looked up, like she was stretching her neck for some form of physiotherapeutic pain relief when she dealt a card to Godara. While everyone's gaze was flying between the table and Rose's hands and the other players, Amrita was focused on Rose and picked up the cue, I hope.

Rose then dealt a card to Anand Kumar and finally, to Rahul. She repeated the process with the second round … and there she glanced at the roof yet again, for a fraction of a moment, when she slipped the second card to Godara. She continued to deal the third card to everyone without any cues.

Now … if you've been paying attention to me all along, you should know what just happened at the table. Do you? No? Let me refresh your memory. *Looking up is looking North. England is located towards the North of India. England had a Queen, which means if you look up towards the ceiling* … remember? Rose had dealt two Queens to Roshan Godara. In a way, it was entrapment, if you know what I mean. With a Queen-pair, Godara would go out guns blazing. He would think he had a winning hand; he would put a lot of money on it. And lose.

Why?

Rose must have dealt Amrita a magnificent hand. I was thinking Aces, but that would be risky unless Rose had also controlled the third card she dealt to Godara. Giving two Aces to Amrita would be pointless if, by a stroke of luck, the third card in Godara's hand also happened to be a Queen. I had warned the croupiers not to deal three Aces to anyone – that would be too much for others to swallow. And imagine if Godara got three Queens and Amrita got three Aces in the same deal? That was beyond a coincidence. That kind of thing only happens in books and films. Or when someone cheats.

'Teen Patti, sideshow on request,' Rose announced.

The game was, once again, afoot.

First round: blind.

Second round: blind.

Third round: also blind. Then Amrita picked up her cards and kept them down quickly. As she moved the chips to the centre to indicate she was not folding, I spotted Godara and Anand Kumar looking at each other. *Shit!* What if Anand Kumar had a Queen and he passed it on to Godara? We'd be screwed. There was a high probability that Rose and Amrita had both missed that Anand and Roshan had sneakily *collaborated* before.

'Boris,' I called right away, 'move towards Table One, keep your eyes on Godara and Anand – if you spot anything suspicious, call it out.'

Boris started moving before I cancelled the call. He was so near Table One that no one could move their hands and cards under the table – which was a strict no-no in all casinos – let alone switch with their buddies. If Anand and Godara had intended to exchange cards in this round, the opportunity was now gone. No such luck if Boris was overlooking the table from such close quarters. Kaput.

Mrs Goenka didn't fold either.

Godara had to be content with two Queens. His demeanour remained poker-faced; nothing suggested that he was holding a brilliant hand, but he remained in the game.

So did Anand.

Rahul folded after seeing his cards. The guy had been having a bad night. Hadn't won a single game.

Boris stood guard.

Another round and no one went out of the game yet. Amrita, Mrs Goenka, Godara … but Anand Kumar wanted a sideshow. His buddy obliged and asked him to fold. Once Anand's cards were back in the deck with Rose, I asked Boris to move on. His standing in one place for a long time could be seen as out of character. In any event, there was little Godara could do now. Mrs Goenka wasn't suddenly going to pass her cards around to him.

In the next round, Mrs Goenka asked Amrita for a sideshow. Amrita declined.

Godara, on his turn, asked Mrs Goenka for a sideshow. She declined too.

Ten minutes later, there was not a single chip left with Amrita, Mrs Goenka or Godara. Each player had chips worth two crores at the table when the evening commenced. They could ask for two more since they had deposited four crores at the entrance. Mrs Goenka decided to fold, which made Godara think, while Amrita confidently let Rose know that she'd like more chips. Which, if you asked me, was a mistake – her only one this evening so far. Her conviction intimidated Godara. She should have waited for him before asking for more chips. Well, that was my assessment. Who is to say what Godara might have done if Amrita had not hastily ordered more chips? In this case, he asked for a show.

The two turned over their cards, one by one.

Amrita: Ace of Spades.

Godara: Queen of Spades.

Amrita: Two of Spades.

Godara: Queen of Clubs.

Amrita: Three of Spades.

Three consecutive cards from the same suit. Pure sequence. Straight Flush.

Godara didn't bother revealing his third card. I could sense the hurt in his eyes – hurt turning to anger, then to hatred. He must have been baying for blood, losing that kind of money. Anand Kumar put his arm around his friend to calm him down.

'Could we get some drinks on this table, please?' It was Kumar, in a loud voice, gesticulating to one of the waiting staff, who rushed to them.

I could see Mrs Goenka congratulating Amrita. I could see Godara burn.

And I was beside myself with joy.

I glanced at Tables Two and Three. Prem seemed to be neck-and-neck with Jinendrabhai. All the others at the table looked broke. Sanjay hadn't been as successful, but it hardly mattered. He would win, I knew he would.

'Time for a drink?' Puja asked.

'Yes, please.'

She wandered off into the kitchen and Chikki gave me a kiss.

'Get a room, you guys.' Puja was back with a chilled bottle of Pinot Noir.

'Cheers!'

FORTY-THREE

'Achcha Sila Diya' – Ustad Attaullah Khan

11:14 P.M. ANAND KUMAR HAD LOST SOME MONEY, BUT nothing close to the blunder Godara had made with the pair of Queens. He had won marginally after that fiasco but was still a long way from recovering his losses. Both looked distraught since they saw there wasn't much time left. As per the rules, the tables would close at 1 a.m. It usually took another hour for the staff to tally the chips and change them back to cash so everyone could depart by 2, leaving them to clean up.

Drinks were being served all round. Everyone took a short break before returning to their tables with new gusto. The next time they take a break would be at the end of the night.

Rose, Vinita and Sid began shuffling cards to deal.

Then.

The police sirens were loud enough to come through the speakers of our computers. There was blue murder all around. If we could hear them, so could the people inside the casino. Puja glanced at me. Chikki, too. We watched the people on the screens looking around, too, bewildered.

Abruptly, Boris's voice loomed large over the microphone. We could hear him loud and clear.

'Ladies and gentlemen, may I have your attention, please … I'm sorry for interrupting what has so far been a magnificent evening, but we have a situation. It might cause anxiety to some of you, but the police are at the front door. This is the first time this has happened in any club that I've worked the security for, but there is no need to panic. We have procedures in place to handle a situation like this. We have an emergency evacuation procedure that we must all follow to be safe.' He had a placatory smile on his face. What else could he do at such a time? The arrival of police had put paid to a brilliant evening.

There was quite a hubbub in the casino after the announcement. Some of the patrons looked like passengers on the *Titanic* who had just heard the news of its sinking. Eager to jump off, without knowing how or where. Although Boris had promised there were lifeboats, there was shock and fear and agony on their faces. Disbelief. They'd been in casinos before, but this wasn't something they were prepared for. How? Why? There were questions on their lips even if we couldn't hear them. While it looked hilarious as a spectator, I could appreciate how horrifying the situation would be for those in the room. Easy to laugh when it wasn't you or your money.

'The front shutters are closed,' Boris continued, 'and it will take approximately six minutes for the police to get them open and march in. That is all the time we require to file out through the rear entrance.

'We apologize for this rather unpleasant interruption, but there is little we can do at the moment. As you all know, in intractable situations like these there are just three actions we can take – fight, freeze or flight. Unfortunately, the first two aren't an option for any of us, so I kindly request you to maintain your calm and presence of mind and move out in a single file. Once outside, do not run, as this will attract attention. Walk to your cars as you normally do and drive away. Leave everything here. If you are stopped, the police will have nothing on you.

'We have guidance from the bosses of the casino that in an event like this, all of you will be refunded the money you deposited at the door. Four crores each. Today's winnings and losses are forfeited and, as a gesture of goodwill, no commission will be deducted. Moreover, you will be invited to play another night, with all commissions waived very soon.

'I request you to please drop all chips and cards at the table and leave now. Stay home and wait seventy-two hours for us to contact you, after which your money will be delivered to you. On behalf of the management, I profusely apologize once again and request you to lie low for the next few days. Be assured that your money is safe. Now, let's move …'

The room, which moments ago was filled with alarmed faces, now contained only an air of resignation.

The curtain came down.

The lights went out.

Our screens went blank. The signal was cut off. Boris, it seemed, had started the evacuation. Before the three of us could talk, I received a WhatsApp message from Ranjit.

Dimpy, are u alone now?

Nope

Can you move away from the girls?

why??

I'll tell u in a min. Just go into the bathroom, NOW!

Something was definitely not right – he was asking me to move away from Chikki and Puja. They were as much part of the team as we were, weren't they? But I didn't make a fuss.

Instead: 'I'll just go to the loo,' I told the ladies, and I rushed out of the room.

I locked the door and opened WhatsApp again.

Yeah, I'm alone now... what's the matter?

U remember the detective I got hired through a Contact to follow Chikki?

yes, a while ago

what happened?

I could see dots appear. He was typing. Then:

somehow I missed one of his emails - it was in my spam folder. It doesn't look good

Shit!

what doesn't look good??

Even as I typed my last message, a chill raced down my spine.

What did the detective find about Chikki that we had missed?

one time, when she went out, she met someone

Who met someone?

Chikki... who else?

she met someone at a hair salon in Cuffe Parade

When was this?

sometime in April

who? who did she meet?

A woman

Did he give u the name of the woman Chikki met?

no

this was right about the time we had asked him to drop the surveillance... remember?

Of course I remember, but that doesn't help now, I wanted to tell Ranjit, but didn't. I had brought Chikki into our plan, so blaming Ranjit or anyone else seemed inappropriate. I had shared everything with Chikki, right down to the last detail. As I looked into the mirror in the bathroom, I could see my face was red. I thought I was a good judge of character. How did I go wrong when it mattered the most?

he's sent me the pic of the woman Chikki met...

do you recognise her?

no, never seen her in my life

send it to me right now

ok

I'll call you the minute I receive it

ok

I heard the distinctive ping. Ranjit had sent the picture of Chikki with the unknown lady, but it took a minute to download – the longest minute of my life.

I called up Ranjit immediately, but it went through to his voicemail.

Before I left the toilet I sent him one final message:

Delete this entire chat from your WhatsApp. I'm leaving the toilet & going back to the girls

FORTY-FOUR

'Poker Face' – Lady Gaga

AS I RETURNED TO THE ROOM TO BE WITH CHIKKI AND PUJA, the two were all giggles, oblivious to the conversation I'd just had with Ranjit. And I had no intentions of letting them in on it – when ignorance is bliss and all that. I kept a straight face like nothing had happened. I could be poker-faced, too. And while a wave of relief had washed over me when I saw the photograph Ranjit sent me only moments ago, doubt and dread still preoccupied my exhausted, un-slept brain.

The next seventy-two hours are crucial. Decisive. The anxiety I feel is overwhelming. Boris has promised the twelve gamblers that they shall receive their money – forty-eight crore rupees – back by that time. A lot can go wrong between now and midnight of Monday. And Tuesday morning ... well, that'll be another story, a guaranteed all-hell-breaks-loose moment.

Boris has to disappear, as per our plan, ASAP. He is booked on a late evening flight out of Mumbai. Where to? I don't know, and I have no desire to know either. As I've mentioned before, sometimes not knowing is better. If all goes to plan, he should be out of the city soon. However, until he takes that flight, a lot is at stake. He has seen me, albeit in disguise; he has interacted with me, although as Michael Ferreira. If, somehow, he and Jasmine get together, it won't require hiring

Sherlock Holmes to put two and two together. Of course, it will still be difficult to find me, but it might get a lot messier than what we have planned.

A lesson for everyone: Plan B is never as good as Plan A, otherwise it would've been your Plan A, wouldn't it?

All things considered, Boris needs to leave town *now*, having discarded the SIM he's been using all this while in Mumbai. He is going to meet someone shortly – I say *someone*, like I don't know who exactly; someone Ranjit will send through a third party. Boris has to give that person his SIM card in exchange for the money we owe him: the balance of three lakh rupees in cash. He will then take the one-way flight. Yes, he can return, and yes, he can still become a nuisance, but that will be a nightmare for another day, and we shall take care of it if it comes to that. We have video recordings of him in the casino, together with other staff who also work for those dangerous elements, whom he was instrumental in getting on board. He had manipulated several high-net-worth clients and orchestrated the entire scam without any knowledge of his underworld employers. Ergo, if he returns to cause us any sort of trouble, he'll be first in the queue to the gallows. We know how to tame him.

Why is it so important that Boris goes away from Mumbai? Simple. People will need reassurance that their money is safe. Boris will be the first port of call for many after seventy-two hours pass, if not before. Who else will they go to when he was responsible for inviting a large majority of the players, including Jinendrabhai Patel, for the big night? He was the one who – when the police arrived – stood there with the microphone and promised people that money would be delivered to them. The rest of the staff never had an inkling that they had been called in to work for the evening at the behest of someone else and not by their usual bosses. They turned up, they played their part and they got paid; for them, it was business as usual. All of them came to work that night because Boris had handpicked those loyal to him and who, he was certain, wouldn't question his judgement or his authority. In life, all you need is a strategy to get the right pieces to the right places on the board at the right time. A pawn's first and foremost job is to safeguard the king, and if they do that as slavishly as they are meant to, checkmate to the opponent is merely a formality. Any of the twelve gamblers who call staff members other than Boris will learn nothing.

Our actors will return to their respective lives, too. This gig is over. The reality TV show they were hired for will never get telecast, as you and I know, which neither adds nor takes anything away from their résumés. If anything, they have gained financially and should now get back to the grind, looking for new roles. And while I wish them luck – they all performed brilliantly – I don't think any one of them will become a superstar by tomorrow or by the next weekend. If someone someday recognizes any one of them, there's very little they know about me, so it's not cause for concern. It will just be another dead end. Yes, they might have questions, but they have no one to ask. I am no longer available to them – if they call, I'll disconnect.

Unlikely though it may seem, there is no guarantee that one of the twelve won't panic before the elapsed seventy-two hours and do something brainless. Their stupidity or haste can damage us all. They might jump the proverbial gun and start making calls to others that they know from the venue. Then to the person or persons who invited them to this big game night. In Anand Kumar and Roshan Godara's case, that will be Jasmine, who had introduced her husband to Chikki. Anand will certainly lean on his wife to call up Chikki and ask to speak to Deep Singh Sodhi aka yours truly. I'm surprised we haven't received a call yet, but we've kept Chikki's phone on. Switching off her phone might ring alarm bells. As a matter of fact, we want Jasmine to call Chikki, as that will release some tension – and give us some info on what they're thinking and planning.

'If Anand Kumar calls tonight ...' I told Chikki.

'He won't call tonight.' She sounded sure.

'And you know that because?'

'Because he doesn't have my number.'

'Of course, *he* doesn't have your number, but Jasmine does.'

'And Jasmine is out for the night with a guy from the gym. She tends to switch off her phone when she's on a tryst.'

'Oh.'

'She doesn't know her husband has had to rush out of the club because of a police raid, so she'll make the most of her night out.'

There was another round of *giggle, giggle* from Chikki and Puja.

'Okay, but if and when he calls,' I explained, 'he will want to know why I didn't meet him at the venue, since I was supposed to be on the invitee list. He must have expected me at the game earlier tonight, that I would walk up and introduce myself out of courtesy. Since Anand Kumar has never seen or met Deep Singh, you should tell Jasmine that I was present at the casino, playing at Table Two – referring to Sanjay, one of our actors – and that I wanted to catch up with Anand and his friend after the game, but the last-minute scampering due to the police raid ruined that plan.'

'Okay.'

'If need be, put me on the line and I will reassure him that

I am waiting for my money too. If nothing else, it will give him some confidence that he and Godara aren't the only ones waiting for payments. And that buys us some time.'

There are still too many balls in the air – and this is before I've told you all that Ranjit needs to achieve in this short timeframe. Hence, the next seventy-two hours can mean all-or-nothing, win-or-bust – choose your phrase. So you see, my friendly diary, it isn't time to celebrate yet.

Chikki and Puja continued to giggle. Too many drinks, I thought. We'd been up all night but none of us wanted to sleep despite our eyes and bodies begging for it. Knowing that caffeine would hit our empty stomachs harder than Mahendra Singh Dhoni hitting a ball with his heavy bat, we ate buttered toast before drinking coffee.

My restless brain sprinted in all directions but failed to come up with further improvisation. There was nothing we could do but wait. Despite the coffee, I was struggling to string my thoughts into anything meaningful. I told the girls that it would be wise for us to take a nap, and they agreed. A few hours' rest and we would be revitalized when Ranjit returned, which we knew wasn't going to be anytime soon – at least not until late in the evening.

FORTY-FIVE

'In The Air Tonight' – Phil Collins

I WAS BEING CHASED BY ANAND KUMAR AND ROSHAN GODARA with a stick in his hands. I was quick, but they seemed to be catching up. In any chase on foot, the person being chased has to be significantly faster than the person or people behind him or else they will catch up sooner or later. And in this open field – only God knows how we got there – there weren't any places to hide. I realized I had run in the wrong direction as I got on the bluff, jutting over the Arabian Sea some fifteen feet down, where angry waves crashed onto the rocks on the shore. It was time to jump, or turn around and face my pursuers.

I took the plunge and a jarring sound pierced my ears.

I woke up sweating. It was my burner phone. Shrieking.

What a nightmare!

It took me a few seconds to realize where I was; in the guest bedroom in Puja and Ranjit's flat. I remembered Chikki and Puja had gone to sleep in another room carrying the half-empty bottle of the leftover bubbly. My head was spinning, hurting as my phone stopped ringing.

What time was it?

I picked up my phone and saw a missed call from an unknown number. The caller hadn't left a voicemail. I called back immediately.

'Thanks for calling back, Mr Ferreira. I was about to switch off my phone.'

'Hi Boris,' I sounded gruff even to myself. 'Where are you?'

'At the airport as agreed. I've given my SIM card to the person who gave me the gift – thanks for that – and I'm about to board my flight.'

'Really?' If I sounded disorientated, I didn't care.

'It's six-thirty in the evening. My flight leaves in thirty minutes, Mr Ferreira.'

'Oh … thanks for everything, Boris. And have a nice flight.'

'You sure you don't want to know where I'm going?'

'I'm quite sure about that; as we discussed previously, it's safer that way.'

'If I want to meet you again, how do I find you, Mr Ferreira?'

'If we are destined to meet, we will find each other.' I had no intention of reuniting with Boris for a long, long time. Neither did I want him to look me up or find me in the foreseeable future. Perhaps one day … hopefully never.

'Ha-ha, I've always liked your positive attitude. *Adios* Mr Ferreira.'

'Bye Boris. Have a great life.'

'You too, Mr Ferreira.'

Cancelling the call, I pulled out the SIM card from Mr Ferreira's phone and broke it into two. Michael Ferreira wasn't expecting any more calls from anyone. He was off the grid from that moment onwards.

I wondered if I should lie in for some more time or get up and wake the girls. I decided on the latter. I went to the kitchen and put the kettle on. A strong coffee was required. Then I knocked on Puja's bedroom door, and heard a groggy, 'Go away, whoever it is.'

'It's me, and the coffee is ready.'

It took Puja and Chikki more than ten minutes to appear in the living room.

'Had a good sleep, beauties?' I asked.

'Yes, but not a proper beauty sleep.' Chikki.

'Isn't Ranjit back yet?' Puja.

'Nope.' I looked at the mobile in case there had been a missed call. No. Not even a message.

'Shouldn't we call him?' Puja.

'We can try.' I called him, but it went straight to voicemail. Maybe there was no signal where he was. I saw no point in leaving a message.

As we looked at each other, sipping coffees, trying to figure out what to do next, the key turned and Ranjit Bhatia walked in. He must have been in the building's lift when I had called a moment back.

'Hello, my dears.'

For someone who had been out for the last twenty-four hours, he looked and sounded quite fresh. Then it occurred to me that our exhaustion was not merely due to lack of sleep. The alcohol and the frustration of being oblivious to what was happening on the ground – after the cameras went off post the police raid – had taken their toll, too. Funny, how the human brain functions. Ranjit gave all of us hugs before slumping on the sofa.

'How are things?' Me.

'All done. Nothing for any of you to worry about.' Ranjit.

'Should we pop the champagne then?' Puja.

'Hang on, girl … it's still early.'

'Let me get you a coffee, and then you can tell us all about it,' I said and went into the kitchen.

'How much detail do you want?' Ranjit asked when I returned.

'Give us a summary. We don't want a migraine.' Puja.

'Almost done.' Ranjit said, and then took a sip while we waited for him to continue. He didn't.

'What's almost done?' Me.

'You guys said you wanted a summary, I've given you what must be the shortest summary in the history of mankind, along with the result.'

'Very funny.' Puja.

'Okay, a little more detail, please?' Me.

'Well, like I said. It's almost done. It will take another twenty-four hours, but I'll get the confirmation on the phone. No need for anyone to fret or worry. You're in extremely reliable hands.' He raised his fists to emphasize.

'Okay by me.' Chikki.

Everyone agreed. We'd never discussed Ranjit's part of the operation – we didn't know the how or the who, so why get into it now?

'When is your flight?' Ranjit.

'In sixty hours, now.' Me. Chikki and I wanted to get away from Mumbai right after the seventy-two hours that Boris had given to the casino punters elapsed.

'Until then, let us party like it's 1999.' Ranjit.

I'm not sure about Chikki and Puja but I was quite surprised by his zeal. Even more so by his physical state. He'd been awake for more than thirty-six hours and he was ready to party.

'Yes, bring it on.' I have to admit his enthusiasm was contagious.

'I'm famished. What's for dinner?'

'Nothing. We'll order something.' Puja.

With Radha having been given the time off, and the three of us busy with the surveillance, there hadn't been time for anyone to cook.

'Why don't we order aloo parathas from the local restaurant close by? We'll reheat them and have them with butter and pickle, if that's okay with you guys. Meanwhile, I'll take a quick shower.'

'And yogurt,' I added.

'Aloo parathas again?' Puja.

'Why not?'

The girls called it a night around eleven. Ranjit and I stepped out for a smoke. We were nearly there now. There was no cause for concern, no need for the butterflies to flutter anymore.

♥

Ranjit received *the* confirmation call after forty-eight hours, a call I'll never forget all my life.

The curtain had finally fallen!

Chikki and I will be on the flight tomorrow morning.

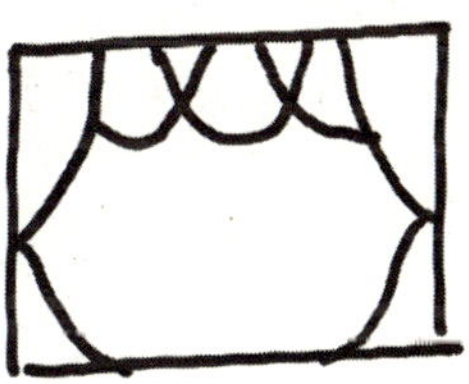

PART FOUR

'When I was young, people called me a gambler. As the scale of my operations increased, I became known as a speculator. Now I am called a banker. But I have been doing the same thing all the time.'

SIR ERNEST CASSEL

Ab Dilli Door Nahin!
ALMOST THERE NOW!

FORTY-SIX

'Lyin' Eyes' – Eagles

I'VE MENTIONED THIS A HAZAAR TIMES, AND I WILL SAY IT again: I completely and utterly trust Ranjit. He's a friend, isn't he? Friends don't cheat friends. Much like spouses – they shouldn't cheat on each other either. Maybe I'm living in some alternate universe or perhaps I'm the biggest fool between the two tropics.

Perish the thought, I keep telling myself. Tomorrow is another day.

I've only ever lived in two cities in my life, and if I were offered a choice, I'd pick – surprise, surprise! – Mumbai, not Saharanpur. The city embodies everything that I consider life. The glitz, the glamour, the spirit of the people, the work ethic, the non-interfering neighbours, unlike Saharanpur or any other small town in India, for that matter. You can be anyone in Mumbai, and no one cares. I am not saying it is all rosy; it has its fair share of unwanted characteristics, but then which city doesn't? Leaving it will bring tears to my eyes, but so be it. That boat has already sailed now.

Before I go to sleep – my last sleep in Mumbai for now – it gives me immense pleasure to say that the long con we planned and executed has been completely successful, and I don't need to conceal anything anymore. There is no cause for concern.

We've got away cleanly without leaving any prints on the knife, as it were. So let me explain how it went down as the seventy-two-hour timeline to return all the money to the patrons came to a close.

Well, the twelve gamblers got diddly-squat. Not a single paisa. We needed seventy-two hours to get away from Mumbai, and will be on a flight soon. Ranjit needed seventy-two hours to clean up, which he accomplished.

Are you familiar with the term gaslighting?

No, I'm not telling you about how to light a gas fire. I'm not your Boy Cub leader. This is not a Scout manual. This is my diary. Remember?

Gaslighting is a form of psychological manipulation. I kid you not. The term was coined in the late thirties of the last century; it's also been used in films and theatre. In plain English, you play with the mind of your subject. It can work at an individual level and equally well at a group level. All you need to do is sow the seed of doubt and water it incessantly.

Misdirect and misinform until the subject starts questioning their own self. Am I here? Is this real? Am I dreaming? The victims are conned into disbelieving themselves. Because what they so vehemently believe to be true has dissipated. The truth that they have been clinging to does not exist. It has vanished.

The rule of the jungle is that the predators stalk the river for the prey, but what if the river vanishes? Anand Kumar and Roshan Godara and Jinendrabhai Patel, or for that matter any of the other nine gamblers who were present in the casino on the night of October 26th, must have returned to the Versova casino when their money wasn't returned as promised – to get answers, to get their money back. But there would have been no one there to respond to their questions, no one there to quell their misery.

Because.

There would have been no "there".

They would have struggled to find the place itself.

Because.

There is no "there". That casino or club or lounge – whatever you might want to call it – does not exist. Period. It never did. It was a temporary structure constructed with gypsum boards, painted and decorated by a builder on an empty plot that was hired for a few months by a production house called *Art Lovers Private Limited.* Which, again, no one will be able to trace. The builder believed he was being contracted by a consortium of artists to construct a reality TV show set. Conning 101: be consistent with your lies. In case the actors had bumped into the builder before the event – although we avoided taking them to the site while the construction was happening – they'd have been on the same page.

Through the builder, Ranjit hired the furniture, the props and created the entire set. I provided the actors. Given the temporary nature of the structure, it took the contractor merely seven weeks to get the set ready – the blueprint of which was fed to us by Boris from Bihar and improvised by Ranjit and yours truly. The exterior was painted like real walls, and Puja and Chikki painstakingly styled the interiors in a sophisticated way by without visiting the site once. It was designed to withstand the visual scrutiny of our twelve patrons, unless one of them went berserk and started smashing the walls. And, if it came to that, we had enough security – led by Shri Boris ji – to take care of the situation.

The contractor was given strict and clear instructions to knock down and cart away every bit of material and equipment from that site within twenty-four hours of the big night. And destroy it. The demolition began in the early hours of Saturday,

27 October, but it took a little over thirty-six hours to ensure the site looked like the unused plot it was before we hired it for the 'shoot'. You see, whatever can be built in less than two months can be destroyed in less than two days. That is why Ranjit wasn't with us on that night. He wasn't directly involved with the contractor, no way. But he was supervising the set being dismantled on camera, leaving nothing to chance.

The arrival of the police couldn't have been timed more perfectly. Then again, what did you expect when it was completely choreographed? It's actually quite a simple thing to plan and execute if you think about it. No one encountered the police at all, not even Boris and the staff. Everyone left the premises as directed by Boris – no one wanted to be taken to a police station for being present at an illegal outfit. Truth is, there never was any police outside the casino; it was only sirens that everyone heard. Heard inside, not outside. We didn't want to wake up the neighbours. The concealed sirens were included in the brief to the builder. They were activated using a WiFi remote that was controlled by Ranjit.

My pad wasn't in Versova by coincidence. I had chosen the same to be in the vicinity, to scout the area where I knew Ranjit had commissioned the structure. I didn't overtly turn up and bark instructions or render unsolicited advice. Ranjit knew what he was doing. But the car I had hired passed the place every time I travelled to and from Versova.

We were extremely cautious. My instructions to Boris had been quite specific. He was told not to invite anyone who had been to the existing Versova casino – neither the customers nor the employees. The real outfit in Versova was a kilometre away from our site and owned by some powerful outlaw(s) from the other side of the tracks. We would never have been able to access it. Do you think such people trust their staff to keep the keys? Essentially, everyone who was in attendance that night had heard about the existence of a real casino in Versova, but they didn't know the exact location, since no one had ever been there. We had mitigated – if not eliminated – that risk in our planning. All twelve gamblers believed they had been invited to an established outfit that had been present in the suburb for a few years.

We did overlook certain things, I admit. For example, we didn't have a liquor license. *Art Lovers Private Limited* would have come on the government radar had we applied for one. Even if we had made an application, there wasn't a chance in hell we'd be granted a license for a temporary, unlicensed structure. So we improvised, and served free drinks as a good gesture. You don't need anyone's permission to serve drinks to your guests at a private party.

If you think what we did sounds nearly impossible, you're correct; it sure was. If I hadn't planned and participated in carrying out the whole con from the beginning, I'd have thought that someone had made it all up. Like you're thinking now. I don't blame you. It's up to you whether to believe me or not – it doesn't matter to me, since I will soon be twenty-three crore rupees and some change richer.

What did the twelve gamblers do in the last three days? Nothing. I'm fairly certain the twelve of them tried to – but couldn't – find us. And they won't be able to, ever. Period.

They must have gone around in circles, failing to find the casino. They must have gathered they'd been conned, that the actual casino is in another location, but the realization had come too late.

They can't go to the police. What will they say? That they went someplace to gamble illegally and lost money? No way – their egos and reputations are far bigger than the money lost.

They will seethe, they will curse, they will point fingers, but they will not go to the authorities. Going against a casino, even a fake one like ours, will upset the business of the three that exist in the city, and we all know what kind of people run them. No, the likes of Anand Kumar and Roshan Godara don't have the gonads to wake such sleeping dogs.

Yes, they will never forgive or forget the night. But losing money was bad enough; they can't afford to lose face telling others they got conned. Each one of them must feel like a total ass.

I can visualize Roshan, Jinendrabhai and Anand losing their shit. Going bonkers, crying, yelling, beating their chests, wondering, promising to teach *someone* a lesson. Baying for blood, probably. Initially, I can imagine they might have thought it was some kind of a joke. If they did, they could wait for the punchline forever.

LOL – remember we agreed I can write that acronym in my diary?

The best part is that they don't even know it was me. Not yet, anyway. I don't think I'll even be on the bottom shelf of suspects; there's no way they can possibly connect me to the con this time. In time, perhaps, one of them might suspect me. If someone mentions Pedder Road, if they come to know I've moved out of Mumbai and that the timing of my exit coincides with the big night – but going to the police and trying to prove anything will be impossible. The saddest part is that I am not able to see the three 'a-holes' in this situation to enjoy their misery. Schadenfreude, as it is known, enhances pleasure, but I don't want them to come looking for me either, so it's a compromise I'm more than willing to make.

I know nine other people got fleeced in settling scores with Anand, Roshan and Jinendrabhai, but I'm not going to lose sleep over it, and neither should you. I'm not saying there isn't one, but I have never seen a book about a gambler's code of ethics. Maybe I should write one. Anyway, who's to say what's right or wrong? It's not like we bankrupted them. Life's not fair. Never was. Never will be. But we know that it's not partial to anyone, you have to give it that. And isn't it life's tendency towards unpredictability that keeps it interesting?

All twelve of them decided to go to Versova that night, lured by the big buy-ins, big money, big stakes, big winnings. It isn't hard to understand why people gamble. Everyone wants to make a free buck. You could double your money overnight. However, when you go out to gamble big, you can win or you can lose. And on that particular Friday night in Versova, all the twelve wealthy gamblers lost big. End of.

Just one more thing before I finish this – you might be wondering about the WhatsApp messages I exchanged with Ranjit on the night, when he sent the photograph of Chikki with someone. My heart had skipped a beat or two until I saw the photograph he had forwarded to me. That *someone* in the photo with Chikki was none other than Jasmine. I asked Ranjit to delete all the messages since I didn't want Chikki to ever know I had doubted her. And don't you dare – if you've read my diary – mention this in presence of Chikki. No insinuations on the sly either. I am guilty of being suspicious of Chikki, I truly am. But I cannot mention that to her now – she might laugh it off and forgive me, or she might feel hurt and kick me out of her life once again, and that is one chance I'm not willing to take. After all, I am not a gambler, I'm just a simple card artist, and I don't even perform for kids at parties anymore. I won't play the violin anymore either … not professionally, not for commercial purposes.

I should go to sleep, so I don't miss the flight to my peaceful future with my wife. Oh and in case you're interested, I want to learn to play the piano now.

♦

When I woke up the next morning, everything had changed. Chikki was missing from the bedroom. She wasn't in the shower; she wasn't anywhere in the Bhatias' apartment.

Poof! She had vanished.

I realized her mobile had been left behind when it rang. It was Jasmine. I cancelled the call. It was now a day past the seventy-two hours that Boris had promised so it wasn't unexpected. However, there wasn't anything to discuss; no need to put on an act, no need to lie anymore.

The phone rang again. I let it go to voicemail.

'Hi Chikki, hope you've been well. Anand wants to speak to you … or your beau, Deep Singh. In any case, it's been quite a while, we should catch up soon. Give me a call when you get this message, please.'

I let the message play, after which I switched off the phone.

Then I woke up Ranjit and Puja. They were equally baffled by Chikki's behaviour. How could she disappear from the apartment without leaving a message? We went around the entire building, but Chikki was nowhere to be found. The watchman hadn't seen her that morning, but he couldn't tell us anything about the previous night. The old man had fallen asleep, like he did every day.

Back at the apartment, the entire energy in the room had changed. Ranjit picked up the car keys, and the three of us drove to Versova, breaking every speed limit along the way.

When we got to our safehouse, we realized we had been fucked. Royally fucked. The van loaded with cash had vanished. Exactly like Chikki aka Zara. Poof! Gone. There was a note – Chikki's handwriting, of course – that simply read: *BYE!*

FORTY-SEVEN

'Ek Akela Is Shehar Mein' – *Gharonda* OST

NEW DELHI.

When Chikki vanished, we had to accept we had lost. Lost big time. All my savings were gone. I had committed to the project a hundred per cent, and to be fair – to all of us – we had pulled it off, hadn't we? We were backstabbed. By the last person I had imagined would dupe me.

But that was not true. I had suspected Chikki; I had even asked Ranjit to do some cursory checks but all had looked hunky-dory. What had happened then? What had we missed?

Ranjit asked some agency to look for Chikki, and they came back with the info that she had left for New Delhi, where we had planned to go together.

History does repeat itself.

Ranjit convinced me to go through with my plan of leaving town. His hired private eye had informed him that the twelve punters who had lost crores were out for blood. With the powers of the twelve of them combined, it was only a matter of time before someone traced the breadcrumbs to me. It wouldn't matter if they had any tangible evidence or not. It wouldn't matter that I had been double-crossed either. That would be my problem, not theirs. They'd break my legs before they even started asking questions. Worse still, they might inform the underworld that I had taken people for a royal ride, indirectly weaponizing the reputation of the casinos they ran in the city. I'd be toast. Limbless toast. It was best for me to go to New Delhi and lay low, change my identity and stay in budget hotels until the dust settled.

And like the last time when I left town, Ranjit gave me the money. Despite having lost crores, due to the partner I had introduced into the mix, he and Puja did not blame me for the swindle. There was no finger-pointing, *gali-galoch* or any such thing. They realized I had lost a lot. I could sense the pain in their eyes, but I could do nothing except apologize. Ranjit – to an extent – knew the security and background checks his contact had done on Chikki had failed. Puja was completely unaware we had ever suspected Chikki, and now was not the time to talk about that.

I had lost the most in the deal.

I had lost all my money and my apartment.

I had to leave Mumbai, the city I loved.

I had to leave my only friends behind.

I had lost the love of my life.

I had lost the life I had built and loved living.

Not to overlook that I had also lost my pride, my ego and bragging rights. Someone – and not just someone, my wife – had outfoxed me.

♣

Delhi, I realize, isn't vastly different from Mumbai. Of course, the pedantic among us will point out a hazaar differences to you, but what I mean is that all big cities represent the same lifestyle. There is one thing that I particularly like about Delhi – the space. Delhi, in terms of area, can accommodate a couple of Mumbais, if not more.

The one big compromise is the lack of the seaside.

Chikki and I were meant to meet estate agents the day after our arrival to find ourselves a new residence here, to make Delhi our new home. Ranjit, being in the property business, had called ahead and booked viewings for us. But it was all futile now. I didn't have the inclination to go looking at houses alone; I wasn't a masochist who sought pleasure in hurting myself. Not to forget, I no longer had the money to set up a home.

I lay in bed licking my wounds for a while, dozed off, woke up, then unpacked, took a shower and, instead of wallowing in my grief, decided to set out exploring nearby Janpath on foot. I wasn't there to shop, but getting out felt good. There was a vibe in the air; there were hazaar vendors and the aroma of fried food filled my nostrils. Before I knew it, I was standing next to one of the hawkers devouring street food – gol-gappes, samosas, kachoris – bring it on! The hawker and I started chatting. Not sure what came over me, but I told him I was from Mumbai and had recently been dumped by my wife (I didn't tell him that she ran away with my money, too). He felt sorry for me and refused to charge me for the snacks. *Bhai bade dilwala nikla!*

DILLI DIL WALON KI!

Food, they say, relieves stress. If there was any truth in that, I would be stress-free for the next week. I ate so much, my stomach hurt as I walked back to my hotel.

♠

My mobile buzzed around eleven-thirty. Number withheld. For a moment, I thought of letting it go to voicemail but changed my mind and took the call anyway. What's the worst that could happen now, eh?

'Good evening,' said the woman on the other side. Polished voice, a whiff of a Punjabi undertone in the accent. Typical Delhiite, then.

'Good evening. Who is this?'

'Laila.'

'Laila, who?'

'I am not here to play knock-knock jokes, Mr Ferreira.'

Crap. She knew my most recent name.

'Who are you?' I was shitting my pants if I'm being honest. How had someone tracked me down here? And what lay in store for me? What you must understand is that I was already out of my comfort zone. I was an alien in Delhi, I knew no one. I was in this hotel which, in the name of security, had only a couple of stray dogs lying down, flat as pancakes, outside the main door.

Oh, I forgot to update you about Zeenat. You might be concerned about where she has been during all of this. I expect some empathy for her, even if you have none for me. She's staying in Ranjit's office because Puja and she don't see eye to eye, and I didn't have the heart to subject either of my loved ones to compromise, even for a short period. And to be honest, who knew how long this phase would last? How long would I need to stay in hiding? Maybe I would need to find myself a livelihood and live in Delhi forever; maybe I'd go back to Mumbai after a few months, when Ranjit thought it was safe to do so.

Anyway, back to the call.

'I just told you I am Laila, didn't I?'

'Okay, so how can I help you, Laila ji?'

'Cut that shit out, Mr Ferreira, because I don't think you can help me.'

'Then why have you called me, if I am of no use to you?'

'Because *I* can help *you*.' There was unspoken glee in the voice. She was mocking me. When your chips are down everyone else thinks they're fuckin' Napoleon's grandchild, don't they?

'And how can you help me?'

'I can help you find your wife.'

This was getting serious now. This person didn't just know my name, but she knew about Zara, too.

'What do I need to do?'

'Meet me.'

'When and where?' I asked, but I had no intention of meeting any Laila or their Majnu. I would fix a date and time and place and leave this hotel forever. I wouldn't even bother to check out since whoever the woman was, she might have been watching the hotel. My checking out might send a signal that I was going on the run, which I would be. I would call Ranjit and let him advise me as to whether I should buy a one-way ticket to Mumbai, or take a train back to Saharanpur.

'Are you there, Mr Ferreira?'

This was a trap. She knew where I was … she was playing with me, but I put up a brave front.

'Yes … yes, I'm listening.'

'Where are you staying, Mr Ferreira?'

'You called me, so I guess you must know where I am, Laila ji.'

'It's a mobile phone so you could be anywhere – maybe in Mumbai, maybe in Delhi, how would I know?'

'But you asked me to meet you if I wanted to know more about Chikki.'

'Chikki or Zara, yes.'

Shit!

'How do you know her?" I asked. My mind raced in all

directions, including *paataal lok.* What if this was someone trying to bait me? My mobile number was the same one I had in Mumbai, so Anand Kumar and Jinendrabhai would have it in their contacts. If they had smelled out that I was behind the entire scheme at Versova last week, then they'd know about Chikki's involvement too. In that case, they might've also found out that I was double-crossed. What better way to incentivize me into revealing where I was than to lure me by promising me the whereabouts of Chikki? Oh, this was a sweet trap, sweetened further by using a girl with a polished Delhi accent. Laila – of course, it was a fake name. After Boris from Bihar, I could bet this was Laila from Ludhiana.

Who named their daughter Laila these days? My best bet was to get off the call ASAP and call Ranjit for an update from Mumbai.

'I'm sorry, Chikki and I broke up, so I don't want to know where she is. If you see her, please give her my love ... and best wishes.'

'It will only take a minute—'

'What will only take a minute?'

'Meeting me.'

'But I don't want to meet you.'

'Why not?'

Another thought crossed my mind. Was this woman keeping me on the phone long enough to find out my coordinates? I was told once – or did I see it in a film? – that you have to keep someone online for three minutes or so for them to figure out your location. Shit. Yes, shit again! I cancelled the call. And then I heard the scariest sound of them all. A knock on my door.

'Who is it?'

'Room Service.'

Room service in this hotel? You'd be lucky if you got the kettle in the room working. But still I said, 'I didn't order anything. Who is it?'

'Laila.'

In that moment, I wondered how many Majnus she had brought along with her. Would the hotel owner and/or manager help me in case these Majnus tried to pack me in a crate and take me away? The least they could do was call the police. I looked around for a window to jump through and escape; all of them had metal bars – the irony was that these bars had been put there for protection. I pulled out my phone and called Ranjit – although how could he help when was 1,500 kilometres away? – but the call went straight to his voicemail. Just my luck! *As you sow, so shall you reap*, the saying came to mind. I was never a religious guy, but I had started saying my prayers now …

PART FIVE

'In gambling, there is a fool and a thief.'

OLD PROVERB

लैला

ONE

'Laila Mein Laila' – *Qurbani* OST

DON'T FRET, DON'T TURN THE PAGES, THIS IS NO CON. THERE is no one conning anyone, anymore. This is my diary, not the conman's.

Who am I?

I am Laila.

But you might know me by my other names, maybe. Zara Khan. Chikki Singh. Yes, I am the one who disappeared on Michael Ferreira aka Dimpy et al. I had to do it; you must understand that there was no other way of stopping him. He has been incredibly lucky to come so far with only one arrest. But good luck cannot be trusted. You cannot depend on luck alone to live a life.

It might have been okay for Dimpy Raja to sail through life when he was single. What's the worst that can happen, he often remarked. While that is a positive mantra, it is no way to live life, taking risks every single day. Dimpy wasn't capable of making this decision on his own. And if I am being honest, I wasn't sure he would have chosen to leave his old ways behind even if I or anyone else advised him. If I had insisted, he might have agreed, but someday he'd go behind my back to get back to his old life in one way or another. And the circle of lies and deceit would start again. Don't they say, *bandar kitna bhi budha ho jaaye, gulati maarna nahi bhoolta*?

Ergo, the only option for me was to use some kind of shock tactic. And I couldn't do it alone, I knew. So I spoke to Puja. Convinced her that Dimpy needed to move on, now that the two of us were together, with a third person on the way. Oh, did I not tell you that I am pregnant? A little Dimpy or a little Zara. I don't want our baby to be brought up by someone else while we, the criminal parents, are languishing in some jail. I want to give my child the best life there is, the life my Dimpy missed growing up, the opportunities he didn't get, the life avenues he never had the chance to explore.

The only good people in Dimpy's entire life were Puja and Ranjit. Puja is a headstrong girl, and once she was convinced, Ranjit understood my dilemma; that Dimpy's current path would led him nowhere. Ranjit arranged for the money truck to vanish, and me with it. Funnily enough, there was no money in the truck – no one in their right mind drove a truckload of cash from Mumbai to Delhi. He had transferred the money using some not-so-legitimate money transfer services into a few *benami* bank lockers in Delhi, which I was provided access to. How he did that, only he knows. He told me he transferred cash for his construction business all the time, and I believed him.

Finally, Ranjit and Puja slipped a sleeping pill into Dimpy's coffee the night I left. *Disappeared.*

❤

They had booked me a room in Le Meridien, Delhi, and put me in touch with a real estate agent in the city. I am not sure what Ranjit told the guy, but he must have thought I was royalty, the way he was dressed in a navy suit over an open-collared pale blue shirt. His name was Anil.

'Hello madam,' he greeted, as he walked up and shook my hand.

'Hello, Anil.'

We walked out of the hotel and into a waiting white Toyota Innova. He had a chauffeur in white livery drive me around.

'How familiar are you with Delhi, ma'am?'

'I can't say I'm familiar at all.'

'Oh, then is it okay if I take you to the properties we've shortlisted for you in any order?'

'I'll rely on your knowledge of the city. How many properties am I viewing today?' I asked as the car rolled down the ramp.

'Four, ma'am,' Anil said, then gave the address of the first one to the driver.

◆

I went to the bar on the ground floor of the hotel on my return. It was stocked with some great whiskies. I was carrying with me the glossy brochures of the four properties we had toured that day. It had taken me more time to cover the geography of this massive city than to actually view the homes, but I guess that is one of the minuses of every metropolis around the world.

Three drinks later, I decided on a large three-bed flat, which occupied the entire ground floor of a private house in Sunder Nagar. I wished Dimpy was there with me to make the decision, but we can't always have our way. Anil had told me that Sunder Nagar was one of the poshest South Delhi locations. Kapil Dev, the erstwhile captain of the Indian cricket team, was just one of its celebrity residents. Knowing Dimpy, that little nugget of info – the possibility of hobnobbing with Kapil – would make him happy. I liked the flat, too. I mean, I wasn't buying it, just renting it. You should know by now that Dimpy – and by association, I – cannot and do not *buy* such expensive things in life because of stupid taxes and proof of income, source of funds and all those undue rules and regulations.

♣

Dimpy was shocked when he realized I was Laila. I wish you could have seen his face. When he opened the door to his hotel room and saw me, Puja and Ranjit, he closed his eyes and shook his head like he was in some kind of a trance. He couldn't believe it. We sat him down, gave him water and then narrated the entire story to him. Poor guy, the last few days had been extraordinarily tough on him.

The car was waiting downstairs, and the four of us drove together to our new house in Sunder Nagar. Puja and Ranjit stayed with us for a couple of days before they flew back to Mumbai.

EPILOGUE

'Heroes' – David Bowie

Three months later

HI ALL,

I am Anjali Ahluwalia. My husband and I were out of the country for ten years, but we decided to come home and settle here three months ago. Yes, we are married. We got married one drunken night by our friends Puja and Ranjit at their place. We never formalized it in a court or anywhere else. It's not a taboo for us – we talk about it sometimes, but neither of us sees the need to involve a priest or a magistrate to put a stamp on our relationship. It's working well and as they say, if it ain't broke … why fix it?

My husband is Vikramjeet Singh Ahluwalia, although most people who know him well call him Vikram or Vicky. Vicky and I are partners; we deal in antiques in New Delhi and no, we don't have a shop in Chandni Chowk for tourists to flock to and bargain. We operate from our residence in Sunder Nagar.

We only work with people we know, and those vetted by previous clients – you just never know who to trust these days. Too many conmen around. The business isn't retail; it's not about footfall, and we don't stock anything. It's about knowing your client's requirements, then sourcing objects from bygone days for them.

The third being in our happy family is our plump ginger cat. We call her Zeenat. She's four years old, the vet recently told us. A cat's first year is equal to fifteen human years; their second year equals nine human years; and every subsequent cat year from then is four human years. So Zeenat and the two of us are approximately the same age now: thirty-two. Surprisingly, Zeenat has the same routine as she did in our previous home: she's found new friends in Sunder Nagar, and she comes and goes at will. We now have a flap fitted for her in our door. But let me not stray from what I was about to tell you as Dimpy used to …

You see, Zeenat, Vicky and I are similar in a way. Like her, we like to think we have nine lives, too. Vicky is on his sixth one, and I'm on my third. Nothing to sweat about, since we have plenty more to go after this one, so let's just pray that we can keep our curiosity in check.

I have become a lot bigger. Twelve more weeks until the baby arrives. We both hope Zeenat will like her hooman sibling.

Pray for us. I sincerely hope we will meet again.

It's time to finish up and get dressed, now. Ranjit and Puja are arriving today. They're staying with us for a week, since we didn't get time to celebrate after a big gig we pulled off in Mumbai last year.

The party is on. And you're invited.

THE IDEA BEHIND THE STORY

AS YOU MIGHT IMAGINE, ALL AUTHORS, AT SOME POINT, IN some interview, get asked where they got the idea for a particular story. It isn't like there is an idea repository that we go to, to check out a few, pluck one and take it home. Ideas come from imagination but, equally, they come from random incidents, anecdotes, conversations and observations we have in our real lives. While this particular story took shape over the years, the idea of gambling as a central theme for the book wormed its way into my brain during one of our holidays in the US.

Due to an unfortunate last-minute change in plans, we got stranded in Atlantic City on New Year's Eve in 2008. Casinos in the state of New Jersey, as you might know, are only legal in Atlantic City. We spent the night in a casino, like so many other tourists, and while my wife decided to try her luck at the slot machines, I wandered around watching the professional gamblers for a few hours. It is an interesting way to spend an evening, trust me.

We had planned to visit Princeton the following day, but we failed to find any public interstate transport between the two cities. The hotel kindly arranged for a cab, and we left Atlantic City in the early morning.

I sat in the backseat, while my wife sat in the front chatting with the lady who was driving us. During the course of those hundred miles, the driver told us about her life. She was about fifty, born in AC and had spent all her life there. She narrated her melancholic story of how she had got hooked on gambling so badly that she had to go to GA – yes, there is something called 'Gamblers Anonymous' – that helps people deal with the addiction. Before that day, I didn't know that gambling was as much an addiction as, say, alcohol or drugs. She was in tears as she admitted that despite spending her days and nights in casinos, and knowing well that she could never win against the house, she couldn't stop herself from being in a casino every waking hour – until her marriage collapsed, she had burned through her inheritance and some distant relative took her to GA.

I had just finished writing the initial draft of my very first book when this conversation took place, in January 2009. At that moment in time, I had no idea that one day I would be writing a book with gambling as its central theme. I still remember the lady's parting words as she dropped us at Princeton: 'Addictions enslave you; every addict thinks they can quit whenever they want … until they try.'

The gambling industry in the United Kingdom warns its customers, 'When the fun stops, stop.' Good luck with that one! A conman is no better than an addict in need of a fix. An addiction is, simply put, an addiction.

Acknowledgements

I recently read somewhere that the 'Acknowledgements' page an author writes is akin to a speech given by an actor at an award ceremony. It can easily get mushy and gushy when the actor goes on blabbering with no full stop in sight. Some even say that it should be eliminated – the author can thank the people personally if s/he so desires. In any event, everyone says that authors should learn to keep it short.

Ergo, I'll keep it brief.

I

thank

all the following.

My only wife: Nidhi Singh

Literary Agent: Mita Kapur of Siyahi

Film Agent: Sid Jain of The Story Ink

My friend & beta reader: Malcolm Lander

Editor: Shreyoshee Bandyopadhyay

Pan Macmillan India team

All My Readers

The Universe

All

Love, lots of it.